Until We Collide

Charlotte Fallowfield

TO ZIII,
WISHING YOU A HEA!
LOVE Charlotte x

ISBN-13: 978-1519156662

Version: 1

I am a British author and write in British English.

Editing by Karen J

Proofreading by Jasmine Z

Cover Art by Kellie Dennis at Book Cover by Design

Book content pictures purchased from Dollar Photo Club, iStock and Shutterstock

Foreword

Written from Paige Taylor's point of view, Until We Collide is a romantic comedy novel, the first by Charlotte Fallowfield.

Her website holds the most comprehensive information about her, as well as her current and up and coming releases.

Dedication

This novel is dedicated to my best friends, Anna, Claire, Deborah, Françoise, and Karen. Every girl needs a best friend to share love and laughter with, as well as to have, and to be, a shoulder to cry on in times of need. I'm lucky to have all five of these women in my life, and I hope that the laughter we've shared has more than outweighed the tears over the years. And long may that ratio remain!

I hope that you enjoy this novel, which was inspired by my very first crush back in the days that I was in a Shropshire Young Farmers Club (YFC). I can still remember it as if it was yesterday.

For those of you who have already found your Prince Charming, I hope that you get your happy ever afters. For those, like me, who are still searching, I keep everything crossed that you get to find him soon and have as many laughs along the journey as my heroine, Paige.

Charlotte x

Chapters

The Cow's Arse

July

'Poppie, you'd tell me if I was about to make a fool out of myself, wouldn't you?' I asked my best friend, biting my lower lip nervously as I waited for her answer.

'Please,' she muttered with a roll of her glossy chocolate eyes as she buttoned up my long, stark white jacket. She stepped back to cast an appraising eye over my new look and giggled. 'You look quite the part.'

'O shut up,' I giggled in response, reaching up to smooth my ponytail and check for any stray hairs. I'd taken extra care this morning, using my hair straighteners to ease out the natural waves in my long brown hair. Then I'd also made sure that my makeup was light and fresh, enhancing my baby pink heart-shaped lips and deep blue eyes.

'I can't believe you actually did it. We're virtually townies now, Paige, not country bumpkins who say "Ooooh, ahhhh," after every sentence.'

'I love that you're so undiscriminating,' I laughed, giving her a shoulder bump.

'Whatever, this guy had better be worth me getting up at this ungodly hour on a Saturday,' she moaned, flicking her long blonde hair over her shoulders.

'It's eleven a.m. Hardly ungodly.'

'It so is. Bloody young farmers my arse. When have you ever stepped on a farm before today? You're all about heels and glamour, yet here you are dressed up like a butcher in wellington boots,' she scoffed, folding her arms across her ample chest as she shook her head.

'Not just wellington boots,' I protested, looking down at my attire. 'These are *Hunters*, the crème de la crème of wellingtons. I even got myself a waxed *Barbour* jacket to look the part. This was a very costly mission.' I'd spent all of my savings on the two items in the hope that they'd get me noticed by him.

'You'll be wearing a tweed skirt and flat cap next, and going out on a weekend fox hunt,' she laughed.

'I'm telling you, when you see him, you'll totally think it's worth it.' I sighed, caught up in a daydream as I thought of Alec Wright, chairman of Young Farmers. At twenty-one, he was four years older than me and, in my eyes, the epitome of male perfection. Six foot three, dirty blonde hair that always looked like he'd just got out of bed, blue eyes I could drown in, and the most kissable lips I'd ever seen. It was obvious he worked out, and he took so much pride in his appearance. I had some stiff competition for his affections though. Since he'd transferred to this club from another on the other side of town, the female membership had apparently exploded, reaching heights the club had never seen. And it was all down to Alec, sex God extraordinaire.

'O, Christ, you're off on one of your daydreams about him again. Hello, earth to Paige,' Poppie called, snapping her fingers in front of my face.

'Sorry,' I grinned, shutting the boot of my car. 'Come on then, let's get this over and done with.'

'*This* I have to see,' she replied, shoving a clipboard and gel pen in my hand. She linked arms with mine as we made our way across the field, heading towards the stables of the large farm that hosted the annual summer country show.

I lived on the outskirts of Shrewsbury, in Shropshire, in a tiny hamlet with my parents. I'd met Poppie at boarding school when we were eleven, and our friendship had continued when we left the security of our all girls' education and ventured into a mixed sixth form college in the town centre. It had been an eye opener. I'd fallen for the hustle and bustle of a town immediately, the constant noise of people talking and laughing, street sweepers and refuse collectors, pigeons in the town square, and cars hooting as they tried to navigate the one-way system. It was such a contrast to the peace and quiet that I'd grown up in. Then there were the shops. I'd seriously found my calling in life. Clothes, makeup, and accessories shopping. Not that you'd be able to tell under this damn outfit.

'I'm nervous,' I whispered as I approached Ruth, the Vice Chairman, who had some of the other team members gathered around her.

'I'll bet,' chuckled Poppie. 'I'm going to record this on my phone, so that I can watch it and laugh again and again when I'm feeling blue.'

'I hate you,' I scowled.

'You love me,' she winked, letting go of me and shoving me in Ruth's direction.

'You're late!' Ruth snapped with an irritated glare.

'Sorry, but it's not like they have somewhere to be, is it?' I cringed as everyone but Ruth sniggered. She'd had it in for me from the moment I'd joined the club.

'Here come the judges. Just remember, even if you don't know what you're talking about, sound confident and fake it. The subject in question today is called Daisy. Don't be afraid to get up close, she's mostly harmless. Emma Parkinson ended up in hospital with a broken nose and two cracked front teeth last year, but I'm sure that was a freak occurrence. Good luck,' she breezed, shoving me through the stable door. I stumbled and landed face first in a pile of straw on the floor, narrowly missing a very wet and sloppy cow pat. Everyone behind me burst out laughing, Ruth's witchy cackle the loudest of them all. I hated her with a passion.

'Paige, are you ok?' came a deep and very sexy voice. Alec. *Great! Way to make a good impression, Paige,* I scolded myself, pushing up and sitting back on my heels with my back to him. I picked up my clipboard and pen and pretended to scribble on my paper.

'I'm fine, thank you, just checking Daisy's feet, and I'm pleased to report that they're hoofilicious. Does she have a pedicure? Are there people who do pedicures for farm animals? Because that pedicurist deserves an award for these alone. I wonder what you'd call yourself if you ran that business? Cowabunga, Trottertasic, Moovellous, or maybe …'

'Did you hit your head?' he interrupted. 'You seem to be rambling.'

'I'm good,' I replied, trying to stand up without looking at him. Nerves got the better of me every single time I was in his presence and I'd babble ten to the dozen, often about rubbish. No way did I want him to see me red-faced. He grabbed my elbow and helped me to my feet, then spun me around. I gulped as I looked up into his blue eyes, which were twinkling with merriment, and felt my legs turning to jelly. He ran his eyes over my face and body, probably checking for damage. He was a good four inches taller than me, which just made him seem all the more masculine. What I wouldn't give to be wearing a pair of my sexy heels and a pretty dress right now, instead of this blinking outfit.

'You look good, very good in fact,' he replied, the corners of his lips lifting into a sexy smile that showed off his symmetrical dimples. I blinked a few times. Was he flirting with me? 'Here, put on these protective safety glasses.'

'Glasses? You don't expect me to milk her, do you?' I looked up at him confused, and he shook his head and laughed.

'Right,' interrupted an older gentleman wearing an outfit similar to mine. 'Are we ready to begin?'

'Are you ready, Paige?' Alec asked in a serious tone. I nearly swooned at that simple question. *So ready*, I wanted to reply, imagining he was here to collect me for a date. I just nodded, knowing my cheeks were colouring up. 'Good luck, I'll be watching,' he whispered. He winked and went to stand outside, locking the lower part of the stable door and placing his elbows on it as Ruth went to stand next to him and did the same. I bristled when I saw her shoulder bump him, laugh, and tuck her hair behind her ear. *He's mine*, I wanted to shout, but I had more chance of Daisy talking me through the finer points of her rump than Alec ever asking me out. I put on the ridiculous glasses, sighed, and turned around to face my audience of three judges, four if you counted Daisy, who was chewing on some hay and watching me with her moist, large brown eyes. I had a feeling she was inverting the task, and I was actually here for a judging of humans by her.

'Right, Miss Taylor, ready when you are,' nodded the eldest judge in the group.

As I'd just joined young farmers club a few months ago, the only event left for me to partake in at this year's show was stock judging. To be honest, I'd been hoping for photography, given it seemed to be Alec's passion. The extent of my knowledge of cows was the beef aisle in our local supermarket. I'd only been told by Ruth on Thursday night that this was what I was being entered for. Evil … *cow*. I said a silent apology in my head to Daisy for tarring her with Ruth's brush, then went to stand in front of her and took a deep breath. I cocked my head as I studied her, sucking on the end of my pen in an attempt to look sexily studious.

'Wrong end, Paige,' Alec called.

'I'm supposed to start at her bottom?' I asked, looking over at him in surprise. I'd been up most of the night, cramming on the notes he'd handed to me after Thursday's meeting, and I was fairly convinced that I was supposed to start at her head. Everyone, including the judges, tried to hide their laughter.

'Wrong end of the pen, you have blue ink all over your lips and tongue,' he indicated with his finger.

'No, seriously?' I groaned, reaching up to rub my mouth with my fingers. I coated them in wet ink too and quickly wiped them on my white jacket, making even more of a mess.

'Miss Taylor, you're on a two minute time limit here,' announced one of the judges, checking his stopwatch. Great, just great. As if being humiliated by my lack of cow knowledge wasn't bad enough, I was now covered in blue ink with Alec and Ruth watching. I saw Poppie give me a thumbs up of encouragement as she and the rest of the onlookers peered through the wooden slats covering the two window apertures. I took another deep, and hopefully calming, breath and turned to face Daisy again. I scribbled some notes, trying to remember the pointers from the cards that Alec had given me, and walked down her flank to her rear, writing as much as I could remember about what a nice cow should look like, regardless of whether Daisy fit the dairy cow bill. I made it around to her rear end, giving it a gentle squeeze and ignoring Poppie's fit of giggles that I could hear in the background. I was doing this for Alec, I wanted to make a good impression. 'Time's up,' called the judge. 'Please give us your verdict.'

'Thank you,' I nodded, feeling a sea of nerves swirling in my stomach. My mind had gone blank. I looked down at my notes, but it was like I'd written them in a foreign language. 'Well, I'm judging Daisy on her suitability to be a dairy cow. She has a very pretty name, very fitting for a dairy cow. A name like Gertrude, Henrietta, or Millicent wouldn't be too far off the mark either. Or maybe a Georgia or Layla. Now a Bob, Gavin, or Bill just wouldn't do, far too masculine, which brings me to a *very* crucial point when it comes to dairy cow stock judging … a very crucial point indeed,' I nodded as I gestured emphatically with my leaking pen. I was losing it. Was I seriously talking about cow names? 'Man cows can't be milked, they don't have these squeezable boobs here.' I pointed to Daisy's udders, as I almost did a shudder of shame to realise I'd just called them boobs. *Think Paige, think*, I ordered myself, desperately racking my brain to get back on track. 'Or udders as they are commonly known in the … cowiverse. That would be the first thing that I'd consider, is this specimen of cow fit for purpose?'

'Excellent point,' called Poppie with a clap, trying to give me some encouragement. I saw Ruth rolling her eyes, and Alec just grinned as he chewed on the end of a piece of straw. Great, I was making a complete tit of myself. The first task he'd entrusted me with and I was blowing it. If I stood any chance of him seeing me as anything but a silly, pretty little girl, I needed to focus. I looked back down at my notes, thankful they were in English again.

'She has beautiful bright eyes, with lashes to die for. Mascara companies really ought to check her out for tips. She has a long feminine head and broad nose, a level top line, and very shapely neck and shoulders,' I announced firmly, some of my confidence returning as I remembered some of my crib card notes. 'Her udders are long and even, with a broad girth, giving a great handful to squeeze. They're a lovely pink colour with a prominent vein. I'd imagine they squirt quite nicely once they've been pulled for a while.' O my God! It sounded like I was talking about penises. I ignored the sniggers that came from my audience, this was serious stuff. I was on a roll now. 'She has very supple skin, I'm not sure if anyone rubs lotion on her, but if they do, they should keep doing it as she's as soft as a baby's bottom. Not that I go around touching baby's bottoms, I might add, I don't, it's just that …'

'Back on point please, Miss Taylor,' coughed the judge.

'Daisy has nice dairy triangles, not *Laughing Cow* cheese triangles you understand, rather the angles of her length and width. She has a very nice broad and meaty arse … shit, sorry, rump, not arse,' I stammered, looking over at Alec for reassurance. I was making a complete pig's ear of this, or cow's arse of it rather. He just gave me a lopsided smile and ran a hand through his hair. I stood for a moment staring at him, mesmerised by how attractive he was.

'The cow's arse,' called Poppie, rousing me from my daze.

'Sorry, yes, a very nice ar … rump. In conclusion, I'd say that Daisy was a very fine specimen of dairy cow indeed. I'd have no hesitation in recommending her to anyone that likes milk, or products of a milk persuasion. Best to be avoided by anyone with a lactose intolerance, a fake disclaimer is no one's friend.' I clutched my clipboard to my chest, wanting to die of embarrassment. Seconds later, there was the swoosh of a tail across my face and the loudest fart I'd ever heard in my life, as Daisy had a bottom explosion, showering me from head to toe in hot, wet, greenish-brown and udderly stinky, prize dairy cow poo.

'Holy shit,' screeched Poppie, unable to contain her laughter, and everyone else seemingly joined in as I stood there mortified, dripping in it. The fact that luckily my mouth had been closed and my eyes were covered in protective glasses was little consolation. So much for a good impression.

I stood in the middle of the yard, fully clothed with my new cow shit accessories, as crowds of onlookers gathered to watch while I was hosed down with freezing cold water by a far too gleeful Ruth. Poppie just grimaced at me as I stood there shivering and dripping when Ruth was finally done.

'Come with me,' Alec ordered, offering me his hand as he appeared at my side with a bundle of stuff cradled in his one arm.

'I'm wet and shitty,' I cringed, beyond mortified. 'I look and smell awful.'

'I've seen and smelled worse over the years. Daisy's known for being a bit of a blaster, you're lucky she'd been on a pre-show diet or you'd have been covered in a hell of a lot more. I'm surprised Ruth didn't warn you. Come on,' he repeated, grabbing my wet hand. Ruth gave me another of her glares, while Poppie gave me a wink and put a hand to her brow, faking a swoon. I knew she'd understand once she saw him. No one could fail to find him attractive. I could feel my cheeks going red as Alec tugged me back towards Daisy's stall, but all I could think about was that he was holding my hand. I couldn't stop the inane grin from spreading across my face. It felt so natural, like mine had been made to fit his. Now if only he'd part my fingers with his own, then weave them between, it would be the best day ever, shit shower aside. He led me back into the stall and pushed the lower and upper door to, giving us some privacy. 'Here, get undressed and put these on,' he offered, letting go of my hand. 'It's just a pair of my gym track pants that I was going to wear later and my gym towel for you to dry your hair with.'

'That's really kind,' I whispered with my head down, too embarrassed to make eye contact. He tucked his fingers under my chin and forced me to look up at him. He took the corner of the grey towel and gently swept it over my cheeks and under my eyes, probably removing the remains of my streaked mascara and eyeliner, as he held my gaze. I wanted to look away, to break the intensity of it, but I couldn't. I could stare into those gorgeous electric blue pools forever. My heart skipped a few beats as he smiled down at me. *Kiss me,* my subconscious was screaming. I had it so bad for this boy. I'd never been interested in boys before, until one of our friends showed me some pictures of the young farmers' group she was in and I spotted him. It hadn't taken much persuasion for me to enrol immediately and fawn over him for the last couple of months.

'There, that's better. You're even prettier without all of that black. Your eyes stand out even more now.' This time I knew I blushed. Alec Wright thought I was pretty.

'I don't ... I don't have a clean top,' I stuttered. He set the towel on a clean bale of straw, his track pants on top, then started unbuttoning his shirt. 'What ... what are you doing?'

'I'm wearing a t-shirt under here. If you don't mind that it's been worn, it's yours until I next see you. Hurry up and get out of those wet clothes, you'll catch a cold,' he ordered.

'Turn around then,' I said, too shy for him to see me in my underwear. First off, I was in virginal white, so not sexy like black, red, or hot pink. He looked like he was experienced, and experienced men would want sexy. Secondly, I wasn't your classic girl from the magazines. I had full breasts, hips, and a curvaceous backside with a small waist. Mum always compared my figure to Marilyn Monroe's, which would have been fine if I'd been born in that era, but not now, when everyone was under pressure to be thin.

'Honestly, Paige, it's no different to me seeing you at the swimming pool in a bikini and I've seen you there plenty of times,' he retorted, tossing his shirt onto the bale. My mouth opened and closed, nothing coming out. He'd seen me at the swimming pool? Why had I never seen him? There's no way I'd have missed him, let alone in a small pair of swimming trunks, dripping wet and … 'Unless you're completely commando under there,' he added with a grin, right before he ripped his t-shirt over his head.

I went into complete overload. I nearly fainted at his feet, I was sure I even drooled as I stared. My eyes were on stalks as I took in his buff body. However good he looked dressed was nothing compared to his bare torso. Ryan Gosling, move over! I quickly turned around and started unbuttoning my soaked white jacket. I peeled it off, then bent over to pull off my Hunter boots, tipping the water out from inside them as I tried to memorise how good his abs looked.

'I'm sure I've never seen you at the pool,' I said, desperate for something to break the tension I was feeling to have him standing so close to me, half naked.

'I'm not really much of a swimmer, but my friend Si is a lifeguard there. I meet him for a coffee from time to time. More often since he told me that there was a blue-eyed brunette stunner coming every Wednesday night who had curves to die for. I had to check her out and see if she was for real.'

'O, right,' I replied, my shoulders slumping at the thought of him ogling other women. I undid my jeans, that were already tight before they were soaked through, and started to shimmy them off. 'Was she for real?'

'Most definitely, I can see why he's got it bad for her.'

'Could see,' I corrected. 'Can see is present tense.'

'I meant can see, present tense. Your backside in those white knickers looks even more sexy than in those blue bikini ones,' he chuckled. I gasped and turned around, forgetting that my jeans were around my ankles. I screamed as I felt myself falling and before I knew what was happening, I was grabbing the waistband of his jeans to steady myself, forcing him to topple too, and we both landed in a heap on the straw. He burst out laughing as he lay on top of me, my hands trapped between our partially clothed bodies, my chest heaving.

'I'm so sorry,' I apologised. I wasn't sure where to look. His lips were so close to mine that I could feel the heat of his breath on them. His firm pecs and abs were pressed against my body, and the sight of his large, toned biceps was intoxicating. I felt lightheaded and giddy, but again I couldn't look away as he gazed down at me. It sounded twee in my head, but it was like I could feel an inexplicable connection to him.

'Paige,' he whispered gruffly.

'Yes?' I replied breathlessly. Was he going to kiss me? My heart and my breathing stopped, suspended in time as my lips pouted, ready for him.

'What the hell is going on?' I grimaced, my whole body sagging with defeat, as I heard Ruth's voice.

'Just giving Paige my t-shirt as she didn't have a top, I tripped and landed on her,' Alec replied. He flashed me an apologetic look as he shot off me and grabbed his shirt, leaving me in my underwear, with my jeans still around my feet.

'Right,' Ruth bit, her eyes narrowing as she looked down at me. 'If this is how she behaves, trying to steal other women's boyfriends, then I'm banning you from spending any time alone with her. As your girlfriend, I won't stand for it.'

'Girlfriend?' I uttered, feeling completely devastated. He was seeing *her?* I'd have been pretty naïve to think a guy as hot as him wouldn't have a girlfriend, but Ruth? She wasn't good enough for him.

'Since we were teenagers, so whatever ideas you have of tempting him away, dream on, Paige. Do you know how many girls join our club hoping to snare him? Not one of them have, so I'd suggest if that's the only reason you joined, quit now, because you'll never be able to compete with me.'

'Ruth, that's enough,' Alec snapped, quickly doing up his white shirt while I lay there, not sure how to get up gracefully, given my feet were still anchored by my wet jeans. I didn't want to humiliate myself in front of either of them any more than I already had today. 'It was nothing, an accident. Besides, Paige isn't like those other girls that only joined looking for a boyfriend. She's got more about her. I'll wait outside and make sure no one comes in,' he added, giving me another apologetic look. I gave him a smile and a wave, before wrapping one arm over my chest and covering my possibly see-through white knickers with my other hand. Could this day get any worse? On top of it all, I was *exactly* the kind of girl to moon over a hot guy. He didn't know me at all. He dragged Ruth out, but not before she tossed a smug look at me over her shoulder. I covered my eyes with my hands and sighed.

'O.M.G! What happened?' came Poppie's voice. I squinted through my fingers to see her standing with her hands on her hips looking down at me. Daisy was just chewing away on her hay in the corner, totally non-plussed by all the action in her stall today. I filled Poppie in as I tugged my jeans over my ankles and pulled off my wet socks, rubbing myself down with Alec's towel. 'He's seeing *her*?' she gasped. 'Ok, I shouldn't be judgemental, I've only just met them both, but *seriously*?! Chalk and cheese. He's hot and she's … not. Talk about the cow's arse, she has a face like a slapped one!'

'Stop it,' I giggled, undoing my ponytail and squeezing my hair to let the towel take away most of the moisture.

'Come on, she has. So, he's been checking you out at the pool? I'd say his time with her is limited. He's into you, big time.'

'He's not.' I rolled my eyes as I picked up his t-shirt and pulled it over my head. It was still warm and smelled of … *Alec.* I felt my stomach flutter as I breathed him in and reminded myself that this material had been touching his naked body.

'So is, I saw him when you turned into a blithering idiot talking about Daisy. He couldn't take his eyes off you and he didn't laugh when Daisy painted you brown, and let me tell you, that was quite some feat. It was seriously funny, if you weren't … well, you. He looked gutted for you. Paige and Alec sitting in a tree, k.i.s.s.i.n.g,' she sang, swinging her hips in time to the beat.

'Shut up!' I laughed. 'He's taken. I'll just have to make do with admiring him from afar.' I stood up and grabbed his running bottoms and pulled them on. I had to roll them at the waist to shorten them and leave them sitting on my hips, then turn up the bottoms to slip on my wet boots again. 'Let's go home. I've had enough humiliation for one day.'

'No way! You dragged me out of bed this morning with no designer shops in sight, so we're going to make the most of it. We're going to look around this countrified show and scoff some beef burgers, sorry Daisy no offence intended, then have an ice cream and see whether the country has any other stock worth investing in, the sort with a rump like Alec's,' she winked. I shook my head as I combed my fingers through my hair.

We dropped off my wet clothes into the back of my rusting old VW Polo and I groaned as I saw the state of myself in the wing mirror. No makeup, unless you counted my blue lips, my hair couldn't be less straight, and I was wearing a baggy white t-shirt and oversized grey bottoms.

'Please, I can't go out looking like this,' I pleaded.

'Paige, you're the most gorgeous girl I've ever seen and I'm not even into girls. You look stunning with or without makeup, whatever way you do your hair, and no clothes can disguise a sexy figure like that. Own it, embrace countryside chic. They don't get that ruddy-cheeked look by using makeup with SPF in it, do they?'

I gave in and we headed off towards the crowds and the main arena, Poppie laughing her head off as my feet squelching in my boots sounded like someone farting every time I took a step. We ended up having fun, checking out some of the local arts and crafts, sampling produce, and having a few rides at the small fun fair. Poppie ushered me towards the fenced-off arena when they announced the stock judging results were about to be awarded.

'Like I'll win after that disaster,' I laughed, shaking my head. I nearly fell over again, Poppie screaming with delight, when my name was announced as the winner of the dairy cow judging. I boot farted my way onto the stage, repeatedly telling everyone it *was* actually my boots and not me, and probably making matters worse. I shook the judges' hands and did my best attempt at a blue ink stained smile as a picture was taken of me receiving my certificate and rosette, with Poppie's whooping drowning out most of the uninterested, polite claps. I wasn't of interest, everyone was waiting for the tractor dancing event, which apparently was the highlight of the show, other than Alec Wright. I headed off the stage and was shown to the exit in the fencing, groaning to see Alec and Ruth standing there.

'Congratulations, first event and a win,' Alec beamed.

'Thank you, I'm quite shocked all things considered. Thanks for the loan of the clothes and towel, I'll bring them to the next meeting if that's ok?'

'I could come to yours to pick them up,' he suggested, then winced as Ruth elbowed him in the ribs. 'On second thought, the meeting would be great.'

'Ok, thanks. I'd better get going, my underwear is soaked. I mean … you know, because of the water, not because we had a roll in the hay, which we *totally* didn't … I'm going now and it's the boots farting, not me,' I garbled, quickly squeezing past them.

'Congratulations again,' Alec called with a chuckle.

'Hardly an achievement when she was the only competitor. No one ever wants to judge Daisy given her reputation,' Ruth scoffed. I stalled in my tracks, clutching my precious rosette and certificate to my chest. I'd had less than a minute to bask in the relative glory of my win. As if I hadn't been humiliated enough today as it was, I'd only won by default?

'Ruth, there was no need to tell her that,' I heard Alec bite. I felt some tears roll down my cheeks as I imagined the smug look on her face. I dumped my winnings in the nearest rubbish container and ran past a surprised Poppie, all the way back to my car.

I threw myself into the driver's seat and cried properly. No wonder I was single. I was a walking disaster, rubbish at everything.

'Paige,' sighed Poppie when she found me.

'I'm so stupid. Look what a fool I made of myself.'

'You didn't, you stayed dignified throughout. No shit,' she winked. I giggled and wiped my eyes.

'I deserve a *cow pat* on the back, don't I?' I sniffed.

'Pull the *udder* one, now *mooove* it,' she teased, dragging me out and giving me a tight squeeze.

'Did I look a complete *teet*?'

'No *bull*, I'm not going to lie, it was hilarious. I'm going to *milk it* forever,' she laughed, continuing our cow-themed banter. 'At least this Alec situation is all out in the open. It's Friesian now.'

'Friesian?'

'*Black and White*, a Friesian cow.'

'I thought they were Herefords,' I frowned, pulling back to look at her.

'Whatever, cowtato, cowtarto, point is you know he's unavailable now. Time to move on.'

'I guess,' I sighed, not sure I'd ever get over him. 'I'll have to go on Thursday to give him his clothes back.'

'Fine, but then you're quitting. You want to join a townies club, let's go wine-tasting or something,' she suggested with a smile.

'We're underage, for a few more months at least,' I reminded her. She sighed with a shake of her head.

'I can't wait until we're legal and I can ditch this fake ID.'

'You're a nightmare, Poppie,' I laughed. 'Thanks for cheering me up. Come on, let's go home, I need to try and get this ink off my face and lips. I've had enough crap today to last me a lifetime!'

'I've had another great idea for mixing with fit, toned guys when we start the new term,' she stated confidently.

'Why do I have a feeling that I may live to regret it?' I grinned, sliding into the driver's seat and taking a not-so-subtle inhalation of Alec's t-shirt before Poppie jumped in and slammed the door. She rolled her eyes when she caught me.

'He was hot,' she confirmed as I started the car.

'Tell me about it,' I sighed.

Stick in the Mud

May

'You have got to be kidding me,' I exclaimed, digging in my heels as Poppie tugged me towards the canoe club's hut in the college grounds. For someone smaller than me, she had alarmingly powerful strength.

'What?' she protested.

'Canoeing?'

'Fit men,' she offered with an unapologetic shrug and a wink over her shoulder.

'You already have one,' I reminded her, struggling to stop my progress towards the rickety, rusting, corrugated metal shack the club called home. Poppie, unwilling to concede defeat, moved behind me and started pushing me towards the red wooden door.

'But you don't. Don't be such a stick in the mud. I need to make you forget all about Alec Wright, it's been almost a year. We need to get you back on the horse.'

'I was never actually on the horse, Poppie. I never rode him. We never even made it out of the stable.'

'So that makes it even easier for you to get on the saddle with another guy, doesn't it? Don't argue with me. This will be fun,' she muttered, with about as much enthusiasm as I was feeling right now.

'Right, like body building first term, then computer programming the second.'

'You met lots of men, the aim of the game.'

'Not men I fancied. Please, it's cold. You could already hang your coat on my nipples and I haven't even got in the river yet,' I moaned, really not in the mood. The only water I liked being around was a hot shower, warm pool, or an exotic clear ocean with a sandy beach and palm trees. A cold and murky river, not so much.

'You could hang my entire summer wardrobe on your nipples even when it's scorching hot, that's how big they are,' she retorted. 'People see them coming into a room about a minute before you arrive.'

'My bus is at quarter to six,' I reminded her, as she shoved me into the inner porch.

'And this finishes at quarter past five, you have loads of time to get to the bus station. Honestly, anyone would think I was torturing you,' she huffed, putting her hands on her hips and blocking my escape.

'You are!'

'You won't be saying that when you see that James McCologh's a member.' She raised an evil eyebrow as I groaned. James was the only guy in sixth form that I found even remotely attractive, but my head was still full of Alec and of what I'd seen in his eyes when he'd been lying on top of me in Daisy's stall. We had a connection, but I had to let it go, he was seeing Ruth. 'Not just a member either, he's the *captain*,' she overemphasized, with a *so there* nod of her head. Like the distinction really mattered to me.

'Fine, but I'm telling you, if there's no wetsuits, I'm out of here,' I warned her as she opened the door.

'Wetsuits? You'll be in a canoe, not snorkelling for buried treasure at the bottom of the River Severn.'

'We'll be in a canoe,' I corrected her.

'Forget it, there's no way I'm getting in one of those tiny floating death traps,' she laughed, pushing me inside. 'I'll be waiting on the bank, watching. Good luck.'

'I hate you,' I muttered under my breath, then sighed as I turned to face the room of expectant faces, all doing up their bright orange life jackets. I was the only girl, it was all guys. What was Poppie thinking?

'Hi, Paige,' James grinned, stepping forward with a vest for me dangling from his hand.

'Hi, James.' I gave him a shy smile and tucked my hair behind my ears. He was quite cute, with his mop of dark hair and cheeky smile, but in all honesty, I just wanted to focus on my last year of studies. There was a lot riding on my exam results and I really didn't want to jeopardise everything for a guy that didn't make me shake at the thought of seeing him, that didn't make my hands tremble or my mouth go dry. Nice as James was, it wasn't happening, but I was going to look so stupid if I made an excuse to back out, now that I was standing here.

'Let me help you with your jacket and we'll head down to the river and run through the basics.'

'Ok,' I nodded, turning around to allow him to slip it over my arms. Poppie wiggled her eyebrows at me as she leaned on the doorframe, watching. I stuck my tongue out at her and spun around as James fiddled with the straps, easily doing up the one around my waist. He frowned in concentration as he tried to secure the one around my chest, but the gap was too big. Everyone started chuckling as he tugged harder and harder, jerking me back and forth like a rag doll as he desperately tried to do them up.

'God, I'm sorry, but they don't make life jackets for women with …' He grimaced and mimicked squeezing with both of his hands as he stared at my breasts, making my cheeks colour up.

'Maybe it's like doing up a pair of tight jeans. Lie her down, straddle her, and get her to breathe in,' offered Poppie behind me. I flung her a scowl over my left shoulder.

'I'm game if you are?' James confirmed, with an obvious twinkle in his eye. I gasped when I saw an obvious reaction in his jeans as well.

'I'm fine, thank you very much,' I retorted, folding my arms across my chest, given the entire club were now appraising it. 'It's done up at the waist and it's not like I need a lifejacket, since I clearly have my own set of buoyancy aids.'

Poppie and I were put in charge of carrying the oars while the eleven guys carried the six canoes down the steps and across the road that ran along the edge of the river. It was really pretty, with oak trees and weeping willows running along its edge, as well as all of the flower baskets that were left over from the annual Shrewsbury Flower Show. No amount of prettiness, however, took away from the dark green water of the river. If Poppie's aim was to get me to mix with men, couldn't she have enrolled me in the photography class? Or even mechanics, what girl didn't like a rough and ready, hands-on guy in a pair of ripped denim jeans, grease-stained white t-shirt, with oil streaks on his face and biceps? Actually, scratch that, *this* girl wouldn't like that. Oil and pretty clothes meshed worse than oil and water. I looked down at my outfit and sighed. Poppie had told me to dress warmly this morning as she had a surprise, but she hadn't warned me what I'd be doing. I had on my favourite pair of grey Uggs, black skinny jeans, and a grey cashmere jumper. If I got wet, I was going to kill her. She grinned at me as she plonked herself on a bench at the top of the steep embankment, while I looked down towards the water, wondering where the official steps were. All I could see were some rudimentary steps that appeared to have been trampled into the grass and mud bank.

'Here, take my hand,' James offered as he stood below me, the rest of the guys already down there and getting into the canoes. 'Just go slowly, you'll be fine.'

'Thanks.' I took his hand and went one step at a time, making sure I didn't slip. Now if it had been Alec's hand I'd been holding, I'd have been so distracted that I'd have shot down that bank faster than a dog on skis. I looked up at Poppie as I made it down to the small wooden floating platform. She gave me a thumbs up and wrapped her arms around herself, tucking her hands into her armpits to keep warm. I watched, alarmed, as James got into the small two-man canoe and it started rocking.

'Sit on the platform and slide yourself in slowly, I'll hold us steady.' He gave me a reassuring smile.

I bit my lip and looked around. Everyone was watching me expectantly, it wasn't like I could back out now. I did as I was told, letting out a triumphant screech as I made it into the canoe without overbalancing us and ending up in the water. It was actually quite fun as he taught me how to paddle, then turn the canoe to face the other way. Some of the other guys were really experienced and shot off up the river, but James said for my first time, he wanted to keep me away from the faster moving water. We went for a gentle paddle, then he got me to turn on my own and head back as the rest of the team caught up with us on their way back. I gripped the edges of the boat as it rocked when James jumped out. He offered me his hand again and I carefully stood up, putting one foot on the jetty. I screamed as the canoe lurched dangerously under my other foot and I felt myself falling backwards. James yanked hard on my hand, catapulting me forwards against his chest.

I blinked hard as he gazed at me. There was barely room for a piece of paper between our lips as he held me tightly, and his breathing seemed to quicken. The second his hands slid down to squeeze my backside, I quickly pushed on his chest with my palms. I didn't want anyone kissing me. It seemed ridiculous, but ever since I'd seen that picture of Alec, I'd imagined he was going to be the first man to kiss me. I was saving myself for him, even though I knew it was never going to happen. My shove didn't seem to have much of an effect, he didn't let me go as his friends hauled the canoe from the water. He dipped his head, his lips parting as he went to kiss me, so I reacted with lightening speed and slapped him. I wasn't sure which of us was more surprised at my reaction, but the second he let me go to rub his red cheek, I lost my balance. My arms flailed wildly as I began tipping backwards. Seconds later, with an almighty splash and a loud shriek, I landed in the water. It was freezing and it stunk of rotten foliage. I could feel it starting to saturate my woollen boots and make my jeans tighten around my legs, but with this lifejacket on, my top half was bobbing above the waterline. I could hear Poppie's screeches of laughter from up on the bank as I tried to paddle my way back to the platform.

'Grab my hands,' James ordered. I didn't argue, too desperate to get out of this stinking cold water, but I grimaced when I saw the outline of my hand glowing like a Belisha beacon on his face.

'Sorry for slapping you,' I spluttered, spitting my wet hair out of my mouth as he hauled me out of the river and onto my front on the platform. 'You kind of took me by surprise.'

'Yeah, not my most subtle of moves,' he replied. I rolled onto my back and quickly undid the strap around my waist, then sat up and shrugged off the jacket. I groaned as I looked down, my boots were ruined. I pulled them off and tipped them upside down, draining them before trying to wring them out.

'You ok, Paige?' called Poppie, trying to sound concerned and failing miserably between her giggles.

'Just peachy, thanks,' I yelled. I stood up and shook each leg, but the only way these jeans were getting dry was once I got them off, washed, and in the tumble dryer. The lower half of my jumper was sodden and now reached down to my knees with the weight of the water. I squeezed the bottom of my hair, which was also wet, and pulled out a load of green slime, shuddering as I flicked it back into the river, then wiped my hands on my calves. I turned around to look up the bank. Everyone else had made it up, canoes and all, it was just James and me still down here.

'After you,' he suggested with a flick of his hand.

'No, after you,' I smiled. Pervert. He only wanted to be behind to see my backside in my jeans.

'I insist.'

'I insist harder,' I replied stubbornly, thinking it might be quite nice to check out his backside and thighs as he climbed ahead of me.

'Are you one of these modern women who hate chivalry?'

'Not at all, but my legs feel a little shaky after my fall. I'd be more comfortable if you went first.'

He sighed and virtually jogged up the bank. I grabbed a soggy boot in each hand, padded barefoot over the wooden slats, and carefully started to make my way up. My wet foot slipped in a patch of mud, so I put my boots on my hands and carried on up using them for grip.

'Come on, Paige, you can do it,' Poppie called. I looked up to roll my eyes at her, and this time both feet shot out from under me. I thudded down onto my stomach with an "oomph", then rapidly slid feet first, bouncing down the makeshift steps back to the platform and getting a face full of mud and grass on my way down. I lay there for a moment, winded by the journey. 'Shit, are you ok?' Poppie yelled, actually sounding concerned this time.

'Best day ever,' I yelled back, spitting out a clump of grass. I could feel slime all over my face, and I dreaded to think what I must look like. I rolled onto my back, lifting my hand to wipe the mud off my face, but totally forgot that I had my boots on my hands and smacked myself in the face. 'Owwww,' I moaned, shaking them off. I heard someone scrambling down the bank and tipped my head back to see James approaching, his eyes on stalks.

'Bra,' shouted Poppie.

'What?'

'Your bra's on display.'

'Great, just great,' I groaned, reaching up to find my jumper ruched up under my chin. I desperately scrabbled to roll it back down as I sat up.

'Are you ok?' James panted, coming to crouch next to me.

'I'm cold, soaking, stinky, muddy, and I hit myself in the face,' I pouted, my shoulders slumping. 'I think it's going to bruise.'

'I wouldn't worry about anyone noticing, you can barely see your face for all of the mud on it. Can you stand up?'

'I think so,' I nodded. I winced as I straightened up, I was going to ache all over tomorrow.

'Right, this time I'm not taking no for an answer, you go first and I'll push you up. At least I can catch you if you fall again.'

'Thanks, that's really sweet of you.' I felt bad for slapping him, he'd been nothing but nice to me from the moment I entered that stupid hut. I was so going to get Poppie back for this. I didn't object when he planted his hands on my wet bottom to help give me a shove over the slippery patch that made me tumble last time, and I eventually made it to the top. Poppie's face said it all as she stood up and ran her eyes over me. This was way, way worse than my encounter with Daisy the flatulent cow.

'We'd better get you back to the hut. We have a shower where you can clean up, but I'm not sure what you're going to wear after,' James said apologetically as he joined me.

'No time, bus,' Poppie reminded me, tapping her watch.

'I can't get on the bus like this. My face is starting to tighten from this mud pack already.'

'How else are you going to get home? No taxi driver's going to pick you up. You stink and you're covered in crap.'

'God damn it.' I turned around to face James. 'Thanks for helping. Again, I'm really sorry I slapped you.'

'I was pushy, I'll ask you on a date first, next time I see you. Will you come on Thursday for the next meeting?' he asked, looking hopeful.

'I don't think so, not after this disaster, but I had fun while we were on the water.'

'Paige, we've got to fly,' Poppie urged.

'See you around, James.' I did my best attempt at a smile, given how stiff my face was feeling. Maybe this was how people felt after Botox, tight and expressionless. I put both of my boots in one hand and reached for Poppie's hand with my other as I approached her.

'No way,' she laughed. 'Who knows what you have all over you.'

'Do I look really bad?'

'I'd be more worried about the smell. I'm going to walk ahead, follow me but keep your eyes on the pavement. The last thing we need is you treading in a pile of dog shit.'

If I thought the walk along the main road to the bus station, with cars hooting and people laughing as they passed, was mortifying, it was nothing compared to the bus driver's reaction when Poppie gave me my bag and I flashed him my laminated season ticket. I was only allowed on after he'd been to the drivers' staff room and returned with two black bin bags. I thought they were for me to sit on, but no. He cut a hole for my head and arms and made me wear one over my jumper, then I had to stand in the other and hop onto the bus and up to the hastily vacated disabled seat, like I was a participant in a sack race. The whole bus was shaking with everyone trying to stifle their laughter and failing miserably.

'Call me later?' Poppie held her thumb and little finger up to her ear as she stood outside, grinning at me through the window. I smiled, then grimaced as the mud on my face cracked and started flaking off onto my bin bag. 'I think you ought to try again on Thursday, he was super sweet with you.'

'Forget it,' I called over the sound of the bus engine starting up.

'Stick in the mud!' Poppie shouted, losing her battle to contain her laughter. She reached up to wipe tears from her eyes. I shook my head and rolled my eyes. The only consolation I had was at least Alec hadn't witnessed that.

'Wait, wait,' someone yelled, banging on the bus door as the driver started to pull away. He stopped and opened the doors. I groaned. It was only Ruth, Alec's girlfriend. My day couldn't possibly get any worse. I put my head down, hoping to get away unnoticed, but luck was most definitely not on my side today. 'Paige Taylor. Well, well, well. Looking as delightful as the last time I saw you,' she scoffed. I lifted my head to glare at her and it took all of my self-restraint not to leap up and slap her when she took a picture of me with her mobile phone.

'This all washes off, Ruth, whereas you're stuck with that nasty personality and a sour face that looks like you've sucked too many lemons.'

'Sling as many insults as you like, but it doesn't change the fact that I have the one thing you want. Alec Wright. Enjoy dreaming about him. If seeing you make a fool of yourself at the show wasn't bad enough, seeing the picture of you looking like this will squash any interest he might have had in you.'

'Why are you so nasty?' I uttered.

'Sorry, I really can't stand to be around you for a second longer. You smelled better when you were covered in Daisy's poo,' she laughed, tossing her hair over her shoulder and stalking up the aisle, leaving me frustrated. I'd really love five minutes alone with her, one on one. I hated her with a passion. I sighed as I looked out of the window, trying to imagine what Alec would think of me once she showed him that picture. But something sparked in my brain. "Any interest he might have had in you," Ruth had just said. Alec Wright had been interested in me. Even if he wasn't now, especially after that disaster of a stock judging competition and now this picture of me, he had been. That was enough to put a small smile back on my face.

Cinderella

July ~ Friday

'I'm so nervous,' I confessed to Poppie as we applied our lip-gloss and checked our reflections in the mirror. It was our farewell ball at sixth form, our last official college experience before we applied to our preferred universities to start in September.

'I'll bet,' she grinned, twirling to check out her gold strapless prom dress. She looked gorgeous and relaxed, but she had no reason to be nervous, not when her boyfriend Reece was accompanying her.

Me on the other hand, I felt giddy with nerves. When Poppie had asked to come and get ready with me, I hadn't thought twice about it. We often did that before a night out, but this time she had an ulterior motive. One I nearly kissed her for when she revealed it. It seemed that Alec had broken up with Ruth in May and had contacted Poppie, through our old friend Bella who was still in YFC, to arrange to surprise me by taking me to the ball tonight. I hadn't seen him since that embarrassing incident at the summer show a year ago. I'd been so ashamed that I'd given his towel and clothes to Bella to return to him at the next meeting, along with my letter of resignation. She'd said he'd been gutted, I thought she was just being nice. I'd even avoided going swimming, just in case I saw him there. I'd not dated at all. I'd been asked out by a few guys, one of those being James, but none of them compared to Alec. I was still infatuated with him, and until I met someone who made my hands shake and stomach feel as if a million butterflies had been set loose, like he had, I didn't want to settle.

'What if he doesn't turn up? I can't go to the ball on my own.'

'Why wouldn't he turn up? He went to a lot of trouble to arrange this without you knowing. I told you last year that he was into you. Besides, you've turned down every other guy that asked you, you'd have been going alone anyway,' Poppie reminded me.

'I was planning on not going at all, but not letting you know until the last minute. I just agreed to go on my own to get you off my back.'

'You minx,' she objected, pulling a pout.

'Like it would ruin your night if I didn't go,' I laughed. 'You only have eyes for Reece.'

'Speaking of, I think he's here,' she replied, shooting over to the window to look out at the drive. 'O wait! Paige, you'd better be ready, it's your Prince Charming that's here and *damn,* does he look fine in a tuxedo.'

'O God, O God, O God,' I moaned, checking myself in the mirror and smoothing my hand over the floaty material of my dress. I'd gone for a jewelled bodice with sweetheart neckline and a cerulean taffeta ankle-length skirt, which Mum had insisted set off my blue eyes. A pair of strappy silver high heels and a small silver glitter clutch complimented my outfit, and I'd done my hair in an elegant loose chignon. Long dark lashes, a hint of silver eye shadow, rosy cheeks, and clear-glossed lips, and my look was complete. Poppie had told me that I looked like a princess. I felt like one, even without Alec accompanying me. But I was determined that there were going to be no disasters tonight. If Ruth had shown him that picture of me coated in mud, then the last two times he'd seen me, I'd looked totally bedraggled. Tonight had to be perfect. There was a knock at the bedroom door and Mum stuck her head around it.

'Your date's here and if you're not ready, I'll go with him. He's gorgeous.'

'I know,' I blushed, secretly pleased he'd obviously passed her stringent inspection. 'And I'm ready, but Reece isn't here yet. I can't go without Poppie.'

'You can and you will. He's always late, go with Alec and I'll see you there,' Poppie urged, her smile threatening to crack her face. She clapped her hands and giggled. 'Don't give him a chance to change his mind. My best friend finally has a boyfriend. I've waited years for a moment like this.'

'You have?' I laughed, kissing her cheek. 'He's not my boyfriend yet, we may not even get on.'

'Please,' she scoffed. 'You're one of the easiest people ever to get on with. See you in a while.'

'You look beautiful, darling,' Mum smiled, linking arms with me as she herded me out of my bedroom.

'Thank you, I just love my dress,' I beamed, so touched that my parents had treated me to it.

'You'd look beautiful in a sack, I meant your face. You're glowing. You really like this boy, don't you?'

'I do,' I nodded, feeling a frisson of excitement run through me.

'He's older than you,' she stated. I detected an element of concern in her voice.

'Only by four years.'

'Do we need to have the birds and the bees talk before I hand you over to him?' She raised her immaculately groomed eyebrows at me as we stood at the top of the stairs.

'Mum,' I moaned. We never discussed boys or sex. She didn't even know that I'd never kissed a boy, let alone anything else.

'Well?'

'No. I know all about sex, thanks to school and Poppie, but I've never slept with a boy and I have no intention of doing it tonight either. Besides, he's not like that. He's too nice to pressure me.'

'I hope so. If he respects you, he'll wait until you're ready.'

'Mum, I haven't even kissed him yet, sex is so not on my mind.' I was being honest, the thought of doing something wrong and putting him off me absolutely terrified me. Kissing though, that was a whole other matter. I couldn't wait to kiss him.

'Good. I know you're eighteen now, but you'll always be my baby,' she reminded me, kissing my temple.

She walked me to the front door, which was wide open. Dad was either talking to Alec or grilling him. Either way, I was too preoccupied drinking in my date to care. I'd challenge anyone to find a man better looking, and that was without a tuxedo to enhance the appeal. He was clean shaven, and his strong jawline and body looked even more masculine than when I'd last seen him. He'd left his blond hair in that surfer's unruly mess that I loved. What was even more breathtaking, if that were possible, was the look on his face as he ran his eyes from my blue painted toenails, up my dress, lingering for a second on my breasts, then up to look into my eyes. My breath hitched to see the expression on his face, and the way his tongue darted out over his soft and utterly kissable lips.

'Paige, you look stunning,' he greeted, pulling a hand from behind his back to produce a silver beaded bracelet with a blue corsage. My eyes widened in surprise as he waited for me to give him my hand so he could slip it on. 'I had a little help from your mum, as well as Poppie,' he smiled.

'Thank you,' I whispered, my normal voice failing me. My skin tingled when his fingers brushed my wrist and I felt my stomach flip.

'What time will you be bringing her home, Alec?' Dad asked, sounding like a strict headmaster.

'What time would you like me to bring her home, sir?' Alec replied. I saw Mum smile out of the corner of my eye. She liked him already, and that question and salutation would earn him some serious brownie points with Dad.

'How about midnight?'

'Dad,' I moaned, at the same time as Mum said, 'Richard!'

‘She’s eighteen, for goodness sake. She’s never given us any trouble, give her a little slack. Two a.m. the latest please, Paige,’ she warned.

‘Two?’ Dad spluttered, his eyes bulging with horror. I could virtually see all of the scenarios fathers feared would befall their virgin daughter flashing through his eyes.

‘Two,’ Mum said firmly, kissing my cheek and shoving me out of the door before Dad had another chance to object.

‘Thank you,’ I grinned. I turned and kissed a still-stunned Dad, then looked up at Alec. Even with my heels on, he was still slightly taller than me.

‘Shall we?’ he smiled, offering me his arm. I took it, trying to contain the ridiculous smile that was threatening to crack my face. He looked and smelled divine. I glanced up at him in surprise as he showed me to the passenger seat of a sleek-looking black car. ‘Toyota GR86. It’s new, I just got a really good job offer. We have a lot to catch up on,’ he advised as he opened the car door for me and helped me in, tucking in my dress before carefully closing the door. I watched him walk around the front of his car, waving goodbye to my parents who stood watching, then he undid the button on his black jacket before sliding into the driver’s seat.

‘I think you ought to start with why you’re here, I thought you were seeing Ruth?’ I asked in a rush as soon as he shut the door.

‘Nothing like easing into casual conversation,’ he laughed, starting the engine. ‘What happened to “Hello, nice to see you,” Paige?’

‘It is nice to see you, but I’m still confused. I only found out you were coming about forty minutes ago. Do you know where you’re going?’

‘I do,’ he nodded, flashing me a dazzling smile. I quickly looked out of the window to wave goodbye to Mum and Dad and Poppie, who’d joined them on the doorstep. I suddenly felt nervous. I was on my own with him. On a date. Paige Taylor, klutz of the year, was on a date with sex God, Alec Wright. ‘You really do look stunning,’ he added, sincerity saturating his voice.

‘Thank you so much,’ I blushed, turning to smile at him. ‘You look really handsome in that tuxedo. Not that you don’t look handsome all of the time, you do, you always have … not that I make a habit of comparing how handsome you look in various outfits, but … I’m going to stop talking. I’m doing that thing that I do. I babble when I’m nervous. Not that I’m nervous because you’re here, I’m not, honestly. God, Paige, shut up. See, I’m doing it already, that thing I do, babbling,’ I uttered, aghast with myself. He laughed as he pulled out onto the main road.

'I like that thing that you do and I especially like the idea that you find me appealing. I've been crazy about you ever since I met you.'

'You have?' I asked, my stomach doing that weird rolling thing again. It only ever happened around him. Did he just use the words "crazy about you?"

'Wasn't it obvious? I was so close to kissing you in Daisy's stable last year, which was so bad of me, I was with Ruth at the time.'

'And you're really not now? You may not have noticed, but she doesn't exactly like me.'

'She doesn't really like anyone, Paige. I didn't realise that she was so horrible to everyone else until that day. We'd been together so long, I guess I was blind to it. No one else interested me enough to make me see that I wasn't actually happy with her, until I met you. But then you vanished.'

'I was so humiliated,' I whispered, dropping my head to my chest. 'Everyone seeing that disaster of a competition, getting covered in cow poo, and then finding out I only won because no one else entered. I couldn't face seeing you again.'

'You still did really well and it only made me want to protect you when I saw you so upset.'

'So, what changed? I saw her in May and she said you were still together.'

'She did something that I found really appalling, so I broke it off right away,' he nodded, with a distasteful look on his face. I twisted in my seat to get a better look at him as he drove.

'What?'

'She posted a picture on Facebook with some nasty comments and got quite irate when I called her out on it. We had a blazing argument and I ended it there and then. I should have ended it earlier, when I knew I liked you, but you disappeared and I had to head back to university. After so many years with her, I guess I just thought better the devil you know and all that. I just can't believe I was with her for that long when she's so hateful.' He flashed me a look of sympathy before turning to face the road again.

'It was me, wasn't it? A picture of me on the bus after I fell in the river,' I sighed. I knew she'd show him, to put me down, but to publically broadcast it? That was really low.

'Yes,' he said quietly.

'You ended your relationship with her because she was mean to me?' I stared at him stunned. He was like some medieval knight in shining armour.

'In part, but also because she was mean full stop, that was just the catalyst for something I should have done a long time ago. Can we make an agreement that we don't talk about her for the rest of the night? It's not exactly first date etiquette to talk about the ex, is it?'

'First date?' I smiled at him shyly, my heart suddenly racing with excitement.

'Yes, ok?' He gave me another of his swoon worthy smiles, making me virtually melt into the cool leather of his passenger seat.

'Yes,' I whispered, astonished that I seemed to have acquired a boyfriend. Not just any boyfriend, the one guy I'd been dreaming about for the last year.

'Great, so tell me all about what you've been up to since I last saw you.'

The journey passed in a blur, and before I knew it, he'd pulled up in the car park of The Domville hotel and was opening my door. I took his hand as I stepped out, praying I hadn't just waffled all the way here and bored him to tears. That habit I had was really irritating and if I felt like that about it, God only knew how much it must annoy people on the receiving end. I gasped as he lifted a hand, palmed my cheek, and ran his thumb over my lower lip. Sparks of electricity ignited all of my nerve endings and sent a shiver skittering down my spine.

'You look like something out of a fairy tale, Cinderella at the ball, but even better. Do you have any idea how beautiful you are?' he murmured, holding my gaze. I swallowed a lump in my throat, my heart soaring at his words.

'Does that make you my Prince Charming?' I asked, a noticeable tremble in my voice.

'I guess it does,' he smiled, slowly lowering his face towards mine. My mouth went dry as I tried to remember all of Poppie's tips for kissing over the years. She told me no guy wanted a girl with a mouth as wide as a guppy, who sucked his tongue with the force of a Dyson vacuum cleaner first time, or licked him to death like an overeager puppy. She'd told me to just purse my lips and let him lead and take control. *Don't slobber, don't slobber, don't slobber,* I chanted to myself as he got closer and closer. Not that it would be an issue, as right now my mouth was drier than a centenarian nun's vagina. My knees nearly gave way as he inched ever nearer, and I quickly reached up to clasp his firm biceps. I was sure that he could hear the drumming of my heart on my ribcage, then the short gasp of surprise when he planted a tender kiss on my … *forehead?* What was that all about? 'Time to head in,' he advised, taking my hand, slightly redeeming himself by lacing his fingers between mine. I tried not to look disappointed as I nodded my consent.

We headed up in the lift, still holding hands and occasionally smiling at each other, then made our way to the ballroom, where we were signed in. The noise of music, chatter, and laughter was deafening. Alec made his way towards the bar, not letting go of my hand as we squeezed our way through the crowds. I recognised a lot of people, but Poppie and I tended to keep to ourselves, we'd never really socialised with many of our peers. Some of the girls from my group, that I saw every school morning for registration, gawped as they saw Alec. It made me stand a little taller, proud to think that of all the girls he could pick from, he'd chosen me. *He was crazy about me.*

'What can I get you to drink?' he asked as we made it to the polished oak bar.

'I'd love a water please.'

'Water? Don't you want a glass of wine or champagne?'

'I'm not really a drinker,' I shrugged, not wanting to confess that the mere whiff of alcohol usually rendered me to a giggling heap.

'Ok, water it is, but you have to at least have one glass of champagne with the meal to celebrate.'

'Celebrate what?'

'You've just finished all of your exams, that's a pretty big deal. I'd imagine you're thinking of going on to university?' He pulled up a stool and helped me up onto it, before clicking his fingers and getting the barman's attention. He placed an order for a glass of water and a glass of soda with lime for himself. At least I was going to be a cheap date. He turned his attention back to me, his face turning serious. 'What are you hoping to study and where are you looking at applying?'

'Poppie and I would like to do modern languages at Cambridge, if our results are good enough.'

'That's great,' he replied, the tension on his face easing immediately. 'If you get in there, it will make it easier for us to see each other. I was hoping you weren't going to be too far away from me in London.'

'London?'

'I just graduated from Leeds university, fingers crossed I'll achieve my BA honours degree in photography. My portfolio was so strong that I've already been offered a job in the fashion industry, training under the prolific photographer John Graves. It's an amazing opportunity. I'll be based in London primarily, but will get to travel the world with him on shoots.'

'A fashion photographer, that's amazing,' I stated sincerely, reaching out to touch his arm as I tried to hide the jealousy I felt at the thought of him around gorgeous, scantily clad models. I gratefully accepted my water as he handed it over, taking a few gulps to ease my dry mouth.

'Thanks, I'm pretty excited about it. I start next month, so I've got to get sorted with looking for somewhere to live. Have you ever considered taking up modelling?' he asked. I did a most unladylike snort of amusement, forgetting I had a mouthful of water, and ended up spraying him when I choked on it and two jets shot out of my nostrils as well as a geyser-like torrent from my lips.

'God, I'm so sorry,' I exclaimed, grabbing a tissue from my bag to wipe my face and then dabbing his jacket, absolutely mortified.

'Don't worry, it will dry, though I'm glad you didn't have a glass of red wine now,' he laughed. 'What was so funny about my question?'

'Me, a model?' I rolled my eyes as I sat back on my stool.

'Why not?' he frowned. 'You're tall, you have an amazing figure, and you're stunning. You'd have no trouble booking lingerie or swim shoot campaigns. You'd earn really good money, get to travel the world.'

'Please, I'm Paige calamity Taylor. You've seen me in action. I'm the girl who gets sprayed with cow poo, falls in rivers and gets coated in mud, and snorts water all over her date. I'm not model material.'

'Yes you are, Paige,' he responded seriously, reaching up to clasp my face and angle it up towards him. 'No one in this room holds a candle to you. You have the most exquisite bone structure, eyes I could drown in, and those lips … you have no idea how badly I want to kiss those lips of yours.'

'Do it,' I breathed, desperate to experience it, to know if it would be as good as I was imagining. He leaned in and kissed the corner of my mouth with a chuckle.

'Not now, not here,' he whispered in my ear.

'Does my breath smell? I had a tuna sandwich for lunch as I had no idea I'd be seeing you. If I did, I'd have avoided fish altogether. Is that why you don't want to kiss me, I have fishy breath?' I gabbled. I was going to have words with Mum. How could she let me eat fish, knowing I had a date due to arrive?

'Your breath doesn't smell, Paige, and you've no idea how hard it is for me to resist kissing you, but I'm going to.'

'Why?' I pouted, beyond impatient to pop my kissing cherry with the man of my dreams. He chuckled and tugged on my lower lip with this finger and thumb.

'When I kiss you the way I want to kiss you, the way I've *dreamed* of kissing you, I don't plan on coming up for air for a very long time. I'd prefer not to have an audience for that, ok?'

'Ok,' I squeaked, gripping the edges of the stool seat to prevent me from melting into an over aroused puddle on the floor.

'Trust me, I promise to make up for it later.' His tone just oozed sex. He was confident, masterful, and damn, he smelled so good.

'Paige!'

I looked around when I heard my name being called, and it took me a moment to pull myself together from Alec's promise and refocus my dazed eyes. I spotted Poppie and Reece heading over. I slid off my stool to hug her tightly and kissed Reece on the cheek. When I straightened up, I felt Alec slip his arm around my waist. Poppie winked at me, making me blush.

'Poppie, Alec. Alec, my best friend Poppie, and this is her boyfriend Reece,' I announced.

'Pleasure to meet you, Reece,' Alec advised, shaking his hand. 'I'm Alec, Paige's boyfriend.'

'Boyfriend?' I looked up at him, shocked. I thought we were just on a first date, see how it went kind of thing. I didn't think anyone used labels like that so soon. Especially when they hadn't even snogged.

'Yes,' he grinned. 'Ok?'

'Definitely ok,' Poppie laughed, answering for me when I couldn't find the words. He'd rendered me speechless for once. 'Though I have to repeat the best friend warning I gave you over the phone, Alec. Hurt her and I hurt you.'

'I have no intention of ever hurting her, Poppie,' he stated sincerely, curling his fingers around my waist and gently squeezing me closer to his side. 'And I believe I owe you a few drinks for helping me out with tonight's plan?'

'You sure do. Is a bottle of wine to take to the table pushing it?'

'How about we have a bottle of champagne?' he suggested, only to be met by Poppie's excited claps and a nod of approval from Reece.

'I love him already,' Poppie beamed at me.

I couldn't believe it was time to leave already. We'd had an amazing night. A delicious four course meal, coffee, and petit fours, and I'd even succumbed and had two glasses of champagne, leaving me feeling more than a little lightheaded. Poppie and Reece had made me cringe, and Alec laugh, with tales of some of my worst disasters. I'd kicked her under the table, worried she was going to put him off me. We'd danced too, and of course he was a great dancer. I doubted that there was anything that he did badly. But other than my unladylike nasal douching of his jacket, nothing untoward had happened, and yet he still hadn't kissed me. I fiddled with my fingers in my lap for the full journey home, neither of us saying a word. The tension in the car was palpable. All I could think about was the kiss. Would he do it when he pulled up on the drive? Or maybe as he showed me to the front door? Would I forget all of those kissing etiquette lessons that Poppie had given me and make him change his mind? It would be par for the course with me to have the shortest relationship in the history of the universe.

Or maybe he'd be about to kiss me and Dad would fling open the door and drag me inside. He was probably sitting there now, with a twelve bore shotgun on his lap, ready to take out the man who dared to defile his daughter. He'd probably been online, perusing all sorts of erotic sites that a man his age should never look at for fear of a heart attack, looking for a chastity belt for me until Alec asked for my hand in marriage. Marriage! Crikey, I hadn't even scribbled our names with a heart yet, or practiced my potential new signature, and I was thinking about marriage? Mrs. Paige Wright. It had a nice ring to it. A really nice ring. Rings! I wondered what sort of ring he'd buy. I had a feeling he'd be a classic sort of guy. A solitaire, probably square, and he'd definitely go down on one knee. He was so chivalrous. I could hear him saying my name now, as he kneeled there in front of me, clasping my hand, tears of happiness in his eyes.

'Paige, Paige. Is everything ok?'

'What, huh, what?' I asked, blinking and looking around. He wasn't on one knee proposing, we were parked on the drive and he was looking at me strangely. O God, please don't let me have said "Mrs. Paige Wright" out loud. I'd nearly made it through the whole evening with only one embarrassing moment.

'You zoned out there for a moment, are you ok?'

'Sorry, I'm fine, really fine. More than fine. I had an amazing evening and I'm so sorry about the snort. I don't usually snort like some kind of truffle pig. I don't know what came over me. It's just you of all people, suggesting I should be a model. You should be a model. You're way better looking than David Beckham, or David Gandy, in fact any David out there who models. Any model, by any name, and I haven't even seen your body, but I imagine it's pretty toned. Not that I mentally undress you with my eyes every time I see you, I mean obviously I've thought about what you might look like naked, but I'm not some obsessive pervert. God,' I groaned, covering my face with my hands. 'I'm doing it again.'

'Why are you so nervous?' he laughed, reaching over the centre console to pull my hands away.

'Because our date is over and you're probably going to kiss me.'

'Don't you want me to kiss you?' he asked, his voice low and husky as one of his hands reached up to clasp the back of my neck, drawing me closer to those perfect lips of his, until I could feel the heat of his breath caressing mine. My chest was heaving, I felt lightheaded, and my hands were trembling. I'd dreamed of this moment for so long, but now that it was here, I was completely terrified.

'So badly,' I whispered, 'but I … I'm worried you won't enjoy it, that I won't be as good as your other girls. I'm not exactly experienced. I don't know how to…' He cut me off by pressing his lips gently against mine, forcing an audible moan from my mouth as it tingled and the hairs on the back of my neck stood on end. He did it again, more forcefully this time, and I felt myself respond. The rush I felt was so much better than the two glasses of champagne that had made me giddy early. He tilted his head, angling his mouth as he started to kiss me properly, the way I'd always seen, and envied, in movies. My body sagged as my lips parted and his tongue sank into my mouth. Fireworks went off behind my eyes, my whole body humming with need. I could die happy right now. Kissing was amazing.

'You're perfect,' he murmured against my lips. He clasped my face with both hands and kissed me again, and I found my hands reaching for his hair, tugging it as I moaned into his mouth. I screamed, and Alec jumped, when there was a loud knock on the window.

'Paige Taylor, if you don't want your dad to ground you, you'd better get inside right now. He's been on the lookout for you for the last hour, you're lucky he just went to the toilet. You have about a minute before he comes out and spots you,' Mum called. I groaned with embarrassment as Alec released me and we watched her walk up to the front door in her dressing gown.

'So, I guess this is goodnight then?' Alec asked, tucking a loose strand of hair behind my ear.

'I guess it is. I'm so sorry.'

'Don't be, they agreed two a.m. and it's five past. I don't want him banning me from coming to pick you up again.'

'So, we're doing it again?' I asked, biting my lower lip nervously.

'We are,' he grinned, leaning forward to kiss me again quickly. 'Can I see you tomorrow night?'

'I'd really love to, but I babysit for this family and they've arranged a meal out as they have some news they want to share with me. I daren't let them down.'

'Sunday afternoon? I was planning on leaving for London straight after a goodbye lunch with my family, but I can leave later if you're free?'

'That would be great. Do you want my number?' I asked, finally feeling brave.

'Poppie's already given it to me,' he smirked. 'Go, before you're grounded and I can't see you for a month.'

'Thank you, again. I had an amazing evening.' I leaned in and kissed him this time, wishing Dad was already asleep so I could just stay in here and make out with Alec all night. I quickly got out of the car before Alec had a chance to come and open my door. I watched him reverse and wrapped my arms around myself as he opened his window.

'Paige?'

'Yes?'

'Best kiss ever,' he called with a cheeky wink. I resisted the urge to whoop, Julia Roberts *Pretty Woman* style. Instead, I just grinned and reached up to touch my lips as he drove off. Lips that were still bee-stung from kissing him. I turned around to see Dad, framed in the open door with his arms folded across his chest.

'Good night?' he asked as I skipped in.

'The best. I'm off to bed.' I kissed his cheek.

'Was he respectful, or do I need to offer to get inappropriately violent to defend my daughter's honour?'

'Nothing but respectful. He kissed me, nothing more.' I raced up to my bedroom. Right now I just wanted to be alone, to relive the night in every minute detail. For a first ever first date, it had been amazing.

The Dilemma

Saturday

I wandered into the lounge in a daze, to find Mum and Dad watching a film.

'What's wrong?' Mum asked, reading the conflicting emotions on my face immediately.

'I've just been offered a full-time job as nanny to Brennan,' I sighed, throwing myself down onto the sofa next to her.

'What about university?' Dad asked immediately. He was so proud that I was planning to attend Cambridge.

'One of the many things I need to think about,' I nodded.

'They want you to live in? In Shrewsbury?' Mum took my hand and squeezed it. She'd always told me she dreaded the day I left to go to university, but that was about two months away. Two more months of us spending time together, trying to adjust to the inevitable separation. She was going to be upset when I broke the news to her about this offer.

'Live in, yes. Shrewsbury, not so much.'

'They're moving?'

'Yes,' I confirmed, dreading the next question.

'Where to?'

'The Caribbean.' I looked up at her as she took a shocked gasp. Dad immediately muted the lottery results, spinning in his leather recliner to face me.

'What?' Mum uttered, her face falling.

'They're moving to Grand Cayman with Mr. Farquar's job. He's accepted a three-year transfer, and they want me to go with them. They already have a holiday home out there to move into. It has a pool house with a one bedroomed suite above it that would be all mine. They're offering a really amazing salary and benefits. I'd have the evenings free once I'd put Brennan down, if they weren't out, plus two days off a week and first class flights when I take my annual leave.'

'What about university?' Dad repeated, impatient for an answer.

'Dad, I don't know,' I moaned, throwing my hands up in the air. 'Four hours ago my future was mapped out, but this is an amazing opportunity that I may never get again. It would include all board and lodgings and I could save a load of money, which would mean no student loans strangling me for the next ten years. But …' I broke off and shook my head, still no clearer what to do.

'There's other considerations,' Mum said softly, squeezing my hand. I bit my lip as my eyes filled with tears. I'd miss her and Dad so much, not to mention Poppie. We'd been best friends since we met at primary school eleven years ago. There was never a day when we didn't either see, phone, or text each other. Then there was Alec. I'd not only found myself a boyfriend, but he was the one guy I'd fantasised about forever, and our first date had gone so well.

'You can nanny anytime, get yourself an education first,' Dad muttered stubbornly.

'Richard,' Mum scolded. 'She's an adult now, it's her decision to make. Paige is right, this is an amazing opportunity. We gave her the choice of paying her fees, or buying her a new, reliable car to get around in, and she chose the car, which we've already ordered. She'd be saddled with debt for years if she goes now, like most students. Wouldn't taking this job for a few years and building a nest egg be better? If her results are as good as we expect, she can always apply to Cambridge as a mature student.'

'How many people plan a time out and end up never going back to their studies?' Dad retorted with a knowing look. He and Mum had met in a gap year while travelling and she'd got pregnant with me, which had put a halt to both of their plans. I think he had all of his hopes pinned on me picking up their mantle.

'That may be true, but you can't tell me that you regret the way things worked out for us. We have a beautiful and intelligent daughter because of it. Don't listen to your dad, what do you want to do, darling?'

'If they'd asked me last weekend, I'd probably have bitten their hand off,' I admitted with a heavy sigh.

'What's changed in a week?' Dad asked. 'What?' he repeated when Mum and I gave him a look, and one of understanding settled on his face. 'Do *not* tell me that you're basing a decision on your future around a boy?' he bit, standing up and tossing the remote on the table. I grimaced, he rarely got angry, especially not with me. 'I thought I taught you better than that, that I'd raised you to be sensible and level headed.' He stormed out of the room and slammed the door, making a few tears trickle down my cheeks.

'Give him time, he's just upset at the thought of losing you, but he's right, Paige. Whether you take this job or not, much as I like Alec, you can't make this about him. You've been on one date.'

'I know,' I groaned, tipping my head back on the sofa. I was so confused.

'When would they want you to start?' she asked softly. I swallowed hard, knowing I was likely to upset her, too.

'Next weekend,' I said quietly, before I burst into full-blown, uncontrollable tears.

'O, Paige,' she sighed, gathering me into her arms. 'Ignore your dad, do what's right for you, for your future. I always wanted to go to university, but life had a different path in mind for me and I've never regretted having you. Neither has your dad. Nothing can ever break the bond you have with Poppie, no matter where in the world you are. And if Alec is really the boy for you, there's nothing to stop you seeing each other when you're home, is there?' she asked.

Sunday

I put the phone down after a long chat with Poppie. Both of us had cried, but she agreed that nothing could get in the way of our friendship. In fact, she'd told me that she'd de-friend me if I didn't take the job. That was Mum and Poppie for me going, I was still undecided, Dad was against, and Alec, well I had to face him later and I had no idea how he was going to react as I barely knew him. If we'd been seeing each other for six months, a year even, maybe I'd have no problem declining a job that would take me away from him, but I had to be realistic. We could split up in a week, a month, a year, and I knew myself too well, I'd always wonder "what if." I could potentially get a boyfriend anywhere in the world, but a job like this would be much harder to find.

I quickly washed the tears off my cheeks and put on a bit of makeup to disguise the fact that I'd been crying. Alec was picking me up in half an hour and I had no idea how that was going to go. In a total contrast to the warm weather of yesterday, it was raining today, so I dressed in my navy jeans and Converses, with a white vest and white crochet jumper over the top, leaving my hair loose. I sat at my dressing table, staring at the pictures of Poppie and me tucked into the vintage white frame of my old mirror. It only made my dilemma harder. I roused myself from my daze when I heard a car pulling onto our drive and checked my watch. He was five minutes early. I stood up and took a deep, calming breath, then blew it out forcefully, grabbed my bag, and made my way downstairs. Dad had gone out to play golf this morning, so I'd not seen him since he stomped out last night. Mum had told me that they'd talked most of the night and she'd calmed him down, but I could really do with his sage advice right now.

'Be honest, with him and yourself, that's all anyone can ask of you,' Mum advised as she kissed me and disappeared, leaving me to answer the door as it was knocked. I didn't need to force a smile, the thought of seeing him again did that for me.

'Hi,' I greeted, suddenly suffering from dry mouth again to see him. He was dressed in black jeans, a white shirt tucked in and rolled at the sleeves, and a grey waistcoat, and had one arm behind his back. When he smiled, I sprung an immediate lady boner and felt my cheeks flush.

'Hi,' he replied, bending forward to kiss me. I flung my arms around his neck and kissed him back, relishing the feeling that surged through my body when his one arm anchored tightly around my back, crushing me to him. Why did I have to be offered this amazing opportunity now? It was seriously shitty timing. 'Wow, I take it your dad's not home,' he laughed, looking slightly dazed when he finally pulled away, leaving me panting and flustered.

'Sunday is golf day.'

'Never seen the attraction myself. You on the other hand, phew,' he whistled, giving me an appraising once over. 'Even casual, you look seriously hot. These are for you.'

'Thank you,' I responded, to his compliment and the hand-tied rustic bunch of the brightest blue flowers I'd ever seen.

'I wanted to get you a fancy bouquet from Parker's Florists, but they couldn't source flowers that came anywhere near as blue as your eyes, so I stole these from my mum's back garden instead,' he shrugged, looking a little embarrassed.

'Then I'll treasure them even more than a fancy bouquet, because you put so much thought into them,' I nodded, lifting them to my nose to smell them and try and hide the tears forming in my eyes.

'Ready to go?' he asked.

'Sure, just give me a minute to put these in water.' I flashed him a quick smile and ran through to the kitchen, filling a glass from the tap and making sure that all of the stems were well immersed. They were a gorgeous colour and I really did appreciate that he'd not plumped for the easy option of ordering a flashy, expensive bouquet. He showed me to the car, leaning in to kiss the side of my neck before I slipped inside. How could something so simple as a kiss on my skin make my body turn to jelly?

'What's wrong?' he asked as soon as he climbed in next to me.

'Nothing,' I forced, trying my best to cover.

'Don't lie to me, Paige. I pride myself on my honesty and I expect the same in return. You've been crying and you look like you're about to cry again. Have you changed your mind about seeing me?' he asked, looking hurt.

'No, God no,' I shot back, swallowing hard. 'It's just ... I don't know what to do.' My shoulders slumped as I looked at him. He was in touching distance again, but I could feel him slipping out of my fingers before we'd even had a chance to see if this could have been something.

'Paige,' he warned, reaching over to take my hand. 'Talk to me.'

'Ok.' I took a deep breath and spoke in a rush, telling him about my offer and my dilemma before I could change my mind. He rubbed his hand over his mouth when I finally finished my monologue, then shoved it through his hair with a sigh.

'Why haven't you already accepted? It's an amazing offer.'

'I know,' I confirmed, feeling myself getting emotional again. 'I just needed some time to weigh up the pros and cons.'

'Tell me it's nothing to do with me,' he exclaimed.

'You're a factor,' I whispered, reaching up to brush away a tear that was clinging to my lower lashes.

'Paige,' he sighed, clasping my face and kissing my forehead. 'Take me out of the equation. Would I be gutted to see you leave? Of course I would, but I have the chance to grasp a great opportunity with my job, I don't want to be the reason that you don't do the same. In fact, if you don't take this chance, I'll break up with you, because I won't have you blaming me for a missed opportunity. If you stayed because of me, you'd end up hating me for not letting you go.'

'I don't think I could ever hate you,' I sniffed, my words full of sincerity. 'What if I went, could we still see each other when I come home?'

'I don't think that would work,' he replied, defeat in his voice, echoing the thoughts that had plagued me all night, that I didn't want to acknowledge. 'I might be out of the country when you were here and vice versa. Plus you'll be living out there most of the year and my jealousy wouldn't handle the thought of guys over there trying to tempt you away from me.'

'So, this is it? We're over before we even started?' I felt my bottom lip wobble as I looked up at him, into his startling blue eyes which looked as full of emotion as I felt. He ran his thumbs gently over my cheekbones as we held each other's gaze. This had to be one of the shortest relationships in the world. We'd not even lasted forty-eight hours.

'I don't think we'll ever be over, Paige Taylor,' he whispered softly, 'but right now isn't our time.'

'What if it never is?' I asked, feeling heartbroken at that statement.

'I refuse to believe that. I'm kind of old fashioned and superstitious. I think if two people are meant to be together, they'll find their way back to each other, no matter what. I have to believe that one day, I'll turn a corner and you'll be there, that we'll collide in a passionate embrace and pick up where we left off.'

'You really believe that?'

'I have to, because I'm going to be full of regret at a missed opportunity, Paige. I need something to look forward to. I'm going to go, you need to start packing and getting ready for one of the many adventures I know you're going to have in life.'

'We can't even go on our date?' I couldn't stop the tears from spilling down onto my cheeks at the realisation that this was it, we were going our separate ways.

'Every second I spend with you will just make it harder for me to say goodbye, Paige. I've never met anyone like you, I don't think I ever will again. I think it's best we don't torture ourselves for any longer than we have to. Just kiss me one last time before I go, I always want to remember it, just in case.'

I did as I was told, one hand slipping up his waistcoat and clutching his firm waist, the other clasping the back of his head as I lost myself in a kiss that was even more perfect than our first. It exceeded everything I'd ever imagined kissing to be. We only broke apart when the need to breathe became an issue, resting our foreheads on each others, his hands still firmly holding my face.

'I'm so sorry,' I whispered, swallowing a ball of acid that was trying to force its way into my throat. 'Good luck in London, I'm sure you'll be amazing. Goodbye, Alec.' I pulled myself from his embrace, not daring to look at his face in case I caved, and swung his car door open to leap out. I ran for the front door and fumbled with my keys, dropping them twice and cursing as I fought to stem the tidal wave of tears threatening to totally overcome me. I heard his engine start as I managed to open the front door, and I couldn't help myself from looking over my shoulder to get one last look at him. I was surprised to see how devastated he looked as well as he leaned out of the open window, the rain dampening his blond hair.

'Good luck to you too, Paige,' he called with a sad smile, before turning to face the windscreen and roaring off up the drive. I shut the door and started sobbing, leaning back on it as I covered my face with my hands and gasped for air.

'O, darling,' Mum sighed as she came out of the lounge and wrapped her arms around me. 'Go and lie down. I'll make you a cup of tea and call Poppie for you.'

I threw myself onto my bed, hugging my pillow as I tried to stop the flow of tears. It was ridiculous. We'd been on one official date. Today didn't even count. You could hardly count breaking up as a date. Part of me was disappointed, the emotional side of my brain anyway. It had wanted him to fight for me, to tell me not to go, or that we'd make it work if I did. The sensible, logical, and rational side though? He'd only said exactly what I'd been thinking, that it would be too hard. Plus he was going to be around gorgeous models all the time, I wasn't sure my jealousy would handle that well either. This was the right choice, but it didn't stop it from hurting like he'd been a massive part of my life for years.

I woke up in the middle of the night with dry, itchy, swollen eyes and a banging headache. Poppie lay curled up next to me. She'd insisted on a sleep over, not wanting to leave me in my hour, or night, of need. I snuck out of bed and went to my en-suite to use a cold, wet flannel on my puffy eyes. I didn't have time to mope. I was going abroad in less than a week, to somewhere really hot and tropical. The thought of having to go shopping for some new outfits and bikinis cheered me up a little. I headed back to bed with my temporary cool pack for my face and saw a message on my phone. It was from him.

Just in case the memory of our last kiss fades, I wanted you to have something so you'd never forget me, just like I won't forget you. Until we collide. Alec x

I scrolled down and promptly started crying again. He'd attached two photographs, both black and white, that he'd obviously developed from the many he'd taken the night of the ball. One was a selfie he'd taken of us laughing. He had his arm around my shoulder, clasping my one hand as our temples touched. We looked so happy. We looked so perfect together. Perfectly doomed, more like. The other was a picture he'd taken of me when I wasn't looking. If it hadn't been for my dress, I might not have recognised myself. I was stunned. I'd always known I was pretty, but this picture made me look beautiful, that's how good a photographer he was. He'd attached a caption to it that tugged on my heartstrings.

Like I said, no one can hold a candle to you, Paige. See yourself how I see you. Alec x

Just Lunch

August ~ Two Years Later

I was home from Grand Cayman for a four-week summer break while the Farquars were on a world cruise, and I was bored to tears. Poppie had gone travelling around Europe with Reece. We'd only had a few days together before she left two weeks ago and I was missing her already. I'd settled into my job abroad really well. It had helped going with a family I knew, and a little boy I adored, but the first few weeks had been really hard without my parents and Poppie close by. It had taken me some time to get over my short relationship with Alec as well. I'd not replied to the message he'd sent to me the last night I saw him. I figured keeping in contact would only make it harder for me to move on.

I felt like I had now, and it helped that I finally had a boyfriend. I'd met him when I'd decided to take scuba diving lessons on one of my regular days off. Toby was the instructor, twenty-six years old, good looking, blond, and super tanned from spending his days in and around the water. We'd been seeing each other for about a year. Summer was peak season for his business, so he hadn't been able to come back to England with me. I was surprised at how much I was missing him. I only agreed to date him after he pestered me non-stop, coming up with increasingly inventive ways to woo me, but we actually got on really well. He was kind, considerate, and funny, and though I had no one else to compare him to, as he was my first, sex with him was great. I'd finally lost my virginity and was inclined to agree with Poppie that I'd definitely been missing out. It just bummed me out that sometimes I'd catch myself looking at him and wishing he was Alec. I just didn't get that sizzle of excitement or butterflies in my stomach with him like I had with Alec. Nor did my body completely go to pieces when he kissed me. I idly wondered how long it would be before I stopped comparing, until Alec was completely out of my system. It had been over two years since our one and only date and I hadn't been able to bring myself to delete the photo he'd sent me of the two of us. I'd even printed it and tucked it into my mirror frame here in England, along with all of my pictures of Poppie. I had one of Toby and me in my bedroom in Grand Cayman, but not here for some reason.

I looked out of my bedroom window, it was a gorgeous summer's day for the UK. I was used to a hotter climate now, but it would do nicely. Bright sunshine, blue skies, with just the odd wisp of a fluffy white cloud. Perfect for shopping and a bite to eat somewhere, with a glass of wine. I had a shower and decided to leave my long wavy hair loose, then got dressed in a loose-fitting, white maxi dress with a pair of flat silver sandals, and filled my white crochet tote bag. Silver accessories, a slick of sheer lip-gloss, and spritz of perfume, and I was good to go.

'Mum,' I called through the bathroom door where she was having a shower. 'I'm going into town for the day, do you need anything?'

'No thanks, have fun,' she replied.

'Will do, see you later.'

I bounced down the stairs and grabbed my car keys. I couldn't help smiling as I stepped outside and saw Fi-Fi sitting on the drive. I was so in love with her. Fi-Fi was the hot pink Fiat 500cc that my parents had purchased for me instead of funding my uni fees. It had been too late for Dad to return it, given he'd ordered it with a custom spray-paint job. He was still a little miffed about my decision, especially as he'd purchased the car and then it had sat unused for a not inconsiderable amount of the time. And it didn't help that he'd had to order a bubblegum pink version, being my favourite colour. He constantly asked if I'd consider having her re-sprayed to something "a little less garish," that wouldn't offend anyone. The only person it seemed to offend was him. Everyone else loved her, me especially. I put on the radio and my sunglasses and retracted the roof. I had a feeling that today was going to be an amazing day.

I parked in Abbey Foregate, eager to make my way to Wyle Cop and meander in and out of all of the boutique shops as I headed up to the town centre, but breakfast was the first item on my agenda. I headed over to The Peach Tree and sat outside with my sunglasses on as I ate a delicious meal of eggs benedict with a vanilla latte and freshly squeezed orange juice as I watched the world go by. Everyone here seemed so hurried and rushed to get to wherever they were going. I'd grown accustomed to a slower pace of life now. I popped over to the nearby hairdressers for my appointment at ten a.m. All the sun and ocean swimming meant that my hair was in desperate need of deep conditioning on a regular basis. I quite liked that the sun had bleached a few blonde streaks into it, but the dryness was something I detested. I had my nails done while I waited, a pretty and natural-looking French manicure, then hit the shops for some overdue retail therapy.

When I finally made it up to the town square, it was nearly two p.m. and I was laden down with bags. I had no idea if I was coming home for Christmas, so unbelievably I'd planned ahead and done most of my shopping in July. I'd never been so organised. My fingers were hurting so much from the handles digging into them that I'd nearly had to put the bags down and slap myself when the thought of heading to buy one of those tartan shopping trolleys on wheels, that pensioners wheeled about, crossed my mind. Crikey, next I'd be looking into the one bootie, fleece-lined, electric foot warmer, or one of those slankets, a blanket with sleeves, or God forbid, a totally unsexy onesie. The thought made me shudder. Maybe even a Motability scooter? They did look like fun though. I could zip in and out of shops, hooting at the annoying women who always congregated right at a shop entrance to chat, that or plough them down. It would really make things easier in the Boxing Day sales to have one of those to get ahead of the pack. I did put my bags down for a moment and rubbed my fingers back to life, wondering if a funky and brightly coloured shopping trolley would really be all that bad.

'Paige Taylor, back away from inappropriate thoughts right now,' I warned myself. I grabbed all my bags and spun around, deciding to find somewhere for a snack and a glass of wine, and bumped straight into someone. It caught me so off guard that I cursed as I felt myself falling and bounced inelegantly on the ground, the contents of my bags scattering out around me.

'Paige Taylor, I know that I said "until we collide," but I didn't mean it literally. You seem to have a habit of falling at my feet,' came a reassuringly familiar, but incredibly sexy, voice. 'Are you ok?'

I managed to get myself into a sitting position, adjusted my dress, which had ridden up to my hips, and looked up at the speaker. The sight that met my eyes made me take in a sharp, shocked inhalation. Alec Wright was crouching in front of me, with a smile on his handsome face as he offered me his hand. I gulped hard. Two years had been generous to him. He'd filled out into an indisputably toned, broad, masculine specimen of perfection. I put my hand in his and he stood, easing me up onto my feet. Neither of us spoke for a moment, nor did he release my hand, and I was ashamed to feel that surge of excitement to be so close to him again.

'Are you ok?' he repeated.

'I am, thank you. A bit shocked from the fall, but I'm ok. The same can't be said for my shopping though,' I grimaced, as I tore my eyes off his and looked down at my purchases spread around me.

'I'll help you pick them up.' He slowly let go of my hand and we both bent down at the same time to pick up the closest bag, with a loud crack as our foreheads clashed.

'Owwww,' I moaned with a giggle, straightening up to rub it.

'Sorry,' he grinned, doing the same. 'Ok?'

'I will be if you stop assaulting me,' I teased. We both let out a peel of laughter as we did it again, him rubbing his head this time.

'Ok, ladies first, or we'll end up knocking each other out.'

I hastily crouched and started scooping various items into whatever bag was lying close to hand. I was too flustered to focus properly on what I was doing. My heart was skipping so many beats I was liable to pass out, then I was going to need mouth-to-mouth to resuscitate me. *Would it be wrong to fake fainting just to feel him kiss me again?* I wondered. I mentally slapped myself, for the second time in five minutes. I had a boyfriend, a really nice boyfriend called Alec. No wait, not Alec, Toby. God damn it, I couldn't even get his name right after a year.

'Hmmm, nice choice,' Alec murmured, forcing me to look up. I cringed when I saw a pair of sexy, lace, electric blue boy shorts dangling from his finger, not to mention the hammock of a bra swinging next to them. It was big enough to carry two large Galia melons. I quickly snatched the personal items off him, my cheeks going pink, and hastily shoved them out of sight.

'Mum's Christmas present,' I lied, not wanting to imagine him imagining me scantily clad in said items. It was bad enough being around him, I didn't need to see him aroused. My eyes automatically drifted up his leg to his crotch. Shit, too late. The sight of what was straining in his jeans set me off balance again and I landed on my backside with a thud.

'Calamity Taylor, some things never change,' he chuckled, hauling me up again. 'But unless your mum has had some silicone implants, no way is she going to be wearing that bra.'

'Ok, ok, the underwear is mine. I just didn't want you getting any visuals in your head,' I protested, forcing myself not to lean in and sniff his pale blue shirt or nuzzle his neck.

'Too late, not that I need any help for that. How are you? You look amazing.'

'So do you,' I replied, with an involuntary sigh. 'I mean … you know what I mean. You look well. How's the job going?'

'Great, I'm just back from a shoot in New York and popped in to see my mum for her birthday. I'm back down to London tomorrow, then off to Tokyo.'

'Wow, it's really going well then?' I gathered up my bags, needing something to keep my hands occupied, as they were itching to touch him again.

'It is. What about you? Are you home for good?' he asked. I lifted my eyes back up to his, wondering if I'd just detected an element of hope in his voice.

'No, another year to go before Mr. Farquar's contract ends. I just came home for a few weeks while they're on a family vacation.'

'Are you rushing off somewhere, or do you have time to catch up?'

'I was just going to go and get something to eat.'

'So was I, why don't we have lunch together?' he suggested, wrestling some of the bags out of my hands.

'I'm seeing someone,' I said in a rush, like that was going to protect me from the raw sexual pheromones Alec was unwittingly spewing in my direction.

'It's just lunch, Paige.'

'His name's Toby and he's really nice. It's been almost a year. It's serious, I think. I mean, we're having sex you know, sex is serious. God, now that sounds like he's a total bore in the bedroom, or that I am. He's not. I'm not. I'm a hellcat when I get going, a real tigress. My God, what am I saying?' I groaned. 'I'm babbling again, you so don't need to know about my sex life.'

'Really don't,' he agreed with a frown. I ran to catch him up as he started walking away.

'How about you?'

'You want to know if I'm having sex?' he asked, one eyebrow raised.

'Well, that wasn't actually where I was going with that question,' I replied, my mind drifting as I tried to imagine him without his shirt and jeans. My memory of his ripped torso that day he'd stripped off his t-shirt in Daisy's stall was fading rapidly.

'So?' he prodded.

'So what?' I asked, shaking my head to rid myself of improper thoughts and look up at him.

'You said "how about you?" and I'm not sure what you were asking.'

'O, right. Are you seeing anyone?' I broke his gaze and looked at my feet as we walked, holding my breath as I waited for his answer. I knew already that if he said "yes", it was going to hurt. Which was ridiculous when I was in a committed relationship myself.

'Not at the moment. I've had a few relationships since I last saw you, but they didn't work out.'

'Too hard with you jetting off with your job?' I asked, totally getting that.

'No, they weren't you.' He said it so quietly I wasn't sure if it was wishful thinking, surely my ears had just deceived me. 'It's a nice day, why don't we grab some food and go and have a picnic somewhere?' he suggested, giving me whiplash from the sudden change in direction.

'Sure,' I agreed, biting my lip as I looked up at him again.

We headed to a deli that was close by and loaded up with freshly baked olive and walnut bread, some cheeses, pâté and grapes, then a slice of tarte aux pommes each. They gave us some plastic cutlery, two paper plates, and two plastic cups, so we could share a small bottle of white wine, and packed it all up carefully for us. Alec grabbed one of those picnic blankets that rolls into a small carry case as well, then refused to allow me to pay when the bill was totted up. He led the way up Swan Hill towards the town park as he filled me in on the apartment he'd purchased in London for when he was home. My eyes lingered on The Domville hotel as we strolled through the park, looking for a quiet shaded spot to sit.

'It was a great date, wasn't it?' he said, flashing me his trademark dimpled smile as he set down the bags.

'It really was,' I agreed wistfully.

'Sucks we never got to go on any others.'

'It wasn't our time,' I reminded him, as he bent over to smooth out the turquoise, orange, and yellow striped picnic blanket.

'Just like it's not now, since you still live away and have a boyfriend. So, without graphic details of this man in your life, who I already hate, tell me how it's going?' he asked.

We lost track of time as we lay there, eating, drinking, and laughing. I filled him in on some of my catastrophes, because with me there were always plenty. He regaled me with tales of his travels. I was so jealous, he'd seen so much of the world already and really seemed to be making a name for himself. He was close to leaving his mentor, at his persuasion, to branch out on his own completely. He handed me a card for an agency in London that he was already working with exclusively, repeating his insistence that I had what it took to get a job. I joked that he'd do anything to see me in a bikini again, which had him turn an adorable shade of crimson and choke on his wine. Conversation with him just came so easily. The silences as we just looked at each other from time to time weren't awkward or uncomfortable, but natural, like they'd be with Poppie or Mum or Dad.

'Shit,' he uttered, leaping to his feet as he checked his watch. 'I didn't realise how late it was, I need to get back. We're going out for a meal to celebrate.'

'God, I'm so sorry to have kept you. I've been waffling, as usual.'

'I like your waffle,' he grinned, bending over to start clearing up the debris.

'And you're very easy to waffle around, I could do it with you all of the time. Ok, that came out sounding a whole lot more risqué than I meant it to.'

'Everything you say sounds sexy, it's that voice and the way your lips move. It's hard to focus on anything else.'

'Ditto,' I replied as we held each other's gaze for a moment. Suddenly the British sun seemed almost as scorching as when I was lying on the fine white powdered sand watching Toby snorkelling. I blushed and Alec coughed, both of us looking away at the same time and hastily clearing up. 'Do you ever wonder whether we'd still have been together?' I eventually asked as he tucked the rolled-up picnic blanket under his arm.

'I know we would, but I think any hope of that happening now has long passed.'

'Why?' I asked, looking at him surprised. What had happened to his romantic notion that one day we'd find each other again?

'Because if I was lucky enough to be dating you right now, I'd never let you go, Paige Taylor. I'm over in Frankwell, where are you parked?' he asked, quickly changing the topic again, while my stomach fluttered at his declaration.

'I'm on the other side of town, Abbey Foregate,' I replied. He grimaced and checked his watch again.

'I should be ok, give me some of your bags,' he ordered, trying to take some out of my hands.

'Alec, don't be silly. You're obviously already going to be late, it's too far out of your way. I'm a big girl and this is child's play. This doesn't even count as a shopping spree,' I smiled.

'Seriously? You can buy more than this in one day?' He looked at me amazed.

'I'm nothing if not a professional,' I stated. 'If you're going to do something, do it well. I may even call into a shop on the way back to get something I saw earlier.'

'Women,' he laughed. 'You're sure you'll be ok? I feel bad abandoning you.'

'Please, like your mother would forgive you for standing her up on her birthday to help some girl with her shopping bags.'

'I'm sure she would if she met you.' He reached up to sweep my hair out of my face, then slid his fingers around to the back of my head. 'It was really great to see you, Paige. I hope it's not another two years before I bump into you again.' He leaned in and kissed my temple, the softest of kisses that made me close my eyes and sigh. I dropped my bags again and quickly put my arms around his neck, hugging him tightly, not wanting to let go. He dropped his picnic blanket and embraced me back just as hard. We just stood there for a while, clinging to each other like shipwreck survivors would to flotsam. My God, he always smelled so good. I'd love to bottle his smell and spread it on my pillows so I could go to sleep surrounded by him. 'Did you just sniff my hair?' he laughed.

'No. Maybe. Yes,' I relented with a giggle. 'In my defence, you smell *really* good. I don't go around sniffing men's hair randomly you know, but yours is like … premier league smelling hair, it's scentsational. It was there, calling to me.'

'God I've missed you, you're a breath of fresh air after all those stuck-up models I've dated,' he sighed, his cheek rubbing against mine for a fraction of a second. I quickly pulled away. I had a boyfriend. How would I feel if Toby was so close to another girl? Seriously annoyed I suspected, but the thought of Alec seeing a bevy of glamour models had my blood boiling. What did that say about my relationship with Toby? Was he just a stand in, a poor substitute for the one man I really wanted?

'You'd better go, or your mother will hunt me down and shoot me,' I advised, quickly bending to gather my bags.

'Jesus,' he gasped as I head butted him for the third time that day as he bent to do the same. 'I swear you'll knock me out one day. Are you ok?'

'I'll be fine,' I winced, rubbing the same patch on my head that now had a small egg-shaped swelling. 'Go, before I assault you again and make you even later. Thanks for a lovely lunch and a really fun afternoon.' I swallowed hard as he looked at me sadly. 'Don't do that, you'll make me cry again and I don't want to traipse back through town crying and getting sympathetic looks.'

'Bye, Paige,' he sighed.

'Bye, Alec.' I attempted a smile and watched him turn and start walking away, cocking my head to watch his peachy backside as he strode off with purpose. It was my turn to sigh. 'Alec?' I shouted, forcing him to turn around.

'What?'

'Until we collide?' I bit my lower lip as I waited for his response. He smiled and nodded, walking backwards, neither of us wanting to be the first to turn around. 'Tree!' I yelled, alarmed as it rapidly approached his back.

'What?' he called, seconds before he bashed straight into it, making the branches shake. He reached up to rub the back of his head as I laughed.

'See, you've spent too much time around me, you're picking up my bad habits.'

'Not as much time as I'd have liked.'

No truer words had ever been spoken. I stayed watching him until he gave me one final wave before he disappeared out of the park gates, and out of my life yet again.

'Do *not* cry, Paige.' It was a futile warning, totally unmanageable. A few tears slid down my cheeks as I made my way back to the car and wondered if my best friend was somewhere with a Wi-Fi signal so I could share my day with her.

A Model Citizen

August ~ A Year Later

I stood in Shrewsbury town square on another sunny day, just breathing in the air and remembering my unexpected meeting with Alec here a year ago. My contract with the Farquars had ended and we'd all moved home. Brennan was seven now and about to start boarding school. I felt he was far too young to be separated from his parents, he was upset enough about leaving the only home he remembered and about saying goodbye to me, but he wasn't my child, my opinion didn't matter. I'd filled in my application to Cambridge, which had thrilled Dad, but I wasn't that enthused about it. Most people went to university to better their education, with a view to getting a well-paid job. I'd already had a well-paid job and I had a glowing reference, which would more than likely secure me another position with a wealthy overseas family, but I wanted a little more excitement in my life. I had no ties whatsoever now. Toby had been upset that I planned to come home, but other than getting married to him and starting a family, which I so wasn't ready for, there was nothing there for me. I'd outgrown it, and him. I think he knew that my heart was never fully in the relationship, but it had been good while it lasted.

'Well, well, well, look who's back!' came a scornful female voice. 'I barely recognised you. Then again, you're usually covered in cow shit or mud whenever I see you.'

'Ruth,' I sighed, turning to face her. She smirked and folded her arms across her chest. 'How lovely to see that you've used the last three years to grow as a person. Tell me what I ever did to make you despise me so much?'

'You know what! I was perfectly happy with Alec until you came along.'

'I wasn't the cause for you splitting up, Ruth. From what I heard, you only have yourself to blame for that.'

'From what you heard?' She scowled at me, her lips turning up into a sneer. 'Of course, I forgot how close you and Alec are nowadays.

Best of friends, aren't you? Remind me how long it's been since you last saw him. A year, is it, on your little ill-fated lovers' picnic?'

'How do you know that?' I demanded.

'Because I'm still the one in his life, Paige. His mother adores me, so everything he tells her, she tells me. It's only a matter of time before he comes around and realises what he's given up with me. We're destined to be together.'

'You may have his mother wrapped around your little finger, you evil, manipulative … cow, but he'll never take you back.'

'And you think you're so special?' she laughed. 'If he wanted to be with you, he'd be with you. He has a certain standard now that he's working with supermodels and you, sweetheart, just don't meet the grade.'

'First of all, he's not that shallow,' I bit. 'And secondly, I could be a model if I wanted. Alec even encouraged me to apply to an agency the last time I saw him.'

'They'd never take anyone with a fat arse and silicone-enhanced tits like that,' she scoffed. I lost my cool altogether and slapped her.

'My arse is rounded and my breasts are natural. Nothing about me is fake, which can't be said for you. I'll prove you wrong, Ruth. You're going to eat your words one day, because I'm going to be a superstar. And while you sit here in this sleepy town, waiting for your Prince Charming to come and rescue you, remember this. I'm the one you sneered at when I was at my lowest. *I'm* Cinderella. You're just one of the ugly sisters, inside and out.' I didn't give her a chance to respond as I stalked away, forgetting my shopping plans for the day and heading straight for the train station.

I got off the train at London Euston station and headed for the underground. I'd only been to London on a school trip in my teens, I felt nervous navigating such a large city on my own, but I was twenty-one now. I was a woman who had so much more confidence than the young girl that had said a tearful goodbye to her parents and Poppie at the airport when I left three years ago. It was amazing to think that I'd eaten breakfast back home this morning, with no real plans for the day, and now I was in London, about to do something really stupid just to prove Ruth wrong. Why did I let her get to me so badly? I still couldn't believe I'd slapped her. Was doing this a stupid move though? If I was lucky enough to get an offer, some models earned really good money. But I had to be realistic, I was Paige Taylor from Shrewsbury. The girl who fell over on a regular basis. My clumsiness and a catwalk weren't exactly an ideal pairing. I pulled out the ModOne agency card from my bag, they were in South Kensington. I had no idea where that was, so did a search on my iPhone and asked it for the best tube route.

I purchased a ticket before I could talk myself out of it and hopped on the crowded train. I looked down at myself, thankful that I always tried to dress smartly. I had on a pair of black tapered culottes, with a white cotton three-quarter sleeve shirt, a thin red leather belt, and red heels and bag. I remembered, from watching *America's Next Top Model* with Poppie, that it was best to have your hair pulled back and minimal make up on. I rummaged in my bag for a hair band and quickly raked my fingers through it, scraping it into a ponytail, then used a tissue to remove the hint of red gloss on my lips. Then again, it wasn't like they were just going to drop everything to see me. They must have a long waiting list of girls wanting to sign up, let alone walk-ins on a daily basis. I made my way up the leafy tree-lined street and stopped just short of the smart entrance, with large Italian-looking terracotta pots either side of the door with shaped topiary trees. The name of the agency, ModOne, was emblazoned in mirrored letters above the glass double doors. I quickly pulled my phone out and FaceTimed Poppie.

'Just got out of bed, lazy bones?' she grinned on answer.

'No, as a matter of fact, I'm in London,' I retorted.

'London? What are you doing there?' She gave me a puzzled look as I grimaced.

'Exactly what I'm thinking, now that I'm standing outside.'

'Outside where? What's going on?' I filled her in, amidst much muttering and hissing through her teeth on mention of my run-in with Ruth, then squeals of delight as I told her my stupid on-the-fly plan. 'O, Paige, this is awesome. Go for it, what do you have to lose? You didn't need Alec Wright to tell you that you're gorgeous, I've been telling you for years.'

'What about uni though?'

'Who needs a qualification when you're the next Cara Delevingne?'

'Please, at twenty-one I'm probably already considered past it.'

'Just go and try, let me know as soon as you're out. We'll have to celebrate when you get home tonight.'

'Or commiserate.'

'Shit, I've just realised that I can't either way. Reece is taking me to dinner, says we "need to talk."'

'O my God, do you think he's going to propose?' I asked, feeling really excited for her. 'Are you going to say yes?'

'I'm twenty-one, I haven't developed early-onset insanity yet, Paige,' she laughed. 'No one gets married at this age anymore. Besides, I've applied for some temping work in London to fit around a bilingual secretarial course I've found down there and he's applying for jobs in Dubai. We have some important life stuff to sort out before we even talk about where our relationship's heading. Go, I want to know the outcome the minute you're out, ok?'

'Ok, but don't get your hopes up. I have a fat arse and fake-looking tits, apparently.'

'She'll have a fat lip if I bump into her,' Poppie muttered. 'And as tits and arse go, so not into girls, but if I was, I'd be all over yours. They're lush.'

'Thank you,' I smiled. I could always count on Poppie to boost my confidence. 'Wish me luck.'

'Sending you rainbows and unicorns,' she replied, blowing me a kiss. I returned the favour and ended the call. After checking myself in the mirror and applying a slick of Vaseline on my lips, I put my shoulders back and held my head high as I approached the doors, determined not to fall over or cause a scene. I made it through the heavy glass doors without incident and tried not to gasp in awe at the cavernous reception. The floors and walls were polished white granite with silver sparkles inset, huge black chandeliers hung from the ceilings, and there were vintage silver ornate mirrors on each wall, interspersed with acrylic shots of the various models on their books. There was a long white leather chaise longue along the far wall, with a row of young girls clutching portfolio documents to their chests. What was I thinking? I was so unprepared. I made to turn around and run back out, but the receptionist caught my eye.

'Can I help you?' she called. All eyes were on me as I stood there, caught in limbo between fight or flight. I could do this, I was going to make Ruth eat her words. I strode confidently to the desk.

'Paige Taylor, I want to be a model,' I advised.

'When's your appointment, Paige?'

'Appointment?'

'Yes, we're an appointment-only agency, I'm afraid. Have you made one?'

'No, I thought ... I'm sorry, it's just my friend Alec recommended that I come and see Jean-Claude.'

'Alec?' She looked up at me, intrigued.

'Alec Wright, he's a fashion photographer.'

'You're friends with Alec Wright?' she gasped. I looked at her in surprise. It was as if I'd just name dropped being best friends with Harry Styles or something.

'I am,' I confirmed.

'I can't promise anything, but take a seat. He's casting today, but if he doesn't like the look of a girl on the couch in person, he won't even see them, so he may have time for you.'

'Won't you get into trouble squeezing me in?'

'Not if he knows you were referred by Alec, they're good friends. Just do me a favour. If Jean-Claude takes you, ask Alec to come for a visit. He's so gorgeous and we haven't seen him here in a while. Is he seeing anyone?'

'I've no idea,' I replied, feeling my hackles rise at the thought of her wanting to flirt with him. 'But I'll certainly ask when I next see him.'

She smiled and gestured me over to the already overcrowded seating. I smiled at the girls, who looked me up and down with contempt. A couple glanced at each other with raised brows, implying they didn't feel I was up to standard. None of them made any effort to move up to accommodate me on the bench either. Instead, I put my handbag on the floor and leaned against the wall. Was this what modelling was like? Catty attitudes and only looking out for yourself? Could I really cope with that sort of behaviour? Who was I kidding. I wasn't going to get a job as a model. I giggled as I thought of what Dad's reaction would be to my outing today. I realised as far as my parents knew, I'd gone to town shopping. I really ought to let them know where I was. I bent over to rummage in my bag for my phone.

'Out, out. Mon Dieu, I am casting for swimwear, not famine victims,' came an irate French accent behind me. 'At last, you, with the Kardashian derrière, you're next.'

'I've been here for hours,' moaned the blonde next to me as I triumphantly retrieved my phone and started sending Mum a text.

'I'm not operating a doctors' surgery here, it's not first come first served. You, brunette in black, white, and red, your phone is more important than my time?' his voice snapped. I looked up in surprise.

'I'm sorry, were you talking to me?' I asked, pausing mid text.

'Do you see any other juicy rumps in this line up?' he asked, folding his arms across his chest as he gave me a disapproving scowl that my dad would have been proud of. I nearly gave him one back for comparing my backside to a piece of meat.

'I'm so sorry, I didn't realise that you meant me. I was just texting my mum.'

'In or out, my time is precious,' he snapped, flicking a hand to the door. I hastily shoved my phone back in my bag.

'In, in, most definitely in,' I confirmed, nodding my head vigorously. 'Sorry, Mum,' I whispered as I trotted over and through the white door into his room. I waited just inside the modernistic-looking office as he shut the door behind me.

'Sit,' he ordered, pointing to the white and chrome leather chair in front of his glass desk. I did as I was told immediately, putting my knees together and resting my hands in my lap as I tried to remember not to slouch. He moved in front of me, leaning back on the desk as he studied my face for a moment, while I did the same in return. He spoke with a French accent, but with his jet black hair and piercing green eyes, he looked more Italian. He was dressed in a pair of expensive, black designer trousers and a bright green shirt. He actually had quite a kind face, or he would if he wasn't so intimidating right now. 'Portfolio, please.' He held out a tanned and immaculately manicured hand.

'I don't have one,' I whispered apologetically.

'A model without a portfolio? You came here to waste my time?' he snapped.

'I came because my friend recommended I see you,' I advised, reaching down to grab my iPhone. 'He took a picture of me, I have it on here.'

'A friend? Do you have any idea how many "friends" recommend me? You have a classically beautiful face and on first glance, a body made for swimwear, but if you are untrained, you are of no use to me now. Go, get some advice from a professional, practice, practice, practice, then get a portfolio made up. Only then come back, I will give you one more chance.'

'I promise I'm a quick learner. I wouldn't have come at all, but Alec was so sure I could do well,' I stuttered, trying to multitask and find that damn photo he'd taken of me.

'Alec? Alec Wright?' he responded, his interest piqued.

'Yes, he took the photograph of me. Here, here, I've found it,' I announced proudly, handing my phone over to him. He raised his eyebrows as he looked at the shot.

'Alec has an exceptional eye. Very well, I need to see you in your underwear,' Jean-Claude advised, handing me my phone back.

'Underwear? O God, I mean, I had no idea I was even coming here today and I've no idea if I've got a matching set on.'

'What's your name?'

'Paige, Paige Taylor.'

'Paaaaige,' he breathed with a knowing smile. He picked up his phone and I watched his thumbs move across the screen with lightening speed. 'I see. Now I understand. Well, Paige Taylor, I want to assess your body, not your delicates, so please kindly remove your clothes.'

'O, ok. Please could you direct me to the changing room then?' I asked, desperately trying to remember when I last had a bikini wax. Flashing my bush hadn't been on the agenda when I got up this morning. None of this was.

'Changing room?' he laughed. 'A model is comfortable in her own skin, she will strip anywhere the need demands. Don't worry, I don't bite, and if you haven't guessed, I'm as gay as they come, so you have nothing to fear.' His phone pinged a response and he chuckled and sent a reply as I stood up and took a deep breath. This was no different to me living in a bikini abroad. I kept myself in good shape, as much as my curvy figure would allow, and my once-pasty porcelain skin was a deep golden brown from days spent lazing on the beach or by the pool. I cringed to see I did in fact have on a black v-string and a white minimiser bra. I really ought to sue the manufacturers because it did nothing to minimise my chest at all. If anything, I virtually had an extra two breasts from where they were spilling over the top of the cups.

'Leave your shoes on and walk to the door and back for me,' he ordered. I did as I was told, swallowing the lump of anxiety in the back of my throat. I'd never been really confident about my body, too many stick-thin girls calling me fat over the years. I turned and walked back towards him, trying to read his reaction. 'Your walk needs serious work, but I see potential, yes. Alec has a very good eye indeed. You may dress now.'

He walked around to the other side of the desk, sat down, and turned to face his screen as I quickly pulled my clothes on. I stood waiting, not sure what to do as his eyes moved back and forth and he muttered under his breath.

'Thank you for your time. Do I leave my number with the receptionist in case you want to contact me?' I eventually asked, but he didn't reply again. It was a good minute before he sat back in his chair and looked up at me.

'Monday, six p.m.'

'I'm sorry?' I looked at him, confused.

'I am a very busy man, but I like you, Paige. You will be here at six p.m. on Monday and every night after that until I am satisfied that I have whipped you into shape. Then, and only then, will I arrange for someone to come and do your portfolio and cast you in your first swimwear shoot. My time and the portfolio I will offer for free, but you won't be paid until I'm confident I can make money from you. Be under no illusions, this is an exceptional offer, one you won't get elsewhere and I need an answer now.'

'Right now?' I looked at him wide eyed. I was shocked enough that he was willing to work with me, to help me, let alone for me to start on Monday. That left me five days to pack up my life and move to London. And I wasn't even sure I wanted to be a model, I'd only come to rub Ruth's face in it.

'Right now. I have hundreds of girls who would chew off their right arm for an offer like this. I will work you hard and I expect the same in return, but I see a promising future for you.'

'I don't even know the salary, I didn't expect … I mean it's just …' I stalled, actually lost for words for once. My jaw nearly hit the floor when he gave me an indication of what I could expect to be paid for each shoot. Even Dad wouldn't be able to complain about that.

'In or out?'

'In,' I replied without hesitation. A Cambridge degree in languages wasn't going to earn me anywhere near as much as I could doing this. Plus, fashion. I might be able to make a hobby of mine into a career, with free clothes, makeovers, world travel. The possibilities were endless.

'Monday at six then,' he smiled.

'Thank you so much, I promise I won't let you down,' I beamed. I grabbed my bag and virtually skipped to the door.

'Paige?' he called, making me look back over my shoulder. 'Say hello to him for me.'

'To who?' I asked.

'Alec, he's waiting for you outside. He lives around the corner and was made-up to hear that you'd shown up in my office.'

'Thank you!' I flashed him my best excited schoolgirl grin and he laughed and shooed me out of the door with a flick of his wrist. Alec was here? What were the odds?

'Rosalie, cancel the rest of my appointments, I've found my girl,' Jean-Claude chirped over the phone system as I shut his door. His announcement echoed over the speakerphone in reception and there was a collective groan from the waiting crowd. I resisted the urge to stick out my tongue, especially when I caught a glimpse of Alec through the window, leaning against a tree with his hands in his pockets. He seriously got better looking with each year that passed. I was so excited that I ran to the exit, and the last thing I remembered was pain radiating through my face and the weird sound of something vibrating as I hit the granite floor.

Nose Out Of Joint

'Paige, can you hear me?' came Alec's voice.

'Hmmm,' I groaned, trying to open my eyes and sit up.

'Hey, hey, careful. You knocked yourself out by running into the glass doors. It looks like you've broken your nose as well, an ambulance is on its way.'

'What?' I asked, feeling completely dazed.

'I told you that you have a habit of falling at my feet,' he chuckled. 'How are you feeling?'

'Like I have the worst hangover ever,' I moaned, slowly blinking and adjusting to the bright light. My nose and forehead were throbbing. Had I seriously run into the glass doors? When I was hoping to make a good impression this time?

'You scared me to death, I heard the sound from outside. Here, lie back down, I've put my jacket under your head. I would say it's great to see you, but I'm not sure it's appropriate when you're in this state and have blood all over your shirt.'

'I need to go home, I'm not supposed to be here.' I tried sitting up again, but felt really dizzy and didn't object when he gently pushed me back down again. I closed my eyes and tried to focus on not being sick. It was bad enough I'd made a fool of myself in front of him again, without vomiting all over him.

'The only place you're going is the hospital. Is your phone in your bag? I'll call your parents and let them know.'

'Yes, Dad's going to be so mad. Please don't tell him about the job, I need to tell him.'

'I won't, I'll say you came to see me, ok?'

'Ok,' I sighed. I smiled when I felt his free hand gently stroking my hair. Was it wrong that the first thing I wanted to tell him, when I could open my eyes and look at him properly, was that I was single again and about to move to London? Maybe fate was on my side after all.

I had to fight really hard not to cry when the doctor came to my bed and told me that I was going to need an operation to fix my nose, to make sure it didn't end up wonky. That would be a great look for the start of a modelling career. More upsetting was the news that Alec had a girlfriend. A model he'd met in New York not long after we'd last seen each other. I mean, what did I expect? That a man that desirable would just wait around in the hope that I'd become free for him? That he'd turn to religion and ensconce himself in a monastery with a vow of chastity until we could be together?

'She lives with you here?' I asked.

'No, she's American, she lives over there, but …' he hesitated and ran his hand over his mouth.

'But what?'

'We have to have the worst timing in the world, Paige,' he sighed, taking my hand in his as he sat at my bedside. 'I just took on a studio in New York to set up my own business.'

'You're moving to New York?' I tried to sound happy for him. His own business was something we'd talked about last year, and he was doing phenomenally well. Part of me was so proud of him, but part of me was dying inside. I was moving to London and he was moving to another continent. And he had a girlfriend! I hated her already. Possibly more than I hated Ruth, which was saying something.

'And you're moving to London. Pretty ironic, huh?'

'When?'

'Saturday. I was just here sorting out my apartment, packing up most of my things.'

'Ships in the night,' I sighed, dropping my chin to my chest.

'Paige! Thank God, I've been so worried,' came Mum's voice. I looked up to see her approaching at speed, Dad hot on her heels, and I burst into tears. Alec let go of my hand and stood up, making room for Mum to barge past and grab me in a bear hug.

'Nose, Mum, nose,' I winced as she caught it on her shoulder.

'You, young lady, have some explaining to do,' Dad warned in his stern voice, but the look of relief on his face said how he was really feeling. He kissed the top of my head when Mum sat up and started blowing her nose.

'I'll leave you all to it and come and visit tomorrow, Paige, ok?' Alec asked. I nodded, wincing again and reaching up to clutch my head, which felt as if it was full of spanners.

'Thank you so much for staying with me.'

'Anytime,' he smiled. 'Not that I want to see you in the hospital again, but you know what I meant.'

'Thanks for looking after her for us, Alec. Really good of you.' Dad shook his hand and slapped him a few times on the back. I craned my neck to keep him in my sights for as long as possible, until he turned and gave me a wave from the ward door.

'Honestly, why you and that boy aren't together is beyond me,' Mum sighed.

'He's moving to New York,' I sniffed, snatching the box of tissues out of her hand.

'Less of Alec, I want to know what my little girl's doing in London,' Dad demanded as he sat on the bed and took my hand.

The Following Morning

I was woken up after breakfast by a nurse checking on me again. I'd hardly slept as they were monitoring me every half an hour, given I'd been out of it for a few minutes. A CT scan had shown no permanent damage, to my brain anyway, so I was likely to be released this afternoon. Dad had insisted that I was having my nose done privately, in case I ended up looking like Frankenstein's bride with a botched job, but I had to wait for the swelling to go down first. He'd taken the news of my job offer better than expected, Mum too. I supposed having already lived away from home for three years, they hadn't expected me to move back in with them permanently. I'd not mentioned the lack of pay though, that might tip him over the edge. I had plenty of savings put by to tide me over, but London was an expensive city to rent in. I'd have to use the next few days to pack up my things and find a hotel down here, then I could try and find a studio or something. I just couldn't believe as I was moving here, within reach of Alec, he was leaving. I grabbed my phone from the bedside table. I'd been so headachy and tired last night, I hadn't even rung Poppie to find out if she was engaged, or to tell her my news. I grimaced when I saw six missed FaceTime calls from her. She was going to be in a mood. I pulled the sheet over my head, not sure if by using my phone to call her, I was about to get shouted at for setting off someone's pacemaker or shutting down the intensive care ward.

'Paige?' Poppie answered immediately.

'O. My. God,' we both exclaimed at the same time, looking at each other horrified. Poppie was hard as nails, I'd only ever seen her cry once, at her beloved family pet's impromptu funeral service in their back garden when she was twelve. But her face was red and blotchy and her eyes were swollen, really badly. 'What happened?' we demanded in unison. 'You first,' we said together again. 'No, you first.'

'For goodness sake,' I sighed. 'Mine's a quick one, I have a feeling yours isn't. I ran into a glass door and broke my nose. I'm in the hospital, but I should be coming home later today. I'm fine. What's wrong? Talk to me.'

'My boyfriend … no scratch that, my *ex*-boyfriend is a cheating piece of scum,' she sobbed, reaching for some tissues off screen, then honking her nose really loudly and wetly. She reappeared with tears pouring from her eyes and I figured it wasn't the time to tell her she had some serious booger leakage as well. A snot moustache was going to be the last thing on her mind.

'Reece cheated on you?'

'More than once. And I'd never have known if his last fling didn't threaten to call me to show me evidence. He only told me first to try and earn himself some brownie points.'

'O, Poppie, I'm so sorry. I'd never have believed he'd do something like that. Not to you. You've been together so long. I'm going to kill him the moment I get home.'

'That's not the worst news,' she snuffled.

'It gets worse?' The mind boggled. What could possibly be worse than your long-term boyfriend screwing around behind your back? 'You're not pregnant, are you?' I gasped.

'No, thank God.'

'He hasn't given you VD or something?'

'He'd better not have, but I'm going to have to get myself tested now, aren't I? What if I have some horrible disease because he couldn't keep his dick in his pants?' she howled.

'We'll go to the clinic tomorrow to be sure and if you have something, we'll deal with it together. Right after I castrate him,' I growled. How dare he put my best friend through this. It was inexcusable. 'So what could be worse?'

'You'll never guess who he slept with.' She blasted her nose again and wiped her eyes on her sleeve. I should be there with her. She needed me and I was stuck in bloody London.

'Who?'

'Only that cow … *Ruth*.'

'Noooooooo!' I exclaimed.

'Yes,' she moaned. 'I could handle it if he'd risked losing me for someone nice, but for her? Am I really so horrible that she was a better choice than me?'

'No, Poppie, no. Never think that. You're a million times the woman she is. She's the reason I'm here in London, because she made me feel inadequate, you'd never do that to someone. You don't have a nasty bone in your body. We obviously misjudged Reece, he's not the guy we thought and you're better off without him.'

'God, here's me waffling on about my troubles, I haven't even asked how the appointment went.'

'Assuming they still want me, and my nose job doesn't leave me horrifically disfigured, I'm starting training on Monday.'

'You got an offer?' she exclaimed, her face brightening immediately. 'In London?'

'Yes.' I fought against smiling, the pain was too much.

'Paige, that's amazing. God, we can find somewhere to live together.'

'Miss Taylor,' came an annoyed voice. 'Simply pulling the sheet over one's head doesn't fool me. Phone, now please.'

'Shit, I've been rumbled. Poppie, I've got to go. I'm so sorry, I'll ring later. If I'm allowed home, come and stay with me tonight, we can talk then.'

'Please come home tonight,' she pleaded.

'Miss Taylor, don't make me confiscate it.'

'Shit, it's like being back at boarding school,' I giggled, then winced as my nose reminded me of its sorry state. 'Love you.'

'Love you, too. Call me soon.'

'Will do,' I nodded. I blew her a kiss and cut her off. 'Ok, ok, I'm sorry,' I groaned as I heard a tut and the sheet was pulled back by a scary-looking senior nurse.

'You have a visitor,' she nodded, flicking her head over her shoulder, before turning on her heels and virtually goose walking out of the ward.

'Jesus, Paige, you look awful,' Alec exclaimed as he approached.

'Thanks ever so much,' I replied, quickly reaching up to try and finger comb my dishevelled hair.

'I'd suggest not looking in a mirror,' he advised, bending over to kiss my forehead.

'Do I have a snot moustache?'

'A what?'

'Never mind. How bad is it looking?'

'I've seen you look better. You have two black eyes, a bruised forehead, and your nose is … I can't lie, it's Pinocchio big.'

'Great,' I groaned, rolling onto my back with a sigh, then turning to look at him. 'Should you be here, don't you have a lot to do if you're leaving in a few days?'

'I do have a lot to do, but I wanted to see you in case you were discharged later. I got you some Belgian chocolate truffles, as I figured you'd be forgoing carbs and sugar like most models from next week.' He set a box on the bedside table and I eyed it up and licked my lips.

'You think I got a figure like this by nibbling lettuce leaves? It takes a lot of junk to put in a trunk this big. Open them up then, I'm starving.'

'Don't ever change, Paige,' he laughed, doing as he was told. He held one in his fingers and frowned. 'I think it's too big, it will hurt for you to chew.' I watched him bite it in half, taking a piece into his mouth, then offering me the other. I carefully took it out of his fingers with my teeth and sucked it, letting the powerful and rich flavour saturate my mouth, while the look on his face saturated my knickers.

He licked his thumb, then swept it over my lower lip. 'Cocoa powder,' he said gruffly.

'Thanks,' I replied huskily. He quickly shoved the box on the bedside table and stood up abruptly.

'I need to go.'

'Already? But you only just got here.'

'It's not good for me to be around you, Paige. I was happy until I saw you yesterday.'

'Was?'

'I am, I meant I am happy. See, being around you clouds things and I can't deal with cloud right now,' he muttered, shoving his hands through his hair. 'I'm moving to New York, I'm going to be travelling around the world, never knowing where I'll be from one week to the next. This is bad timing, as ever.'

'Don't go.'

'I have things to sort and your parents will be here soon,' he sighed, missing my point.

'I meant don't go to New York,' I whispered. 'Stay, in London, with me.'

'Paige, I ...' He shook his head and blew out a deep breath. 'You're drugged up and emotional, you have no idea what you're saying. I'm going to go, but I have a proposition for you. I'll message you later, but I think it's best I don't return.'

'I think it's best you go, too,' I replied, a wave of hurt crashing into me. I'd just put myself out there and he was rejecting me. 'Of course I don't know what I'm saying. I seem to have no control over my balance around you, so why should my emotions be any different, right?'

'That's not what I meant. Christ, Paige, this isn't easy for me, you know!' he snapped.

'It's not easy for me either.'

'I've just invested all of my savings in this studio, made commitments that I can't back out of. Don't you think I would if I could?'

'I don't know,' I sniffed, wiping some tears out of my eyes. 'I've just asked you to stay for me, you never asked me to stay for you.'

'Because I knew you'd go anyway, Paige,' he bit, a look of anger crossing his face. 'You weren't in love with me, I was just a crush and I could see in your eyes that you weren't going to choose me, so I tried to make it easy for you.'

'I'm choosing you now, Alec, and you're rejecting me,' I cried out, pain crushing my chest, like he'd just eviscerated me. 'Or maybe it is just me, maybe I'm in this on my own and you never really wanted me.'

'Of course I bloody want you,' he roared, making me jump. 'I've always wanted you, but sometimes it's not that easy, Paige. Sometimes life and adult responsibilities get in the damn way.'

'What the hell's going on?' bit Dad as he strode up to the bed. 'Why are you yelling at my daughter?'

'I was just leaving, sir. Paige is tired and upset and I think my being here is making things worse.'

'Alec!' I tried to sit up as I lost my battle to stem my tears.

'I'm inclined to agree. Thanks for all of your help with her, I really appreciate it, but I think she needs to rest now,' Dad replied, shaking his hand.

'Bye, Paige,' Alec sighed, throwing a quick glance in my direction before turning to walk away.

'Alec!' I shouted, but this time he didn't turn around and I started sobbing uncontrollably as the last forty-eight hours and the pain in my nose, and my heart, hit me.

A Pain In The Neck

June

'See you tomorrow, Poppie,' I called as I rushed to the front door with a piece of toast between my teeth and a travel mug of black coffee in my hand.

'Hey, not so fast,' she yelled, appearing in her bedroom doorway. 'You're not coming home tonight?'

'No,' I mumbled as I took a bite and looked for my keys.

'No way! After eight months of dating, you're finally going to do it?' she giggled, pelvic thrusting to hammer home her point.

'You're so crude,' I laughed, swallowing the last of my breakfast. 'I didn't want to rush it, but it's been long enough. I haven't had sex in nearly a year and I *need* sex.'

'Tell me about it, I have to listen to the various symphonies of your army of plastic boyfriends most nights. You really need to ask our landlord to put in some decent-quality soundproofing.'

'Like I'd ask *him* that,' I scoffed.

'Are you still not over him?' Poppie asked, a serious expression settling on her face.

'Can we save the complicated questions for when you grill me tomorrow please?' I pleaded.

'This Marc better blow your mind, Paige, because someone needs to pull you out of this Alec fantasy you've been living in from the moment you met him. Tomorrow, sofa, wine, Chinese, chocolate, we're talking,' she warned with a pointed finger. I rolled my eyes and blew her a kiss.

'Got to go, photo shoot, can't be late.' I rushed out, with her yelling something about moving on to me.

I sighed as I pressed the button for the elevator. I'd been devastated when Alec left the hospital last year. I hadn't seen him since, but true to his word, he'd sent me a message that night. His proposition had been a financial one, for me to rent his apartment here in London. He'd offered me a really fair deal, so I was saving loads of money and he was making some with someone he knew and trusted to look after the place. Our messages to set it up, and for me to ask if Poppie could move in too, giving him more income, had been polite and courteous, nothing more. I'd have liked to have been in a position to not accept his help, to cut all ties so I could try and get over this infatuation I had with him, but I'd underestimated how expensive properties in London were. His two bedroomed apartment was immaculate, in a great, safe area in London, around the corner from the agency, and came with parking for Fi-Fi. Poppie and I would have had to live right on the outskirts without his assistance, and we'd have paid a fortune in travel costs. My career was starting to pick up, but I was a long way from being able to afford paying big bucks for a house.

The trouble was I hadn't got over him. I was living in his house, sleeping in his bed, using his shower. Everywhere I turned, even without pictures of him, there were reminders. Jean-Claude, my self-appointed mentor and agent, was one of his best friends and kept in regular contact with him. Sometimes he'd let slip that he'd been to dinner with Alec and that he was having the time of his life, enjoying being single, serial dating some of the top models out there. It seemed that he was having fun, that he had no intention of settling down, which was so far from the Alec I'd known, the Alec I'd wanted.

I wondered if he really was the man for me after all, but my heart hadn't got the message. I still wanted him, and Jean-Claude had no idea how much it cut me up inside to hear his stories about Alec, because I'd shared it with no one. Not even Poppie. I was faking it every day, even with my boyfriend Marc. I'd been on a kind of rebound, feeling low about Alec leaving, when I agreed to start dating him. He was a male model from the agency, great looking with a fabulous body, but ... same old story, he wasn't Alec. I'd persevered, hoping in time he'd grow on me more and more, until yesterday I'd asked if I could sleep over tonight, figuring maybe sex would clinch the deal. If I had really great sex with him, he could literally screw Alec, as well as me, out of my mind.

'I know, I know, I'm cutting it fine. I had to pack an overnight bag at the last minute. I promise I'm not going to turn into a diva,' I laughed as I stepped out of the car to find Jean-Claude waiting for me.

'I promise I'd turn into Jean-Claude Van Damme and kick that perfect rump of mine if you did,' he grinned, looping arms with me and kissing my cheek.

'First of all, it's mine, not yours, and it's not a rump. At least call it a derrière, use a little of your French sophistication and class. I mean, I don't even get a kiss on each cheek.'

'I've lived in London longer than France,' he reminded me.

'Why would you leave Paris?' I asked, completely perplexed. I'd only done a couple of shoots there, but I'd fallen in love with it.

'Why would you leave London? You fall for a city's charms because it's something new and exotic. People around the world romanticise living in a foreign city or country, but home is wherever your heart is. Pascal wanted to move to London when we fell in love, and where Pascal goes, so my heart follows.'

'I'd never have pegged you for a romantic that first day I met you,' I smiled.

'And I'd never have pegged you for a confident, skilled model, let alone the sexy woman you're turning into. Sometimes people can surprise you if you give them a chance.'

'They really can,' I agreed. 'But I owe it all to you. If you hadn't taken a chance on me, taken me under your wing, I'd never have made it. I'd have been chewed up and spat out. People are too scared of you to cross me.'

'You owe it to Alec. He saw the potential, I just shaped it.'

'Who's the photographer today?' I asked, steering the conversation away from Alec for the second time that day.

'Why do you avoid any discussion about him? Have you not forgiven him yet?' Jean-Claude sighed.

'Of course I have, I was being unreasonable that day.'

'Does he know that you've forgiven him? He was really hurt at the way things were left.'

'He knows. He knows, right?' I asked, frowning at Jean-Claude.

'I don't think he does, Paige. Maybe you should tell him. He still asks me if I think he made a mistake.'

'No, he was right to leave. I was tired, emotional, and needy, and I had no right to ask him to stay, not when he was already taken and making plans to settle down in a new city.'

'So you didn't mean it?'

'I meant it, I was just out of order. Rubbish timing, as usual.'

'But you're happy now? With Marc?'

'I am,' I said firmly, making sure not to look at him and give myself away.

'You're a terrible liar, Paige Taylor,' he laughed. 'You have a bad neck this morning, I take it?'

'No, why?' I asked, giving him a puzzled look.

'Aren't you and Marc doing it yet?' He wiggled his eyebrows as he mimicked thrusting his fingers.

'Actually no, I didn't want to rush it.'

'You've been dating for eight months, Paige!' He looked around, then leaned in and whispered in my ear. 'Are you frigid?'

'No!' I replied, thumping his arm.

'Vagijawsitis?'

'What the hell is vagijawsitis?'

'Where your piranha vagina is so tight, it bites off his head. It puts a lot of women and men off, so I hear.'

'That's not a real word, surely?' I laughed.

‘It’s vagi-something. I have no idea, I’m all about cock, darling. So what’s the problem?’

‘He’s great, but I’m just cautious. If it makes you feel any better, tonight is the night.’

‘You have a shoot tomorrow,’ he advised, flashing me a concerned glance.

‘I’ll be fine, I promise not to be up all night.’

‘Hmmmm,’ he frowned.

‘Ok, what’s wrong?’

‘O, look, Dominic’s in hair and makeup already, go and get changed. See you in there.’ He darted off, making me chuckle. Dominic McQueen was a well-known male model, gorgeous looking, with the most unusual amber eyes. We were shooting a swimwear campaign together for the next few days. Sadly he wasn’t into women, a fact that wasn’t lost on Jean-Claude, who went to pieces every time Dom was on set. Jean-Claude was madly in love with his partner Pascal, but even I could see Dom’s appeal. I doubted many people would say no if he clicked his fingers and asked them to join him for the night.

I slipped into the white bikini, covered up with a dressing gown, and headed to hair and makeup. I still couldn’t believe that this was my life. Two months of nightly training sessions with Jean-Claude had paid off. I had so much more confidence, and instead of feeling like a klutz most of the time, I now felt like a sexy, desirable woman. I’d been taught how to hold myself, different positions to make my body look its best, angles to ensure the light hit my face correctly to show off my best features, and a proper walk for fashion shows. Obviously I was still learning something every day, but I had enough skills to not completely frustrate photographers and to ensure I’d be booked for jobs I went on castings for. Jean-Claude had told me that my name was already getting out there, that if I continued to do well, I’d be called for jobs, instead of auditioning for them.

My curves meant I was unlikely to ever hit the heights of a runway supermodel, but it was a growing industry. More women were rebelling against the slim, airbrushed image of perfection the media perpetrated. They wanted real women that they could relate to, and that, said Jean-Claude, was where my appeal lay. I was in a world that most girls only dreamed of. I was looked after with mani-pedis, facials, body scrubs, wraps, haircuts, colours, and treatments. I’d be having spray tans too if it wasn’t for my Caribbean colour that hadn’t yet faded. My main speciality was swimwear and lingerie, and I got to keep some of those items. I’d travelled to Paris a few times and was due to go to Tokyo next month. It was fast paced and exciting.

And, if all of that wasn't enough, I had my best friend here with me to share the ride. Poppie had been devastated at Reece's betrayal of her, but she'd decided that dating was like riding a horse and that she needed to get back in the saddle as soon as possible or she could be put off for life. She was casually dating, seeing a few guys at once for drinks, meals, and dancing, nothing serious and no sex. She'd decided that until she found a guy that she wanted to see exclusively, that was as far as she was taking anything. She'd secured a full-time job working in administration for the Home Office and was taking evening classes for her bilingual secretarial diploma. Being in London was amazing. We had a whole new world of cuisine, fashion, and culture to explore, and we were making the most of it. We were rarely in. While my metabolism had always handled me eating what I wanted and not putting on weight, I had started going to a gym around the corner to make sure I stayed toned and in shape. My new career depended on it. A career I owed to Alec. I closed my eyes for a second as I thought of him, then picked up my phone. It was the middle of the night in New York, but I needed to clear my conscience.

Alec, it's Paige. I hope this won't wake you. I just wanted to say how sorry I am for the way we left things when I last saw you. I should have been supportive of your venture and plans, but I was selfish, only thinking how they would affect me. It was a great and exciting opportunity for you and I only hope that it's all working out just as you'd hoped. I also owe you my undying gratitude for helping me get into this industry. I'm simply loving it and Jean-Claude has been an amazing mentor and friend. I'd never have done it without your faith in me, so thank you from the bottom of my heart. I owe you so much more than thanks for everything you've done for me, including renting your home, which I promise Poppie and I are taking excellent care of. Wishing you every success, Paige

I stared at the screen for a while, wondering if I should put a kiss at the end, but I decided against it. What was the point, he was there and I was here, there was an ocean between us, and we were obviously looking for different things right now. I pressed send and tucked it back in my bag before heading over to the green screen set, where I shrugged off my dressing gown and went to cosy up to muscular perfection Dom, who was wearing the tiniest swimming trunks I'd ever seen. Life was good. And tonight I'd be having amazing sex. Maybe I'd set my expectations too high. Great sex. In fact, right now I'd be happy with just plain old boring sex, it had been that long.

The Next Day

Poppie drove Fi-Fi to the shoot for me, giggling all the way there, while all I could do was roll my eyes and sigh.

'Please take care of Fi-Fi, no speeding,' I warned when she pulled up outside the studio.

'I do know how to drive, it's not my first time, thank you very much. Wind your neck in,' she winked.

'Very funny,' I muttered, awkwardly getting out of the car.

'Good thing you're not a porn star, all of that thrusting would be a real pain in the neck today.' She burst out laughing when I bent down to give her my best unimpressed scowl. 'You'll see the funny side later.'

'I really doubt that,' I replied. I headed inside, straight to hair and makeup, to find Jean-Claude leaning back on the long dressing room countertop, while Dom sat having his hair styled.

'Mon Dieu!' he exclaimed, quickly standing up when he saw me. 'What happened?'

'I'd rather not discuss it, if you don't mind,' I replied, putting down my bag and gingerly sitting on one of the barbershop-style chairs.

'Can you work?' he frowned, walking over to place a reassuring and concerned hand on my shoulder.

'I'm not letting anyone down. I'll do my best, but I was warned to keep this on as much as possible for twenty-four hours, so if you don't mind me bringing it on set and just taking it off when Daryl's ready to shoot, that would be great.'

'Can I get you anything?'

'I'd love a strong coffee. I was at A&E for five hours last night, I've barely slept. A mountain of concealer is going to be needed for these bad boys.' I pulled a pouting face as I pointed to the bags under my eyes.

'Here, take these,' Dom offered, heading over with two teaspoons.

'You want me to make you a coffee?' I asked, twisting around to face him.

'No,' he laughed. 'I carry a set with me on every shoot and put them in the fridge. They're great for reducing puffy eyes if I've had a late night. So, bad neck, huh?'

'How on earth did you guess?' I mocked with a roll of my eyes, making Jean-Claude laugh. The thick, soft, and squishy beige neck collar was a dead giveaway.

'I bet I can guess what happened to you first time,' Dom smirked.

'I bet you can't,' I replied.

'Care to lay a wager on that?'

'Game on. I'm so confident you won't guess that I'll bet £100.'

'I'm in, I'm in,' Jean-Claude clapped. 'I can guess, too.'

'Ok,' I smirked, seeing an easy way to win some money here. 'Answers to be written on a piece of paper. If you're both wrong, I get £100 off each of you.'

'And if we're right, you pay us £100 each,' Dom nodded. 'Trace, grab some paper and a pen and get Paige a cup of coffee, will you,' he called over his shoulder to his assistant. I wondered if I'd ever be that big in the modelling world that I'd need an assistant. Dom reclined my chair and stood behind me, holding the spoons over my eyes as we waited, while Jean-Claude headed off to speak to Daryl, the photographer, to warn him of my predicament.

'Ok, ok, let's do this,' he announced when he returned. I sat up as the three of us scribbled our answers.

'Mine first,' chuckled Dom. I opened his piece of paper and smoothed it out on the counter top, my jaw dropping when I saw the three words written on it.

'No way!' I exclaimed as he burst out laughing. I grabbed Jean-Claude's off him to see the same three words and he bent over double, he was laughing so hard at the look on my face. I stared at both identical phrases, virtually matching mine.

Sex with Marc!

'How did you know?' I moaned as I watched their reflections in the long mirror opposite.

'Same thing happened to my best friend, Coco,' Dom grinned, 'not to mention a whole string of models he's dated.'

'He's fondly known in modelling circles as the "Jack Hammer,"' Jean-Claude added, trying to keep a straight face. 'Goes at it like a pneumatic drill on speed. He's never screwed a woman without ... well you know, screwing up her neck.'

'Why didn't you tell me?' I exclaimed, glaring at him.

'I had a lot of money riding on it. There's been a pool running since the moment you agreed to go out with him, and given you made him wait so long, the odds shot up in my favour.'

'You ... I can't think of a word to say to you right now that wouldn't involve me getting fired. And you can stop laughing, too,' I warned Dom with a pointed finger.

'No way, I'm going to enjoy this for the rest of the day. Get your purse out, Taylor, that's my meal out with Calvin covered for tonight.'

'With the money I've made, I'm booking The London Domville for the night for Pascal and me, with dinner,' Jean-Claude nodded. They both high-fived each other as I groaned and reached for my bag. A bet was a bet, even though technically they'd cheated, given they knew the outcome before I even slept with him.

'Seeing him again then, Paige?' Dom teased.

'No, I'm not,' I answered firmly. I just had to tell Marc that now. 'My God, why hasn't someone told him how bad he is?' I asked.

'Did you?'

'Well, no, but I didn't want to hurt his feelings after he had to take me to A&E. I thought maybe it was just a one off, that we weren't compatible. It was *so* bad. I was clinging to the railings of his headboard trying to anchor my arms to stop him knocking me out, he was shunting me up and down the bed so fast. I swear I have friction burns on my back and … you know … down there. It hurts to pee.'

'It's not all bad,' Dom advised as he wiped some tears of laughter from his face.

'Are you kidding me? Where's the good? I'm wearing a collar and I'm in real pain.'

'At least I can spread a rumour that you've got a flaming hot pussy.'

'Dom!' I exclaimed, turning around to whack him and moaning as the movement hurt my sore neck. I paid up and knocked back my black coffee, letting out a sigh of resignation. I was doomed when it came to men. I was just going to focus on my career for now. I should have trusted my gut. Until I found a man who stirred the kind of excitement, passion, and need in me that Alec did, I wasn't ever dating again.

The French Connection

January ~ Six Years Later

I virtually skipped out of The Paris Domville to a clear, crisp, and chilly day. My lingerie shoot wasn't until this afternoon, so I had a few hours free. I pulled my cashmere beanie hat down over my ears, tightened the cashmere scarf around my neck, and put my hands deep into my wool coat pockets. I needed some fresh air. I'd only flown into Paris yesterday morning, after spending a few weeks out on the Gold Coast in Australia shooting a swimwear commercial, then doing a fashion show in Seoul.

My life was now a blur of exotic locations, rushing to different destinations and working nearly every day. I hadn't had a holiday in forever. Not that I was complaining, it was my choice to work so hard. I was going to be twenty-eight this year, there was a limit to how long my body and appeal would keep me this busy. Jean-Claude was already encouraging me to move towards beauty campaigns. It wasn't like I was desperate for the money anymore. I'd been so in demand over the last five years, been on the cover of so many magazines, done public appearances, talk shows, the whole nine yards, I could retire if I wanted to. But I'd miss the buzz, and I wanted to make sure that I'd saved enough to set up my parents, and Poppie, for life as well.

I walked along the Seine, grabbing a hot coffee from a street vendor on the embankment and just enjoying a bit of quiet time. I didn't often get to be alone. I was accompanied everywhere by my PA Shauna, hair and makeup stylist Vivian, and Jean-Claude, whenever he wasn't busy in London casting for his ModOne agency, that I was still a part of. He'd taken a chance on me, I owed it to him to stay with him, and he was one of my best friends now. I adored him. I still lived in Alec's apartment with Poppie, though she spent a few nights a week over at her boyfriend Justin's. They'd been seeing each other for two years now. Poppie had even told me that he was the one, something she'd never said about Reece. I'd asked her how she knew that and she'd told me that while she thought she was in love with Reece, what she felt for Justin was so different, and so much stronger, she'd realised now what love really was. I'd never seen her so happy. She'd even turned down an incredible job in Brussels because she hadn't wanted to be away from him, or me. That's how sure she was. That's how happy she was.

I sighed as I sipped my drink. I wanted that. I wanted someone to love and to love me in return. I wanted to get married and have a family. But over the last six years, I'd built up a wall around my heart so high that no one could climb it. I was my own worst enemy. I'd make excuses that I was too busy, or too focussed on my career, to date. It was sort of true. But I knew for the right guy, I'd find the time, he'd become my priority. The trouble was I'd found that guy, it was just that he was happy with his single life. I hadn't seen Alec in years. Not since that day in the hospital. He'd replied to my apology, thanking me and apologising as well. We sent Christmas cards and the odd message of congratulations for a job well done, but it was all very polite and civil. He'd moved on, he was one of the world's top fashion photographers now, jet setting around the globe, rarely in one country for long, or with one woman for long. He was happy.

I was happy for him.

I was miserable for me.

'Paige, you look stunning,' Vivian exclaimed, her fingers steepled over her lips as I stepped out of my dressing room in my lingerie and a pair of elegant high heels. The designer was up and coming for exclusive, and very expensive, lingerie for women who had curves, and I was the face of his campaign. The body, too. I'd already shot the TV commercial and now we were doing the photography close-ups for the magazines. I was in a custom-made, gorgeous lace bra that had been inset with hundreds of tiny diamonds that glittered under the ceiling lights. The tiny low-rise French knickers and suspender belt matched, and the sheer stockings had diamond-encrusted lace tops. I dreaded to think how much money I was wearing, when I was actually wearing so little. As usual, Vivian had done an amazing job with my makeup and hair. It was looking thick and glossy, my natural waves enhanced to give it body as it hung down to my waist. My long black lashes were embellished with silver crystals, and she'd been asked to painstakingly glue tiny diamantés to my lips, creating a shimmer of sparkle as if I was wearing a silver lip-gloss. I wasn't too keen on those, my lips were tingling and I wanted to scratch them off.

'I feel stunning,' I agreed with a smile, twisting to look at my reflection in the mirror from behind. Wow, these knickers didn't leave much to the imagination, more of my bottom cheeks were out than in. The client had requested a full wax as well, something I'd been thinking I needed doing permanently as it was becoming more fashionable to be hairless, but it never got any easier each time I had it done. I winced as I remembered the first time. The degradation of having a total stranger looking at my privates, then the scream I'd let out as the strip had been pulled away. I'd reacted badly to the wax the first few times as well. I'd come out in pimples that had itched like crazy, leading to rumours of me having crabs from scratching myself that much on set. Dom had come to the rescue, ever the professional who'd seen and done everything. He had some cooling antiseptic gel he always travelled with, which had soon done the trick. I bulk ordered it in now.

'Magnifique,' Jean-Claude clapped as he wandered in munching on a croissant.

'Me or the food?'

'Both,' he grinned, indicating with a turning finger for me to swivel. I did as I was told and he nodded his approval. 'How are you feeling?'

'Excellent and raring to go. Is Juan on set?' I asked.

'Hmmm, about that,' Jean-Claude nodded. 'I may have told you a little white lie. Juan will not be shooting you today.'

'Daryl?' I asked, adjusting the cups of my bra, making sure the girls were as pert as they could be.

'Please do not get angry with me, darling,' he sighed, folding one arm across his chest and reaching up to rub his mouth with his hand.

'Who's the photographer, Jean-Claude?' I demanded, my heart and stomach sinking. There was only one reason he'd lie to me, if he thought I'd back out of a job. And the only reason I'd refuse to do a job was if Alec was the photographer. I'd refused a few in the past, knowing it would hurt too much to see him.

'You know who,' he confirmed quietly.

'How could you?' I gasped, my stomach dropping like a stone. 'You know our history, how hard it would be for me, especially when I'm … barely dressed.'

'I'm sorry, Paige, but this is a huge campaign. The client wanted the best and right now, that's you and Alec. This is part of life, working and dealing with people we don't want to on a daily basis. No one is immune.'

'Does he know it's me?'

'Of course he does. A photographer of his calibre has his choice of models, he only works with the ones he wants to. It was him that insisted on you being hired for the job when the client approached him to do the stills.'

'Alec requested me for this job?' I asked quietly, knotting my fingers together to stop my hands from shaking. I hadn't experienced nerves in a very long time, but suddenly I felt like that eighteen year old, waiting for her first date to pick her up for the ball again.

'He did. He's a professional, Paige, as you are. The two of you are just going to do your jobs, then you can go your separate ways and back to your lives. It's too late to back out now.'

'I'd never back out,' I responded, 'I can't believe you think I would, but I'm not happy that you kept this from me. I could have had time to prepare.'

'You'd have been even worse, stewing on it for days. It was my decision. Alec knows I kept it from you so he's prepared for you to need to relax a little.'

'O God,' I moaned. I wanted to flop onto the comfortable sofa and bury my head in my hands, but seeing as though my diamond-encrusted arse cheeks were worth a fortune right now, I had to be careful, delicate, and graceful. I had to be the new Paige, not the old one. Was I really ready to face him again? Scantily clad at that? I looked down at myself. At least I was in matching sexy underwear, not like that time in Daisy's stall. 'Let's get this over with.'

'Please don't let the client hear your over infectious enthusiasm,' Jean-Claude teased with a shake of his head.

'Dressing gown?' Shauna offered, holding it out to me.

'Everyone's going to see me like this shortly, I've got used to it, thanks,' I smiled. I pursed and relaxed my lips a few times, dying to scratch them.

Jean-Claude led the way, with me sandwiched between Shauna with her iPad, which was constantly beeping with bookings, and Vivian with her custom utility belt to hold her brush, clips, hairspray, and makeup. A maintenance guy stumbled past, rubber necking at my backside, and got a mouthful in French from Jean-Claude, which made me giggle. He was so protective, but it wasn't like my body wasn't public property now, everyone had seen it. Dad had got over his rage at people seeing his daughter scantily clad, he was just grateful "parts" were always covered. I'd kept reminding him of the offers I'd had to move into the porn industry, which I'd declined, and that soon stopped his moaning.

Jean-Claude opened the door to the first set and we all squinted at the bright lighting. A bedroom scene had been recreated on the stage, which looked contemporary and sexy at the same time. The walls were painted grey with white skirting, and there were silver accents in the mirrors and frames that were hanging up. There was a black chandelier above a huge bed covered with black furs. A silver dressing table and stool and black and white chaise longue flanked the bed, and there was a walk-in wardrobe, filled with designer clothes and shoes. I wanted to move in. There were lots of people milling around, fussing over the set and adjusting the lighting, but I hadn't spotted Alec yet. I took Jean-Claude's hand as he helped me up the steps onto the stage. He walked around me, adjusting the straps of my bra while Vivian fiddled with my hair, spritzing it into place while she shielded my eyes. I suddenly felt all of the hairs on the back of my neck stand to attention. He was here. I could sense him.

'Good afternoon everyone, it's a pleasure to be working with you all,' came his deep, husky voice that made my skin goose up. He sounded different, more mature, and he had a slight American twang to his well-spoken English accent. Vivian dropped her hand and moved away and my breath caught in my throat as my eyes locked with his, just like it always did. 'Paige, it's great to see you,' he advised as he strode over, leaned in, and kissed my cheek.

'You too,' I managed to say, as I tried to focus on staying upright as all of the feelings I had repressed for him suddenly rushed back and sucker punched me right in the chest. He frowned as he looked at me, biting his full lower lip. I wondered how he was feeling, seeing me standing here with so little on. Did I affect him at all anymore? The way he affected me? I was hoping no one had noticed that I was finding it hard to breathe, that my nipples had suddenly swollen and that my cheeks had coloured up. His eyes suddenly shot down, scanning me, and I saw his nostrils flare and his pupils expand. What was that?

'Jean-Claude, a word,' he bit, quickly spinning and marching over to the relative privacy of the fake walk-in dressing room. Jean-Claude raised his eyebrows at me and I shrugged, I had no idea what I'd done wrong. I watched as he headed over to where Alec was pacing, running his hands through his hair. They started talking, too quietly for me to hear, but there were lots of emphatic gestures going on and glances being tossed my way. Their voices suddenly raised, and I caught snippets of words. "Unacceptable," from Jean-Claude, "impossible," from Alec. What was going on? Like I needed to feel any more nervous. Jean-Claude came out and clapped his hands sharply, and loudly.

'I need everyone's attention right now, maintenant,' he yelled. The set went quiet and everyone turned to face him. *Breathe, Paige, breathe, you've done nothing wrong,* I told myself. 'This is highly irregular, but today we will be shooting a closed set, just myself, the photographer, and model. I need everyone out immediately.'

'What?' I exclaimed. I'd never experienced that before.

'Well I'm not leaving,' announced Vivian. 'Where Paige goes, I go. What if she needs a touch up or her hair adjusted?'

'Then I will look after her. Leave your belt with me.'

'With all due respect, Jean-Claude,' she started, but he silenced her with his authoritative palm in the air.

'I have been in this industry since before you were born, darling. I can apply blusher or lip-gloss and tease hair with the best of them. Out, now.'

'Paige?' She looked at me for confirmation, as did Shauna. I held my hands in the air and shook my head.

'He's in charge, do as he says,' I sighed. They both nodded, Vivian slipping off her belt and setting it on the dressing table before they scurried off with the rest of the crew. 'What's going on? What about lighting? What about the client? He's due at any moment.'

'Alec will deal with the lighting himself. As for the client, I will go and tell him. When you hire someone of Alec's calibre, you are handing over your trust that they know what to do to enhance your brand and make it shine. He will be pissed off, but this is how it will be.'

'Why?' I asked, still none the clearer.

'For gay men, seeing a scantily clad woman does nothing, but for red blooded men, like the maintenance man, it has a certain effect. Are you understanding me?'

'You're closing down the set because the maintenance guy was aroused by me?' That made no sense at all.

'Paige, Paige, Paige,' Jean-Claude sighed. 'It has never happened to him before, but he is worried about how it will look if this news spreads. He has settled in New York now, clients come to him instead of the other way around, and he is living with his latest girlfriend, Tiffany.'

'Alec's living with someone?' I gasped. For six years, I'd consoled myself with the fact that he wasn't the settling-down type, that this was why he hadn't come back for me, but he'd moved in with someone? I swallowed down the pain, still not sure why that would mean the set would have to be restricted like this. 'What does me being in lingerie have to do with this?'

'Word travels fast and I know that Tiffany is already unhappy about this situation, of the two of you working together.'

'Why would she be unhappy?' I frowned. None of this made sense.

'It's Tiffany Beauchamp.' He raised his eyebrows as he looked at me, as if he was waiting for the penny to drop. But nothing was dropping, except for my heart. Tiffany was gorgeous, a tall, slender, blue-eyed, brunette stunner. 'Do I really have to spell it out, Paige? The resemblance to you is uncanny, albeit she doesn't have your sexy curves. But she does have jealousy issues as she knows that you and Alec have history. She asked him not to work with you, so news of an erection on set would be the nail in the coffin.'

'Alec has an erection from looking at me?' I whispered, my eyes widening as I glanced over at Alec still pacing, then back to Jean-Claude.

'Darling, don't look so shocked. The two of you have always had this chemistry, but he's with Tiffany now and doesn't want to create waves, so he felt it would be better if no one were witness. Now, do you think you can continue to be a professional, despite this knowledge? He is rather embarrassed.'

'No kidding,' I uttered, flicking my eyes over to him again and gulping to see that his predicament hadn't … deflated.

'Good. I'll return shortly. I have a feisty Italian to placate now, and stop worrying your lips, you're making them swell,' he muttered, full of frustration, as he marched off towards the exit, leaving me all alone with Alec. I hopped from one foot to the other, fidgeting with my fingers, trying to decide what would be a good icebreaker in this sort of situation.

'So, you've been busy I see,' I called. He stopped pacing and lifted his head to look over at me. He was captivating. His azure eyes shone with life and vitality and his strong jawline had a dusting of designer stubble. He was in dark navy jeans, with a pale blue shirt and navy waistcoat, which hugged his broad muscular body perfectly. I felt something stir deep in my core as I looked at him, focussing on his face, rather than what was going on below the trouser line. It had been so long since I'd had sex, I'd forgotten what it was like. But right now my body was screaming its hunger at me. This was a recipe for a disaster.

'Yes,' he replied. 'It's nice to finally put down some roots in New York. I've barely been home for the last six years, I was constantly on the move. I shouldn't complain, it's everything I ever dreamed it would be.'

'Must be hard though,' I nodded, then pulled a face. 'Sorry, no pun intended. I know you're hard, which must be … hard. Wow, I was going to try and breeze through this without bringing up erections and I've already said the word hard three, no four, times now in one breath. So, you're turned on because I'm standing here in sexy lingerie, with stiff nipples in an inviting bedroom, who wouldn't be turned on? I'm fine with it, totally fine. I mean, I'd be insulted if you didn't have an erection, quite frankly. Penises are just programmed to spring at the hint of anything sexy, aren't they … O God, I'm waffling, I'm waffling about erections and penises and sex. With you! I'm sorry, what was I saying? I've lost my train of thought.' I wrapped my arms around myself, suddenly feeling vulnerable as he started walking towards me.

'Yes, men are programmed to respond to sexy images, but I'm a professional, Paige. Over the years, I've learned to switch off my feelings, to not be distracted by what I'm photographing. But when the most beautiful girl I've ever seen, the only girl I've ever had regrets over, is standing in front of me in the flesh, dressed like *that* .... I'm only human,' he rasped. I stepped back as he moved closer.

'Most beautiful?'

'Yes, no one holds a candle, still.'

'Regrets?' I whispered.

'Yes, regrets,' he said softly, stepping forward again and reaching out to tuck my hair behind my ear. I heard a gentle whimper leave my lips to feel the pads of his fingers graze my cheek, to be within touching distance of him, kissing distance, to catch a scent of that masculine aroma I'd always found so appealing. The straw-chewing boy I'd fawned over at the farm was gone. This was a confident alpha male at the top of his game, and I was making him react. The feeling was heady, but wrong. He was with her, he lived with her. Our chemistry and attraction was undeniable, but our hearts hadn't been in the same place since that day we split up. 'I have so many when it comes to you, Paige.'

'Life's full of regrets, no one is spared them, but we're both happy now and we've moved on. Why don't we do this shoot as fast as we can, get it over with, and we can get back to our new lives instead of dwelling on the past?' I suggested. Really I wanted to bombard him with questions. I wanted to know what he meant. Did he regret walking away from me, of not giving us a chance? Was he really ready to settle down? Did he see marriage and children in his future? Did he see that with Tiffany, or me? In fact, sod the questions, I wanted to drag him to that bed not two feet from where we stood and see if our chemistry there was as good as I'd always imagined it would be. But he was taken. Much as I wanted him, still, much as I'd always want him, I'd never interfere with another woman's man, that was despicable. I'd seen first-hand what it had done to Poppie. If he was faltering, I had to be the strong one today.

'Are you happy?' he asked, cocking his head to study my reaction as he shoved his hands in his jeans. Damn it, that only made me look down to see nothing had changed. He was still aroused.

'Yes,' I replied as I looked back up at him after a few seconds hesitation. 'Why wouldn't I be? I have an amazing career, thanks to you and Jean-Claude. I'm set for life financially, I travel the world, meet new people, experience different cultures, get bombarded with clothes and accessories. What girl wouldn't be happy with that?'

'They're all things, Paige. Superficial things. That's not what I asked. I meant are you happy here?' He gently placed his palm flat on my chest, right above my breast and my heart. It was like a defibrillator had suddenly jolted a high voltage charge through me as I gasped and heat tore through my veins. I reached up to cover his hand with mine, my breathing coming hard and fast and my chest heaving. He licked his lips, his eyes moist with what seemed like unspoken emotion as he looked deep into mine and opened his mouth to say something.

'Two minutes, two minutes I leave you alone,' barked Jean-Claude. 'We are here to work, or have you both forgotten that?'

We broke apart, and the loss of contact with him was as if someone had just ripped a precious newborn from my arms. God damn him, what was he doing to me, what was he trying to say? We quickly switched into professional mode, but the tension hung heavy in the air and neither of us could look the other in the eye as I moved through a number of poses and positions on the stool and chaise while he clicked away, adjusting the lighting with Jean-Claude tweaking my hair and makeup when required. He left me lying on the bed and went to stand with Alec to look through the shots they already had, and I could see them both shaking their heads.

'What's wrong?' I called, propping myself up on my elbows.

'They're missing something, they're all flat and lifeless. For any other model I'd be satisfied, but this is you, I hold you to a higher standard,' Jean-Claude admonished with a shake of his head. 'You need to bring it, Paige, you need to show your emotions. People need to be buying into sex and glamour and right now, sexy and glamorous as you look, your face and eyes tell me that you could be concentrating on revision for an exam.'

'I'm really trying,' I replied, biting the inside of my mouth. I was holding back, I knew I was. The poses were perfect, but I was bottling up my emotions because Alec was here, because I didn't want to admit how badly he got to me. I was trying to repress the sexual magnetism between us, when ironically it was just what was needed to elevate this shoot. And my lips hurt!

'Darling,' Jean-Claude sighed as he came to sit next to me. He squeezed one of my hands between his as I blinked back some tears. 'I get how hard this is, for both of you, but if we really want this range to fly, women need to open the magazine, see you with a look of ecstasy on your face, and imagine the kind of sex they'd have if they were wearing this lingerie. Men need to imagine *they* are the ones putting that look on your face, that if they bought their old, fat, and ugly wives this underwear, she'd magically turn into you,' he teased, making me smile. 'You *are* a sexy woman, Paige, but right now you're not selling me sex and I need it.'

'How do I do that when I'm feeling so tense around the photographer?' I whispered.

'You become an actress, as all good models do. You tune into your real feelings and emotions for him, use them to imagine he's making love to you on this bed, and the camera will ignite. Do this and we'll nail it.'

'That's not fair, you know how attracted I am to him. You're asking me to let that all out, but what about after? When he packs up and walks away again, back to his life in New York, with her?'

'Life is harsh sometimes,' he sighed, lifting his hand to run his knuckles down my cheek. 'But you chose this job and you excel at it, don't back down now. The Paige I know is a fighter, she does what it takes to be the best. How many times did you fall off my practice catwalk while you learned? How many times did you grit your teeth through the pain of a swollen ankle and do the walk again just to please me? You can do this,' he urged.

'I do this, then you promise me that I never work with him again, Jean-Claude. I keep trying to move on and we keep getting drawn back together, I need a clean break. Any job that involves him, I'm out.'

'We still need to shoot next door on the blocks of ice, then in the pool room with the beach, but when we're done, I think that would be best on both sides,' he confirmed, leaning down to kiss my forehead. 'You can do this, make me proud.'

I looked over at Alec, who was studying us intently, out of range to hear our discussion, then took a deep breath and nodded. The three of us resumed positions and started again as I tried to imagine Alec was on the bed with me, his fingers and lips caressing my skin. I arched my back and reached up to touch the irritatingly itchy diamantés on my lips, letting out a huff of air as I stared down the lens, picturing his intense blue eyes.

'Yes, yes,' Alec called gruffly as Jean-Claude clapped his hands.

The next three hours were torture. I may as well have been doing porn for the images running through my mind. No one who saw my pictures was going to mistake exactly what I'd been thinking about while they were being taken. I'd never felt so alive, so free and uninhibited. So damn horny. Not even draping myself over huge blocks of freezing cold ice dampened the longing in my body. And my muse was right in the room with me, hovering over me at times taking close ups, right within touching distance, but once again he was untouchable. It was like being taken into Chanel, being shown all of the wonderful things they had to offer, but not being allowed to touch or buy them.

'We're done,' Jean-Claude announced gleefully as I emerged from the pool and smoothed my hair back. I wondered where the poor guy in charge of counting the diamonds on loan was right now. He'd be having kittens at the thought of one having fallen off in the pool, or worse, on the sand. Jean-Claude applauded us both. 'Phew, the sexual tension in here is off the charts. Even I have an erection.' His joke didn't raise a laugh from either of us.

'Excellent work, Paige, I have some incredible pictures,' Alec added, his tone low and husky. He coughed as our eyes locked for a moment.

'Can I go now?' I asked, my eyes darting for the exit.

'Will you join me for dinner?' he asked, the hope in his voice evident. I blinked a few times as I looked at him and shook my head. I knew where dinner was likely to lead and if it got that far, I didn't trust myself to say no. I didn't want to be something crossed off his list of regrets before going home to his girlfriend. I wanted to be his everything, or nothing. And once again, it seemed I was the latter, as there could never be any middle ground for me.

'Alec, I don't think that's a good idea, you're both tired and she has a shoot in London tomorrow,' Jean-Claude warned. Alec turned to face him and said something I couldn't hear, and Jean-Claude whispered something back with a shake of his head. I quickly ran to the exit as they were distracted. I raced up to the dressing room, where Vivian and Shauna were sitting talking. Both of them jumped up as I streaked in and grabbed my bag.

'I need to go, now. Shauna, can the driver be ready?' I asked as I stripped out of my expensive items.

'But you're soaking wet, we need to get you dry.'

'No time, I need to go,' I snapped, then flashed her an apologetic look. It wasn't her fault that I was stressed out.

'I'll make him ready,' she nodded, quickly disappearing.

'What's wrong?' Vivian asked, picking up the discarded lingerie and carefully squeezing out the excess water before folding it back into the velvet and tissue-lined custom wooden cases.

'I can't … I'm sorry, I just can't. I need to go.' I pulled my knee-length sweater dress on, which clung to my damp body, but didn't bother with my underwear, shoving it hastily into my bag instead. I didn't have time to pull on my boots either. I grabbed them and tucked them under my arm. 'I'll send the car back for you and Shauna, I just need to be alone tonight.' I kissed her cheek as she stood there stunned, then ran out, racing barefoot up the corridor towards the main reception area and exit.

'Paige, Paige!' Alec's voice echoed behind me, urging me to stop, but it made me run faster. I bolted out of the studio door, skidding on the polished oak floor as I turned and fled to the front door. I could see a black town car waiting, Shauna holding the back door open. This time the glass doors in front of me slid open as I approached. 'Paige,' Alec yelled, sounding far too close as I threw myself into the car. I didn't look back as Shauna shut me in and tapped on the roof. I was lurched backwards as the car accelerated and pulled away from the curb. I could hear Alec shouting at it to stop and covered my eyes with my hands as I burst into tears.

The Following Afternoon

'Paige?' Poppie's voice startled me and I jumped, pulling the duvet down to peek out from under it. She'd obviously nipped back during her lunch break for something to eat, as we weren't supposed to be seeing each other until tonight. 'What's wrong? Why are you hiding in here in the dark? It's after one, I thought you had a shoot today?'

'Ma whipz uh throwern,' I mumbled, not needing to pout. That bloody glue had reacted with them and I looked like I'd had a quadruple course of lip fillers at once. 'Ma dong do.'

'Ma dong do? What the hell are you saying?' she giggled, as she padded across the room and flicked on the bedside light, then gasped as she saw my face. 'O. M. G! Your lips are super swollen and blistered.'

'Datz wah ah zed. Ma dong do,' I nodded, sticking it out for her to look at. I'd had to call out an emergency doctor in Paris for an allergy shot and he'd prescribed medication and called Shauna for me, who let Jean-Claude know I'd need at least a week off until my face returned to normal.

'Ahhh, "my tongue too."' She put her hand in front of her mouth, but I could see her shoulders shaking. I giggled when she finally burst out laughing. 'I'm so sorry, I know it's not funny, but have you seen yourself? What happened?' She plonked herself on the bed next to me and gently ran her hand over my hair.

'Gwoo, on da whips,' I pointed.

'Glue on the lips?' she chortled. 'O dear. Have you had an allergy shot?'

'In ze zazz.' I nodded and pointed at my bottom. 'Tabiz do.'

'Tablets as well? I think you need one now, as you look like hell.' She shook her head as she gazed down at me with pity in her eyes. I nodded, so she reached over to get one, popped it, and handed it to me with my water, which had a straw sticking out of it. 'Did you get glue in your eyes too? They look really puffy.'

'Awick made me qwhy.'

'Awick,' she frowned. 'Alec? Alec was there? What did he do to upset you?' she demanded, anger suddenly flashing in her brown eyes. I shook my head. It wasn't his fault, he'd not done anything wrong, it was me. Me and my messed-up emotions. I felt tears stinging my eyes again as I looked up at her.

'Nuffin, Pwoopie.'

'Pwoopie,' she giggled. 'I know it's not funny really, but Pwoopie?'

I startled giggling again, she started laughing, which made me snort, and she laughed even harder. Before I knew it, I'd forgotten all about my tears of sadness and the two of us were in stitches with tears of laughter rolling down our faces. She decided it would be fun to ask me to repeat things she knew I couldn't say properly and we spent the next twenty minutes howling with laughter, but eventually my melancholy caught up with me and I started crying for real. Proper sobs like a tiny child who'd hurt their knee and thought they were dying. That was how I was feeling right now. I'd let down my barriers and acknowledged my feelings, and it was both shocking and painful. More painful than my poor lips and tongue right now. She captured my hands and squeezed them tightly.

'Talk to me, I promise not to laugh again.'

'I wuv him, Pwoopie. I'm in wuv whiff him.'

It was four days after my shoot with Alec. Four days since I finally admitted to myself just how deeply my feelings for him ran. The night I had my allergy shot in Paris, Vivian told me that rumour had it Tiffany was telling everyone that she and Alec were serious, that she thought he was going to propose to her soon. That had been the icing on a seriously shitty cake. So when I'd seen a text message from him sent not long after I fled back to The Paris Domville in tears, asking if he could see me before he headed back to New York, I'd replied to say that it was best that he didn't. I'd also lied and told him that I was seeing someone and was very happy. I hoped he'd believe it, because I wasn't fooling myself, but his life was over there, with her, mine was here, alone.

Poppie had taken advantage of my inability to talk properly the day I'd confessed that I was in love with him and had given me a stern lecture. She knew how badly I wanted to find someone and to have a baby, and she'd warned me that life was passing me by as I pined for him and approached thirty. I'd argued that I needed time to get over him, she argued that I never would if I didn't start dating again, and that the fantasy in my head of a life with him could never be matched. She said that I needed to keep dating, see as many men as possible and imagine I was trying on a bra. Throw away the ones that didn't fit or make me look my best, and keep the one that made me standout, made me look and feel amazing. It kind of made sense, though I wasn't sure I'd ever find a sexy, pretty, supportive, and cleavage-enhancing man who was up to handling me.

I'd told Vivian and Shauna to take the week off while I was recovering, they were in as much need of a break as I was, so I'd missed my spray tan after the last shoot and was in need of a top-up for the shoot tomorrow. I talked Poppie into a day away from Justin so we could help each other with some bronzing body lotion and have a pamper night. I never did my face, as sometimes my natural skin tone was needed, so I usually went with a soft body glow and makeup was applied to match. We took a shower and exfoliated each other, in a scene that wouldn't have been out of place on Pornhub.com if we weren't wearing G-strings and laughing so much. I wrapped my conditioned hair in cling film, then a hot towel, and hip bumped

Poppie out of the way of the mirror to apply my nasal, chin, and forehead pore strips.

'What's that?' Poppie asked as I pulled a tub out of my bathroom cabinet while she cleansed her face.

'A new masque that a beauty company provided. It has oils, some metallic mineral, and Dead Sea salts, and you need this weird magnet after to pull the gunk off your face. Want to try?' I offered, holding it out to her.

'What if I don't take it off in time, will it set and I'll end up looking like Iron Man?' she giggled.

'It's great, honestly. I've tried it once and it left my skin glowing and soft. I had no adverse reactions either.'

'Ok, I'm game, but what about getting these pore strips wet?'

'Just go around them,' I told her, carefully applying a slick of thick gel under my eyes to help with my "few days worth of crying" bags, then slathering on the dark grey face mask. Poppie copied me, then we washed our hands, and she put on some gloves and started applying the fake tan to my front.

'Wow, this is dark, should it be this dark? Are you doing a shoot as a non-Caucasian model?'

'It's dark so you can see where you've applied it,' I laughed as I set the timer on my phone. 'You leave it on for twenty minutes, then shower and all the dark comes off, and in six to eight hours, you're left with soft, golden brown skin. It's a near-perfect match to the spray tans Vivian does on me and they look natural, don't they?'

'They do,' she admitted. She finished my front and moved around to do my back and the backs of my arms and legs for me.

'You're sure about this?' she asked, looking sceptical as she pulled off the dark brown-stained gloves.

'I'm sure.'

'Well I'm not. Can I skip the tan and see how yours turns out in the morning?'

'Sure, chicken.'

'I'm not a chicken,' she objected as she pulled on her dressing gown. 'But I have a romantic weekend away planned with Justin next week, I don't want to turn up looking like I sunbathed in hell for a year.'

'Chicken,' I giggled, flapping my arms as I squawked and chased her out to the lounge.

'Stop it,' she screamed. 'Don't touch me or I'll be covered in it as well. Go and sit on a bin bag or something. I'm putting on some music and opening the wine.'

'I can't sit, I need to stand until the timer goes off, then I can shower and we can order a takeout.'

'What?' she shouted, cupping her ear as she cranked up the *Now Dance* one million and one, or something ridiculous, on the sound system. They did pick good tracks though. She started dancing crazily in front of the TV, so I went to join her, putting my phone on the side to make sure I didn't over bake myself. With four minutes to go, the two of us panting and screeching as we tried to outdo each other with increasingly bad dance moves, we both jumped and screamed as there was an almighty crash and the front door caved in and landed on the floor, framing a fireman with a large axe in his hand. Even the mask over his face couldn't disguise his fury. Poppie quickly turned off the music, as I tried to cover my bare breasts without actually touching them. We both grimaced when we heard the unmistakeable noise of the fire alarm going off in the corridor. 'Shit, I can smell smoke,' Poppie gasped as she looked over at me, right as I noticed it too.

'This isn't a drill, out now,' he barked, as another fireman appearing at his side. 'Follow Spence here and I'll bring up the rear.'

'But I have fake tan on! If it doesn't come off in one minute, I'll turn orange,' I cried, rooted to the spot as Poppie ran for the door.

'Lady, if you don't move it, in one minute you're liable to turn to ash! Shift.'

'Clothes, I need clothes,' I pleaded, my eyes darting to my bedroom. All I needed was a dressing gown, it wouldn't take a second. I screamed again as I suddenly felt myself being lifted and hoisted over someone's shoulder, with an arm between my legs.

'Sorry, sweetheart, no time,' came the mumbled voice of the man carrying me. 'Grip my wrist and keep your head down.' I did as I was told and saw the oak of Alec's lounge floor change to the cream travertine tiles of the communal hallway.

'Poppie, where's Poppie?' I cried.

'I'm here, right beside you,' she replied. 'God, Paige, it's serious, there's smoke billowing under the door of the stairs. How will we get out?' she asked, a tremor in her voice.

'Same way we came in and got your neighbours out, through that window up there. Here, put these over your mouths and noses and breathe through it.'

'Ok.' I was handed a damp piece of cloth and did as I was told with one hand, clinging for dear life to the fireman's impressively toned backside as they headed to the front of the building.

'Spence, you take Lady Godiva down first. I'll follow with this one, she's the last,' I heard the one say. Lady Godiva? O Jesus Christ, I was virtually naked, going butt first out of a window onto a busy street, with a brown-stained body, grey face, and white pore strips. And I was going to turn bloody orange! Not to mention Alec's apartment might burn, along with all of our belongings. I felt the cold air on my cheeks, all four of them, as the window ledge appeared. I banged my head on the edge of the sash window frame and gasped as I saw the towel from my head floating down three stories to the ground below. Wonderful. Now I had a shrink-wrapped head as well. Could this be any more mortifying? I dropped the wet cloth once this "Spence," who was carrying me, started shaking his way down the ladder, so I could grab his arm again and tightened my grip on his backside. I quickly closed my eyes, feeling dizzy from all of the drama and being carried like this.

'I usually go on a date before I let a woman grope my arse,' he chuckled.

'So do I,' I retorted, smacking his as his fingers moved up my legs slightly to brush against mine.

'Naked and feisty, just how I like them.'

'Them? Opportunistic, chauvinistic, and pervy, just how I *don't* like,' I retorted. 'Are we down yet?'

'Nearly, grope me a bit longer.'

'Pun intended, you caveman. I bet you've got longer from seeing me half naked and getting to put your big mitts on my backside.'

'Happy to let you do an inspection, sweetheart. I assure you, I'll pass with flying colours. I was Mr. December in last year's firefighters' calendar.'

'Well, I was on the cover of Men's Illustrated last month,' I bit.

'Wow, the red lingerie shoot? O my God, you're diamond ... girl. Paige Taylor,' he gasped.

'That's me. You should know that my body and face are heavily insured, so don't you dare drop me.'

'Hey look, I didn't know it was a full moon tonight,' a man yelled, as a load of whoops and hollers filled the air.

'Shit, do we have onlookers staring at my G-stringed brown bottom?' I groaned.

'Yup, plenty of them. Open your eyes, I'm going to put you down and I'll give you my jacket to cover up.'

'Thank you,' I whispered, dreading seeing how many people were out here. Fingers crossed the press hadn't arrived already, they'd have a field day seeing me looking like this. I opened my eyes to find us at the back of the truck, and he crouched and gently set me down. 'Did everyone get out?' I asked, quickly glancing up to make sure Poppie was ok. I could see her coming down on the back of the other guy.

'Yeah, you two were the last, my colleagues are working on the blaze as we speak,' he confirmed, ripping off his jacket and draping it around my shoulders. I quickly pulled it around me, covering my breasts as I noticed a crowd behind a police barrier staring at me. 'What the hell have you done to your face?' he asked. I looked back up at him as he pulled off his mask, and caught my breath. He shouldn't be December, he should be every month of the year. He was gorgeous. Grey eyes that sparkled as they scanned my face with amused interest, short dark hair, shaved like Jake Gyllenhaal in *Jarhead,* that made him look even hotter, and biceps that bulged under a tight navy t-shirt, phew.

'What?' I asked, my wandering mind taking me off target.

'What's on your face? And your head?'

'Crap,' I moaned, reaching up to tear off my pore strips. 'Do you have a hose I can use?'

'Is that your way of asking me on a date?' he grinned.

'No,' I exclaimed, whacking him, then tearing the cling film off my head. 'I'm about six minutes over on a fake tan, I need a shower, now.'

'It's cold water.'

'Well I didn't think it would be heated with massage jets. I'm being serious.'

'Chunky, can we spare some water to hose Miss Taylor down?' he asked, as his colleague reached the bottom of the ladder with Poppie.

'Who the hell is Miss Taylor?'

'Diamond tits,' Spence coughed, flicking his head at me and having the good grace to at least look embarrassed. I rolled my eyes. Someone at Alec's office had leaked a shot of me in my luxury lingerie and it had spread on social media like wildfire, leading to the unfortunate nickname. I wondered if it had been done deliberately to create a buzz.

'Diamond … *that's* Paige Taylor?'

'Yes, yes it's me. I'll sign a photo for you to put up in the station if you want, but please, I need to wash off this fake tan, right now. For a model, this is like … defcon one, it's serious.'

'She's not joking,' Poppie added, checking that her dressing gown was secure.

'Strips.' I pointed at her face, reminding her to take them off. Then I giggled when she was left with white streaks in the grey mask instead.

'Razor, how are you looking in there?' Chunky asked over the walkie-talkie contraption on his jacket.

'All under control,' came the static-sounding voice.

'Do it,' confirmed Chunky, with a disapproving shake of his head, 'but I didn't approve it if he bollocks you.'

'Follow me,' Spence grinned, grabbing my hand. He led me around to the other side of the fire engine, where a fat grey hose came up from the street and ran towards our apartment block. It was writhing with the force of the water being pumped through it. We still had an audience, but right now I didn't care. I watched him unravel the other hose and go and secure it to another mains further along the street. 'Jacket off and brace yourself, it will be cold and forceful.'

'Not my first time,' I sighed, thinking of my cow shit shower. At least that time I'd had some clothes on.

'Give me the jacket.' Poppie held her hands out and I slipped it off and passed it to her as I heard a load of whistles and claps going up from the crowd. I nodded at Spence and he turned on the water, obviously not full force, but I still screamed as it hit me.

'Don't stop, please don't stop,' I yelled, shoving water out of my eyes as I hopped up and down, my breasts bouncing so hard I was liable to end up with two black eyes as well. He burst out laughing and I tried not to focus on how many people were watching as I scrubbed myself down and let the water rinse my hair and my face. I wondered if not using the special magnet would have a detrimental effect. Not that a messed-up complexion was going to matter. By bedtime tonight, I was likely to have a glowing body that you could spot from Mars. Spence turned off the water and grabbed me a towel from the truck when I was done. Poppie held up his jacket as I rubbed myself down, while he used his frame to shield me as well. 'I don't know why you've turned your back now, you've already had a good eyeful.'

'I'm not a total arse, thanks,' he replied. Poppie raised her eyebrows at me and grinned. She was like a shark sensing blood when it came to men flirting with me. She always knew before me.

'Really?' I mouthed at her.

'O yeah,' she mouthed back with a nod. 'He's hot, too.'

I shook my head and turned around, slipping my arms into his jacket and rolling up the sleeves before doing it up, then used the damp towel to squeeze as much water as I could out of my hair. Poppie grabbed it off me to wipe my face for me, before starting to try and get the grey mask off her own.

'You can turn around, I'm decent now.'

'Paige Taylor in the flesh, no pun intended. You realise I'm going to be a rock star at the station now?' he winked as he checked me out all fresh faced.

'I'm a model, not a Playboy centrefold,' I reminded him.

'Trust me, you're the top fantasy with most of the guys,' he nodded. Poppie elbowed me in the back.

'Am I your top fantasy?' I asked with a blush.

'Are you flirting with me, Miss Taylor?' His lips stretched into a smile, and I felt my cheeks colour up even more. He had nice teeth. I liked a man with nice teeth. He really was pretty hot.

'If she was, would you ask her out on a date?' Poppie asked before I had a chance to reply.

'Miss Taylor, can I take you out to dinner tonight?'

'If I'm allowed back in my apartment to put some clothes on, yes,' I replied. Poppie was right, I needed to get over Alec. I found Spence attractive, he was funny, and I liked the banter with him. Why not?

'Hallelujah!' cried Poppie.

'Sorry, there's no way you'll be sleeping there tonight. It looks like the fire started in the boiler room and spread to the stairs. Until they've been made safe, no one's going home.'

'Let's ring Jean-Claude,' Poppie suggested. 'We can book in at The Domville until we're allowed back, and he can provide you with clothes, and underwear,' she giggled.

'Great idea, but I don't have a phone, or any money.'

'They know you, Paige, they'll put the hotel bill on account. Look, there's Bill and Nora from next door, we can use their mobile.'

'It looks like we have a date then,' I advised Spence.

'I'll be in the Champagne Bar of The Domville at eight tonight then. You can bring my jacket back with you.'

'Thanks. Will our belongings be safe? Your friend Chunky did knock our door down.'

'We'll secure it before we leave. Ring your insurance firm to get a replacement sorted.'

'Why's your friend called Chunky?' Poppie asked, as she linked arms with mine.

'Weird looking balls,' he chuckled. 'I haven't been able to eat pineapple chunks since I saw them.'

'Ewwww,' I groaned with a giggle.

'See you later, Paige,' he winked.

'See you later, Spence.'

'O my God,' Poppie exclaimed as we gingerly walked barefoot up the road towards the barrier. 'Drama, drama, drama, flashing, then a date!'

'I know. God, I had the fright of my life when that door caved in.'

'Your face was a picture,' she laughed. 'So proud of you, he's a great-looking guy. Funny, too.'

'I know,' I grinned, looking over my shoulder to see him watching me as he wound up his hose. I was actually quite excited at the thought of going out with him.

'Poppie, Paige,' greeted Nora. 'Thank goodness you're both safe. It's so good to see you.'

'We didn't expect to see quite so much of you,' Bill chuckled, then groaned as Nora cuffed him around the back of the head.

The Italian Job

August ~ Sunday

'Baby, come back to bed,' Spence groaned as I wriggled out of his embrace.

'I've got to shower and go. My flight to Rome leaves in three hours.'

'We could have a quickie in the shower then. I'm not going to see you for a whole week.'

'We had sex most of the night,' I called from his en-suite. 'Are you never satisfied?'

'Insatiable when it comes to you,' he murmured into my ear as he pressed up behind me and nipped it.

'Spence,' I laughed, trying to detach his roaming hands from my naked body. 'I'm serious.'

'So am I, baby. I'm really going to miss you,' he sighed, tightening his grip.

'I'll miss you, too,' I replied, tipping my head back for a kiss. I was surprised at how genuine that statement actually was.

We'd been seeing each other for six months and I was staying over at his regularly. He shared a terraced house out in Fulham with Chunky and Nobby, another of his colleagues. I felt kind of weird about him staying at Alec's place, in Alec's bed, so Spence had never spent the night there with me. We'd had a great first date, though I'd had to wear a cat suit with long sleeves, along with gloves and a scarf, as my "golden tan" had, as feared, blossomed into something akin to a hot orange that even Vivian couldn't tame. I really had looked a sight, but it hadn't put him off me.

I relented in the shower, unable to resist his firm, muscular, tattooed body, especially when it was wet and soapy. I finally had a boyfriend, and he amazing in bed, so much better than Toby had been. I mean, Spence could hold me up with those biceps, without the shower wall supporting either of us. We were getting on great, I felt so relaxed around him, it was the happiest I'd been in a long time. I had to forgo doing my hair and makeup, as his idea of a quickie was a half hour ride. Rita Queen of Speed he certainly wasn't. I pulled my wet hair into a ponytail and dressed casually for once, in jeans, a t-shirt, and my Converse trainers. I tried to go incognito as much as possible. I loved my life, but sometimes it was nice to go somewhere without being recognised. I grabbed my handbag and large sunglasses, and sighed with frustration as I watched him leaning against the doorframe with a small towel around his waist. He was so ripped.

'I'll call you when I land.'

'You'll call me incessantly,' he ordered. 'I don't like the idea of you being away, surrounded by hot male models.' His brows knitted together in a severe frown as his bottom lip pouted adorably. My boyfriend had a jealous streak. I laughed and went over to give him a chaste kiss.

'I'm already dating a hot male model, he just chose to be a firefighter instead, which is so much more sexy in my eyes.'

'I mean it, Paige.'

'I know. I promise, I'll pester you until you want to dump me.'

'Never,' he uttered, yanking me close and kissing me properly.

'Spence,' I moaned, my legs turning to jelly. 'I've really got to go.'

'I'll see you to the front door,' he advised, grabbing my hand. I giggled. He was really protective and didn't like it if he found Chunky or Nobby sitting too close to me, or "looking at me the wrong way." He opened the front door and kissed me again. I dropped my shades down onto my eyes and stepped onto the pavement, then screamed in surprise as a guy wearing a balaclava jumped in front of me. I barely had time to react before he tore open his long coat to reveal he was naked, and hard, then raced off up the street. Seconds later, a nearly naked Spence hared past me, chasing the flasher with just his towel from the shower wrapped around his waist.

'Paige, what's happening?' yelled Chunky, his voice full of concern as he raced out to join me.

'Some guy just flashed me,' I uttered in disbelief. 'Spence is chasing after him.'

'Jesus, not again,' Chunky groaned.

'He's done this before?'

'You don't watch the news, I take it? They're calling him the Fulham Flasher. He's been terrorising the neighbourhood for the last few weeks. Did you get a good look at him? The police are desperate to identify him.'

'O yes,' I nodded. 'A young, white, toned male, about six foot tall in a balaclava and long green mac. Let's ring them now, have them hook me up with a sketch artist and I can direct them to draw a picture of his cock and balls. That'll be a real help in narrowing down the search.'

'No need for sarcasm, I was only trying to help.'

'Sorry, I'm just a bit shocked, but seriously, that's about all I saw. I need to go or I'll miss my flight, I'll ring the police when I land if they need a statement from me.'

'Here's Spence now,' Chunky nodded.

'Lost him, he's a nippy bugger,' he panted as he joined us, putting his hands on his hips and bending over to catch his breath.

'Don't do that in the street with no underwear on,' I warned, 'or they'll be arresting you by mistake. That's all I need after the pictures in the media of you carrying me, practically naked, out of a window and then hosing me down, not to mention the shot someone got of me looking like an Oompa Lompa on steroids.'

'That was funny,' he chuckled as he straightened up.

'If I come to the fire station and find any of those shots up, there'll be hell to pay. Kiss me, I have to go,' I ordered as I clicked the button to unlock Fi-Fi, who was parked outside the house.

'You need a new car, that thing's not safe,' he warned as he clasped my face and lay a trail of kisses from one side of my mouth to the other. 'Can't you afford a new one?'

'Yes, but she's special and there's nothing wrong with her. I have parts repaired and replaced on a regular basis to make sure she's in good condition. There'll be newer cars out there that are more rusty and worn than she is.' I never wanted to part with her. She was my gift from Mum and Dad and I'd always treasure her. Her hot pink colour did make it hard for me to zip around London or up to Shrewsbury to visit them unnoticed though, so I'd had to take on a driver for most travel. I slid into the driver's seat, buckled up, and started the engine. Spence knocked on the window, so I lowered it.

'I mean it, Paige, call me the minute you land.'

'Will do. Bye, Chunk.'

'See ya, Diamond,' he called, earning himself a punch in the arm from Spence. I laughed and headed off. I had to get back home, say bye to Poppie, and grab my prepacked suitcase before Jean-Claude came to pick me up.

'Come on, Fi-Fi, let's live a little dangerously and do the speed limit,' I suggested, patting the dashboard as I put my foot down. I giggled, wondering if other people talked to or stroked their cars. Everyone had quirks in them. Mum always leaned forwards when she was accelerating, like she was giving her car forward momentum. Nana had a dish fitted to her dashboard as she liked to remove her dentures when she drove and needed them somewhere handy to pop back in her mouth "in case she was pulled over by a dishy policeman." Poppie liked to sing at the top of her voice and head bang to rock songs that she'd never listen to in public. And Bella, our old school friend, had rather disturbingly admitted that she only ever picked her nose in the car, always wiping her finger clean under the driver's seat. I pitied the poor person who unsuspectingly purchased that car from her. I wonder if piles of aged, crusty snot would go mouldy?

'When ... the ... moon's in your eye, like a big piece of pie, or whatever the lyrics are, that's ... amore,' I sang as I danced across the room, threw open the balcony windows in the lounge of my suite at The Rome Domville, and looked out across the city. I leaned on the ornate railings and rested my chin on my knuckles to soak in the view and atmosphere. 'Hello, Rome, I do love visiting you.'

The noise was insane, the chatter, the whizz of mopeds zipping up the narrow streets, cars and taxis honking. I loved it. I breathed in deeply, I could smell garlic and steak cooking. I was famished. I quickly headed through to the bedroom to unpack. Jean-Claude thought that it was hilarious that I was the most undiva-like model he'd ever worked with. Other than Vivian and Shauna doing the essentials, I packed and unpacked myself, ordered my own room service, made no demands, and had no required list for when I travelled or stayed in hotels. He was also infuriated at my refusal to have a bodyguard. It was complete overkill in my eyes. When I dressed down with my shades on, virtually no one recognised me.

I showered and washed my hair again, taking my time to dry it, and applied a little mascara and Vaseline. I was only going to dinner with Jean-Claude, to an amazing little trattoria off the tourist track, not too far away, so there was no need to get glammed up. I had on a strapless, shirring maxi dress in black with blue flowers growing up from the hem. It was just a cheap thing I'd seen in a supermarket back home, but the flowers had reminded me of the cornflowers Alec had given me on our one and only date. I slipped on a pair of flat black sandals with a large rose bud on the thong and a load of silver bangles, then a silver lariat and a pair of big hooped earrings. My favourite perfume dabbed here and there, and I was good to go. My phone rang, so I bounced over to get it, hoping it wasn't Spence again. We'd already spoken twice since I landed and he was worse than a woman for chatting on the phone, I'd never get out in time.

'Paige,' came Jean-Claude's gorgeous French accent. 'I'm outside on a hot pink moped, just for you. Get your rump down here, let's go.'

'Moped? I have a dress on!'

'Hitch it up, show off those pins of yours. When in Rome,' he laughed.

'I'll be down in a moment. If I get helmet hair, I won't be impressed,' I warned.

I grabbed my small bag and chewed my lip as I looked at my phone, which was a bit too big for my bag. I didn't really need it, so I decided to leave it behind. I slipped in my Vaseline and room key and headed out towards the lift, humming Dean Martin's *That's Amore* as I descended. When I ran out of tune, as I'd forgotten the rest, I renditioned myself with *Just One Cornetto*, laughing as I spotted the black domed camera above me and wondering if they had sound too. I could just imagine the next headlines about me.

Daily News

Paige Taylor's no Taylor Swift!

I nodded and smiled at a few people who did a double take as I crossed reception. I thanked the doorman in Italian for gesturing me out with a tip of his hat, then put my sunglasses on as the early evening summer sun dazzled me. I spotted Jean-Claude on the vivid pink moped, complete with a matching pink helmet, waving to me. I laughed and skipped down the stone steps and ran towards him. Weirdly, it was a proper motorbike helmet with a black visor, rather than the open, strap under the chin one. He was taking my safety very seriously indeed. He held out another pink visored helmet for me and I groaned as I had to take off my glasses and squash it down over my head. Definite helmet hair. I scanned him quickly. He was looking very stylish in black boots, black jeans, a grey shirt, and a black bomber jacket. I nodded my approval.

'How do I look?' I laughed, doing a twirl. He put his thumbs up and flicked his head to the small section of seat behind him. 'Honestly, you go to all the trouble of a proper helmet and I'm going to be balanced on the back of this death trap?' I shook my head and inched up my dress, nearly flashing everyone a glimpse of my knickers, then swung my leg over and shuffled down into the seat, squeezing up behind him and putting my arms around his waist. 'Wow, someone's been working out,' I shouted as he turned on the engine. I'd fallen asleep on him during a plane ride a few months ago and his stomach had been soft and squidgy, not hard and rippled like the one he had now. I wondered if everything between him and Pascal was alright. Why would he suddenly be getting buff? I hoped he wasn't having an affair.

I shrieked with laughter and screamed with fear intermittently as he sped along uneven cobbled streets, weaving through traffic, mounting the pavement and hooting walkers out of the way as was the apparent unspoken custom out here. Despite a few heart-stopping moments, it was fun. I felt like I was on a ride at Disney. I had a few days off before my TV commercial started shooting, the weather was amazing, and I was going to be able to eat some delicious Italian pasta, pizza, and ice cream. Life was good. Jean-Claude pulled up outside a trattoria and I pulled off my helmet, trying to tame my hair as I frowned. This wasn't where we usually went. He stood up and offered me his hand. I started reaching for it, but halted as something registered in my brain. Jean-Claude hadn't been working out, because the stomach I'd been clutching, and the tall man standing in front of me now, wasn't Jean-Claude. He was a good three inches taller, with a far more lean and muscular body.

'Who the hell are you?' I bit angrily as I snatched my hand away and tried to get off the moped quickly in case I needed to run. My dress got caught and the moped wobbled and crashed to the floor, throwing me off it and into the street. 'Shit,' I cried as my elbow connected with a hard, flat slab under me and I lay there stunned.

'Christ, Paige. You've rarely stayed upright all the times I've met you,' came a muffled, but familiar, voice as the person stepped over the moped lying next to me. He quickly stood it back up, then yanked off his helmet, revealing his gorgeous mop of blond hair and those dazzling blue eyes.

'Alec? What the hell?!' I snapped, sitting up and rubbing my elbow, then scrunching up my eyes as everything started to spin.

'God, you're bleeding, you've hurt yourself.'

'No shit,' I moaned, reaching up to pinch my nose.

'You look like you're going to pass out. Hold onto me,' he ordered. I felt myself being lifted up and was too dizzy to object, so I put my arms around his neck and lay my head on his shoulder as he started walking. I heard excited chatter and him replying in Italian. I had no idea he spoke Italian, but then again, why would I? I also had no idea what he was doing here in Rome, or why he was kidnapping me. I'd warned Jean-Claude I'd never work with him again. I heard footsteps on stairs, then wooden floorboards, then more stairs as he carried me up. I wanted to open my eyes, I wanted to ask lots of questions, but I still felt a bit shaky. 'Ok, I'm going to lie you down. Rosita is getting some water, a cloth, and a bandage to clean you up, and some grappa, that should have you feeling more with it.'

'Alec, what's going on?' I asked, slowly opening my eyes to find I was on a small roof terrace, under a canopy of grapes and fairy lights, lying on a cushioned black rattan sun lounger. I tilted my head to see that a dining table for two, with candles, had been set up. 'Wow, this is some kind of romantic proposal setting, but I think you're here with the wrong woman. Tiffany's your girlfriend, not me.' I tried to sit up again as I grasped my throbbing and bleeding elbow.

'Paige,' he sighed, gently pushing me back down again. 'Lie still, you just had a shock. Let's get you treated first, then we can sit, eat, and talk. Ok?'

'I'm not hungry. I'd like to go back to the hotel please.'

'Not hungry? Right,' he laughed. I silently cursed him. That sound, his laughter, his voice, made my toes curl. 'So you're going to tell me it's my stomach that's going off like a pneumatic drill?'

'It's not that bad.'

'It is. Relax, will you? You were going out to dinner with Jean-Claude, what's the difference having dinner with me? If you feel more comfortable eating downstairs with the locals, I'm sure they'll find us a table, but I thought given how recognisable you are, you might like some privacy, so they set up the terrace for me.'

A withered-looking old woman with a permanent stoop appeared, dressed in black from head to toe, and gave me a smile full of gaps where some of her teeth were missing. She looked riddled with arthritis, some of her fingers stuck out at odd angles, but her eyes looked like those of someone much younger and she had incredibly sharp cheekbones. I had a feeling she was quite a stunner in her youth. I smiled back at her as she set the tray down on a small table next to my sun lounger.

'Grazie, Rosita, grazie,' Alec nodded, grabbing her hand and squeezing it.

'Prego,' she grinned.

'Grazie,' I added, giving her a grateful smile. My Italian was rusty, but I knew hello, goodbye, thank you, and enough to order food.

'Bella ragazza,' she replied, winking at Alec and kissing the tips of her fingers before whipping them away from her lips.

'Sì, lei è,' he smiled. She disappeared and he picked up a cloth and dipped it in the bowl of water, squeezed it, and held out his hand. I put mine in it with a wince as my scuffed elbow stretched out, followed by a gasp as that familiar crackle of energy that happened whenever we touched shot through my body.

'What did she say to you?'

'Beautiful girl,' he replied as he carefully dabbed my wound.

'And what did you say?'

'I said yes, she is.'

'Why are you here, Alec? Are you involved with my commercial?'

'No, don't worry, I got the message from Jean-Claude that you don't want to work with me again,' he said sharply. It was obvious I'd offended him and I wasn't in the mood for an argument. He was right, I was starving and right now, I just wanted something in my stomach to take away the nausea I was feeling. We both stayed silent as he put some cream on my elbow, then wrapped a bandage around it, securing it with a safety pin. 'There. I'm not exactly a trained medical professional, but it should hold up until you get it looked at by the hotel doctor tonight or tomorrow.'

'Thanks, it will be fine.'

'I don't want you getting an infection. Here, drink this,' he ordered, passing me the small shot glass. I knocked it back and shuddered, sticking my tongue out and pulling a face. Crikey, that burned. He laughed and took the glass off me and set it back on the tray.

'Then I'll see a doctor. Were you always this bossy?' I asked.

'I like to be in charge,' he smiled.

'Hmmm, yes you do, don't you? Chairman of YFC and now world-renowned independent photographer who snaps his fingers and everyone jumps.'

'Except for you. You run, or fall, frequently. At least you don't seem to have broken anything this time. How's your nose? You'd never know,' he said, his eyes inspecting it.

'It's fine,' I blushed, embarrassed to be reminded of that whole meeting. I groaned as my stomach vocalised its annoyance again.

'My God, woman,' he laughed. 'It's a good thing I took the liberty of ordering for you when I booked the table. It should be here any minute. Can you stand?'

'I fell off a stationery moped,' I laughed in return. 'It was hardly a fast-action movie collision.'

'You look pale,' he commented as he helped me up and led me to one of the dining chairs. 'Then again, after that "you've been tangoed" look, I bet that you get that comment all of the time now.' I looked up at him with my mouth open and he burst out laughing. 'Please, a world-exclusive photo and you thought I wouldn't see it? I'm just miffed I couldn't claim credit for that one.'

'So not funny,' I giggled.

'It kind of was, and the other shots of your rescue.'

'God no,' I groaned, covering my face with my hands. 'How mortifying.'

'I'm glad you and Poppie were ok. How is she?' he asked as he opened a bottle of still water he extracted from an ice bucket at our side.

'She's great, got engaged recently as a matter of fact.'

'Reece?' He started pouring my water for me.

'You didn't hear?' I asked, looking at him in surprise.

'Hear what?'

'He cheated on her, with a number of women behind her back. She only found out because one of them threatened to tell her, so he confessed, hoping to salvage the relationship.'

'What a shit, I never saw that coming,' Alec stated, shaking his head. 'Bit of a bitch to try outing him and upsetting Poppie, too.'

'Yes, I thought so. You know her actually,' I nodded, grabbing one of the breadsticks from the glass in the centre of the table. 'Your ex, Ruth.'

'Really? Actually, I can't act surprised, I told you I realised she was a nasty piece of work after what she did to you. I'm glad to be rid of her. She still keeps in contact with my mother, hoping one day I'll change my mind.'

'What's going on here, Alec?' I asked, chewing on my bread as I held his gaze. 'Sitting here chatting like we're old friends?'

'We are old friends. We've known each other for over ten years, Paige.'

'Sporadically,' I reminded him. 'I've spent more time with Jean-Claude's chihuahua Chi-Chi than I have you and that nippy little bugger let's no one near him.'

'He really doesn't,' Alec chuckled. 'We may not see each other often, but I follow your career, and I ask about you whenever I have dinner with Jean-Claude. I care about you, Paige, I always have, always will.' He picked up a breadstick and put the end in his mouth, slowly biting it. My eyes lingered on his lips as I imagined him doing that to one of my suddenly swollen and aching nipples. Crap. He was some kind of Hogwarts graduate, with a magic power to make me horny. I was Wright horny. It happened every damn time I saw him.

'I'm seeing someone. He's really nice. His name is Spence. You'll have seen him too, in that rescue photo. He was the firefighter who carried me to safety and hosed me down, trying to stop that tan from developing, but of course you know that failed. Anyway, we went on a date and he made me laugh, he's really funny, I think you'd like him. I like him. He's super fit, in that really toned and muscular way, like you, but a bit bigger, but not bulky, you know? I hate bulk. He was December in the calendar last year. You might have seen it. Ha! Wouldn't it be funny if you'd shot it and you'd both actually already met? Anyway, I'm really happy with him, the sex is … whooo,' I exclaimed, shooting my hand off into the air. 'A-ma-zing! He has so much stamina. I had no idea sex could be so good, you know? I mean, there were only two before him. Toby in Grand Cayman and Marc, you know Marc, apparently he's called *The Jackhammer*, but of course no one told me and, my GOD! I bet you had a bet on it too, didn't you? Jean-Claude made a mint out…'

'Paige,' Alec interrupted softly, reaching over the table to clasp my hand, which I realised I'd been rapping up and down on the table in time with my twitching foot. 'You're babbling, like you're prone to do.

Why are you suddenly so nervous? I'm here for work and I already knew you were dating.'

'You did? Of course you did, Jean-Claude told you. He loves to gossip.'

'Is it serious?'

'It can be. I mean, if you tell him a secret and he lets slip to the wrong person. You know what our industry is like.'

'I meant is your relationship serious?'

'Yes, I really like him.'

'Does he make you happy?' he asked. I looked down to see he was still holding my hand. I quickly snatched it away and put it on my chest.

'You mean happy in here?'

'Yes.' He sat back in his chair and lifted his water to his mouth, taking a sip as he watched me over the rim of his glass.

'Yes, he does,' I nodded with a smile. I had feelings for him, not intense feelings like I'd had for Alec, but feelings all the same that I could see growing the more time we spent together.

'Good.' I saw Alec swallow hard and nod. But a strange look crossed his face right as I registered that I'd thought "I'd had for Alec," not "I have for Alec." Was I really getting over my deep-rooted feelings for him? Was this thing between us just sexual attraction now? 'I just want you to be happy,' Alec added.

'I am and I'd like the same for you. How about you and Tiffany? I hear marriage is on the cards.'

'Look, here comes our first course. I hope you were serious about being hungry, as I ordered a lot of food, not sure what your favourite was.'

'I'm really hungry,' I grinned.

'I'm hoping we can do this again, whenever we're in the same city. I like spending time with you. To friends,' he toasted with his water.

'To friends,' I replied, clinking his glass.

'You're not staying in the hotel?' I asked as I removed my helmet and put it on the seat and he pulled off his.

'No, I have an apartment here. I bought one in most of the cities I work in regularly, it made more financial sense than staying in The Domville each time. What are your plans tomorrow?'

'A well-overdue lie in and just some sightseeing. I never seem to have enough time usually.'

'Let me pick you up, I know the city inside out. We could do a walking tour and grab some lunch,' he suggested.

'Aren't you busy?'

‘Not tomorrow. It’s easy to get lost if you don’t know where you’re going. I’ll be waiting down here at ten-thirty.’

‘I haven’t actually said yes,’ I reminded him.

‘Jean-Claude is holding castings for his own line all week. You really want to hang out with your two assistants for the next few days? Don’t you see enough of them? Ten-thirty, don’t be late.’

‘Yes, sir!’ I saluted. I leaned in to kiss his cheek. ‘Thank you. Other than scaring me to death by making me think I was being kidnapped for ransom, I had a fun night.’

‘Me, too. Night, Paige.’

‘Night.’ I ran up the steps, rubbing my sore hip which I was sure was going to be bruised. I turned and waved to him before heading in and up to my suite. It had been a fun night. It would be nice to spend some time with him now and then, especially when I was away from home. I cleaned my makeup off, brushed my teeth, and climbed into bed. I checked my phone to see three missed calls from Spence. I thought about ringing him back, but it was late and I wasn’t going to get the ridiculously long lie in I’d planned, so I sent him a text, letting him know that I was ok, that I missed him, and that I’d ring him tomorrow night. Working so hard without a proper holiday was starting to catch up with me.

Monday

‘Alec, stop,’ I screamed as he splashed me with water from the Trevi fountain, laughing his head off. I giggled and splashed him, making him dart a safe distance away with his precious camera around his neck. I couldn’t believe how much we’d fitted in already in one morning, with him taking non-stop pictures, quite a few of me. He insisted they were for work purposes, but I couldn’t help wondering if that were true. It was like we were young again, back in the Quarry Park in Shrewsbury. I just felt so relaxed in his company. Conversation came naturally, we were always laughing, and it certainly didn’t hurt that he was incredibly easy on the eye. But I was with Spence and he was with Tiffany. We were just friends with a past, that was all.

‘Come on,’ he called over the heads of tourists surrounding me. ‘We haven’t eaten yet and I’m starving.’

‘Me too,’ I confirmed, standing up to find I’d lost sight of him. ‘Alec?’

‘You take picture?’ asked a Chinese tourist as he stood in front of me with a hoard of his friends standing behind, watching me expectantly. I smiled politely. I knew it was a mistake putting my shades on top of my head, I’d been recognised. If I agreed to a picture with him, then I’d likely never get away, but it would be rude to refuse.

'Sure,' I smiled. I stepped up to him and put my arm around his waist, leaning in as I tried to find his friend with the camera.

'What you do? Han my boyfriend!' hissed an annoyed-looking girl as she shoved me off him and thrust her camera in my hands. 'Just take picture already.'

'I'm sorry,' I exclaimed. 'I thought he wanted a picture with me.'

'Crazy British woman, why he want picture with you? Give me camera back,' she scolded, snatching it off me as I stood there flabbergasted. 'Wait, I know you,' the Chinese girl scowled. 'You been seeing Han?'

'No!'

'Then why you want picture with him and why I know you?' she demanded, hands on her hips with fury seeping from her eyes. There was a sudden babble of excited voices, talking in Chinese so fast, my eyes couldn't dart back and forth between their lips fast enough, but I was sure I heard my name being said as the group surged forward. 'You Paige Taylor, supermodel! Why you not say, me and Han have picture with you,' she nodded, her face changing in an instant from one of a scorned girlfriend to one of excitement.

'No, me, me first,' shouted another of the group. All of a sudden, all hell broke loose as all of the tourists started to look and I was recognised. I stepped back, trying to get some space as they all started to crowd me, but there was nowhere to go. I had the smooth travertine wall of the fountain behind me, and if they didn't back off, I was going to end up floating in it.

'Paige, quick, grab my hand,' I heard Alec's voice yell.

'Where are you?' I called, looking around frantically.

'Behind you,' he laughed, tapping me on the shoulder. I looked around and gasped. He was standing in the fountain, holding out his hand. 'Quick, I can hear the police coming, I don't want to get arrested.'

I grabbed his hand and he pulled me up the low wall and into the freezing cold water, which reached just under my knees. I was grateful I was dressed in flip-flops and a pair of denim shorts, and I giggled as we tried to run through it, me nearly pulling him down as I slipped on all the coins lying under the surface. I could hear the whistles of the police being blasted behind us as they tried to break through the crowds, but Alec leapt out, dragging me with him and squeezing through a small gap in the crowds at the side, and we started to run. We darted along the narrow streets, dodging our way through the insane amount of people strolling along, and I dropped my shades down to cover my eyes and hopefully disguise myself a bit better.

'Slow down,' I laughed, 'I'm going to pass out.'

'Can't, the police are still chasing us. I could carry you,' he grinned, his blue eyes shining with mischief.

'Because that won't slow you down at all! I'm serious, I can't keep running.'

'Ok, quick, in here,' he ordered as he pulled me into a narrow alley between two shops. He pushed me up against the wall and grabbed my face in his hands.

'What …. What are you doing,' I whimpered as he pressed up against me.

'Pretend to kiss me,' he ordered as the noise of police whistles got closer.

'I beg your pardon!'

'The best way to go unnoticed is to blend in. Pretend to kiss me, like we're a couple of young Italian lovers.' He didn't give me a chance to object to his crazy scheme, as he dipped his head and planted his lips at the corner of my mouth. I felt my stomach flutter, just the way it had all those years ago, and found my hands moving to clutch his slim waist as I closed my eyes and breathed him in. I could feel my chest heaving, rising and falling in unison with his, and it took a moment to realise that the police had shot past and were moving further away. Neither of us let go, until I felt Alec's nose graze my cheek and I quickly pushed him away from me.

'Do you think it's safe to go?' I asked, trying not to look at his face. I was with Spence, I was happy. I shouldn't be reacting like this to Alec being so close to me.

'Let's risk it,' he confirmed after a momentary pause. 'Take my hand, I don't want to lose you in the crowds.'

'Alec, I …'

'It's just a hand, Paige, you'll get lost if we get separated. I know a great restaurant not far from here where we shouldn't be bothered, we can eat then head on to the Coliseum. You don't want to miss seeing that, but you may want to keep your glasses on, to avoid us being mobbed again.'

'Ok,' I nodded and put my hand back in his, trying to ignore that rush of excitement I got again as our skin touched.

Alec walked me back to the hotel in the dark. I was tired after such a long and eventful day, but I'd had so much fun with him. We'd seen most of the key sights and had had a delightful pasta meatball lunch, followed by ice creams as we strolled through the city. I was too full to even think about dinner, and too tired to want to do anything but have a nice hot bath and curl up in my comfortable super king-sized bed.

'I had a fun day,' he confirmed as he walked me across the lobby to the lifts. 'Even though we nearly got attacked by a Chinese mob and arrested for paddling in the fountain.'

'Me too,' I laughed. 'Thanks so much.'

'What are your plans tomorrow?'

'I don't know, I wasn't sure whether to hire a car and head out of the city, or to go to The Vatican and browse the museums, see the Sistine Chapel, and wander the grounds.'

'I'll tell you what. The weather is meant to be amazing tomorrow, why don't I pick you up? I have a car here, we can go to Lake Martignano, there are hammocks in the trees along the shore. We can take a picnic, swim, and chill out. On Wednesday, I can take you to Vatican City. It's been a while since I went, it would be a nice change.'

'Don't you have work to do?'

'Not for the next couple of days, just like you. Say yes, save me from the boredom of my own company. I'm not like you, I don't travel with an entourage of assistants and beauticians,' he grinned.

'What about Jean-Claude? He'll be upset that he hasn't seen you.'

'I'm having dinner with him here in the hotel tonight actually, I'd better hurry up and go and change. Flip flops, board shorts, and a t-shirt won't cut it in here,' he confirmed, looking down at his watch. 'Why don't you join us?'

'You enjoy a boys' catch up,' I smiled, grabbing my room key out of my bag to access the lift. 'I'm beat and I really need to ring Spence, he'll be worrying that he's not heard from me all day.'

'O, ok. How about tomorrow's day trip?' he asked. I bit my lip as I considered his request. What was wrong with two friends having a few days out? It wasn't like we were doing anything wrong and all I did lately was work or stay in having a "work out" with Spence. It would be nice to get some fresh air and a change of scene.

'Ok, count me in.'

'Great, pick you up at nine, it's about an hour's drive. Make sure you pack a bikini and bring a towel and change of clothes. I had a great day, Paige. Thank you,' he smiled, leaning in to kiss my cheek.

'I did, too,' I confirmed, kissing him back, then swiping my card to access the lift. 'I can get the hotel to sort a picnic hamper.'

'Don't worry, my apartment is above a great little store with a range of fresh meats and cheeses. I'll pull one together.'

'Great. See you tomorrow then,' I smiled, stepping into the lift and turning to face him as I pressed for my floor.

'See you tomorrow, sleep well,' he smiled in response, his adorable dimples coming out. He stayed watching me until the doors slid closed. I grinned. I'd forgotten how sweet he could be. I pulled my phone out of my bag and cursed. I had ten missed calls from Spence and eight text messages. He was going to be so mad I'd been out all day and not been in contact. I hurried back to my room, figuring I'd ring him once I was in the bath to apologise. I also decided it was best not mentioning I'd been out with Alec for the day, or had more day trips planned. There was nothing to it, but Spence already had a jealous streak, I didn't need to upset him.

Saturday

'See you tomorrow, baby, I can't wait,' Spence smiled as he blew me a kiss.

'Me neither,' I grinned. I really had missed him, though he was driving me insane ringing every few hours, like an insecure teenager. 'We're leaving at 4 p.m., so I'll see you around seven.'

'Paige?'

'Yes?'

'I just wanted … I just thought you should know … well … I love you,' he mumbled, his cheeks turning slightly pink. I felt my stomach do a somersault, something it had never done with anyone but Alec, and put my hand on it as happy tears filled my eyes.

'Spence, I…'

'No, don't,' he replied quickly. 'I don't want you to say it just because I have. Say it when it feels right, any day but today.' We both jumped as the sudden blaring of the fire station alarm sounded. 'Shit, I have to go,' he yelled over it.

'Be safe,' I called, blowing him a kiss just before the screen went blank. *Please be safe*, I thought as I set my phone on the dressing table and looked at myself in the mirror. I hated it when he was on duty, the thought of what could happen to him doing such a dangerous job. He seemed extra stressed this week as well. He was ringing me constantly, getting snappy if I'd been out of contact too long. I didn't like the idea of him not being focussed when he was going into a burning building.

I grabbed my bag and headed down to the dining room. I was meeting Alec for an early dinner before he headed back to New York late tonight, plus I was looking forward to an early night and a lie in tomorrow. With all the sightseeing and work I'd done this week, on top of my previous relentless schedule, I was absolutely exhausted. I found him pacing in the corridor, dressed in a dark grey suit with a black shirt. I sure picked some handsome men to be attracted to. He lifted his head and smiled as he saw me approaching, but he looked on edge.

'Hi,' I greeted, kissing his cheek.

'Hi,' he replied, putting a palm on my waist and kissing me back. 'You look beautiful, as ever.'

‘Thanks.’

‘Shall we?’ He gestured for me to go first and the maître d’ showed us to a smartly dressed table for two. ‘A bottle of still water, please,’ Alec asked as we were handed our menus. ‘Unless you’d like some wine or champagne?’

‘No, water’s great, thank you.’ I looked down at the menu, mentally picking some dishes and discounting others as I came up with a short list. I looked up in surprise to see Alec hadn’t moved his from where it had been placed. He was just staring at me. He’d not really been himself all week, and each time I asked about New York, or Tiffany, he either avoided the question or ignored it. ‘What’s wrong? You seem tense.’

‘I’m fine, I just … I need to talk to you about something.’

‘Me too. Talk to you, not to me, obviously,’ I smiled. ‘Spence just told me that he loves me and I’m not sure if I should say it back yet. Is there some kind of unspoken rule where it’s romantic if a guy says it, but it freaks him out if a woman says it back?’

‘You love him?’ Alec uttered, looking at me aghast.

‘What? Is it too soon? You think it’s too soon to tell him, don’t you. But it’s been six months, what if I don’t tell him and he gets upset and leaves because he thinks I don’t care? I need your advice. How long did you wait to tell Tiffany? And when did she tell you?’

‘Paige, I don’t … from what you said, I thought this was just a casual relationship, sexual. I had no idea you’d fallen for him so hard. Are you sure he’s the guy for you? He seems a little clingy, constantly calling you and leaving messages while you're out. He even rang Jean-Claude when he couldn’t get a hold of you.’

‘He cares, what’s wrong with that?’

‘I’m just not sure he’s right for you, Paige.’

‘Why would you say that?’ I asked, feeling hurt. ‘You don’t even know him.’

‘I didn’t ask you to dinner to sit and talk about bloody Spence,’ he huffed, shoving a hand through his hair.

‘Ok, what’s going on with you? You were on edge when we had dinner last night and you’re being weird now.’

‘I lied to you, Paige, ok? I lied and it’s eating me up inside because I never lie, I hate lies,’ he said in a rush. ‘I didn’t come here for a job this week. I haven’t been on a shoot while you were doing yours. I came because Jean-Claude told me that you were getting serious with the firefighter and that you’d be here all week without him.’

‘I don’t understand. You’re saying you only came to Rome because I’m here?’

‘Yes.’

‘Why?’ I asked, feeling perplexed.

'Isn't it obvious?' He let out a nervous laugh.

'Not exactly, no,' I replied. Surely he couldn't have come to say he finally wanted me? Not now, not today. I couldn't believe what I thought he was trying to say. I must be imagining it. We were finally in a good place, we were friends, we had partners we were happy with.

'Paige, come on. I came for you, to be with you. I'm sorry it took so long for me to get here, to realise that I wanted you, but I'm here now and I'm ready.'

'Well I'm not,' I bit, suddenly unbelievably angry with him. 'I was and you weren't and now I'm with Spence and you're with Tiffany. We're both happy.'

'I'm not, I haven't been for a very long time, Paige.'

'You're living with her!' I tried to take some deep breaths to calm down as I noticed people turn to stare at us. I needed to bring my voice back to a level that was acceptable for an exclusive establishment.

'I am,' he agreed, 'but lately I've realised that my feelings for her just don't compare to how I feel about you, Paige. I told you I wanted you when you asked me to stay in London all those years ago, but the timing was so wrong. Your career was about to take off, mine too, they were amazing opportunities that we couldn't afford not to grasp. I was also scared, I couldn't handle you choosing your job over me for a second time.'

'You told me to go to Grand Cayman, Alec. You said you'd break up with me if I didn't. You may have done that out of noble intentions for me, but you still broke up with me and you chose your job over me too, when I asked you to stay in London.'

'And I'm admitting that I made a mistake, Paige,' he urged, reaching across the table to clasp my hand. 'No matter what success I've had, if I had the chance to go back in time, I'd give it all up for you.'

'So what changed? Why now?' I asked, feeling the sting of tears forming behind my eyes.

'My feelings for you were always there, I just didn't realise how intense they were until that shoot in Paris. I dated so many women trying to get over you, I really thought I had, but seeing you again …' He broke off and shook his head. 'I wanted to tell you that I was ready to settle down, to ask you to give me a chance when you were ready, but you ran from me, ignored my message, and hooked up with the goddamn firefighter. Jean-Claude told me that you were happy, so I tried to stay away, but I couldn't. I needed to know if I was too late, if this thing with him was serious, and I don't think it is, no matter what you say. I don't believe you.'

'It is too late, Alec,' I whispered, my heart aching to know how close we'd come to getting together. I pulled my hand out of his grasp and wiped some tears from my face.

'I'm sorry, but I really don't believe that. You haven't once said that you're in love with him, and look how well we got on this week. It's not too late,' he repeated stubbornly.

'It is, Alec. He loves me and I think I might be falling in love with him.'

He took a shocked gasp, his mouth opening and closing as he tried to form words. The pain on his face forced the tears I'd held back to start rolling down my face. He shook his head as his eyes welled up. Then he slowly placed his napkin on the table, stood up, and buttoned up his jacket. I swallowed hard as I looked up into his blue eyes. I'd come away last week so sure of my relationship with Spence. Even on Sunday night, I'd imagined that I'd got over Alec, but after spending a week with him, feelings that I thought I'd got over had started re-emerging again. I felt like I'd been ripped in half, caught in the void between the man I'd loved, who suddenly wanted me, and the man I might love, who I'd been so happy with. What was I supposed to do? Go backwards or move forwards? Was it possible to love two men at the same time?

'Alec, I …'

'I hope you'll be very happy. Goodbye, Paige,' he interrupted, then turned to leave, without even giving me a kiss or a chance for us to discuss what this all meant.

'Alec? Please don't go,' I called. But just like in London, he kept walking and didn't look back. I was left sitting, stunned at his reaction, and then mine as I started sobbing, with everyone staring at me and a waiter awkwardly holding the bottle of water, not sure whether to pour or walk away.

Sunday

I'd convinced Jean-Claude to bring the flight forward, seeing as though we'd come on his private ModOne jet. I wanted to get home. I'd barely slept all night, so confused at whether my ten or more years of love for Alec was stronger than my feelings for Spence after a six-month relationship. Right now I wasn't sure if I'd been using my relationship with him as a mask, to try and cover up how I felt deep inside. We had fun and our sex life was incredible, but now I wondered if that was all it was. Not to mention that Spence's increasingly obsessive need to keep tabs on me this week had highlighted concerns that I'd already acknowledged at the start of our relationship, but had not really given much consideration to since. He was always checking up on me, ringing me constantly, getting annoyed when he saw other men talking to me. It wasn't normal relationship behaviour. I'd seen it all too often with some of the models, who ironically lacked self-esteem. They'd date guys who started out seeming sweet and concerned, but quite often it turned to excessive jealously, then controlling behaviour, and was a short hop, skip, and a jump to mental, then physical abuse. I couldn't believe I hadn't realised until now how bad it had become, so I'd decided that I needed to see Spence immediately. If he threw open his front door and I was hit with a wave of love for him, or just the overwhelming need to have sex, I'd have my answer as to where my feelings for him were really at.

I'd dropped my case at home, Poppie was out, probably over at Justin's, so I grabbed my car keys and headed over to Fulham. I parked up and headed to Spence's door. I had my key, but I still didn't feel comfortable using it, not when he shared with other housemates. So I knocked on the door, biting my lip nervously, wondering what my gut reaction would be. There was no answer. I looked up and down the street. Chunky and Nobby's cars were nowhere to be seen, but Spence's was parked a few up from mine. I stepped back and looked up at his bedroom window to see the curtains were still closed. He was a creature of habit, flinging them open was one of the first things he did when he got up. I checked my watch, it was just after three o'clock. Either he'd been on duty all night for an emergency and was catching up on some sleep, or he was sick. I let myself in, dropped my handbag on the hall table, and made my way upstairs, opening his bedroom door and putting on the light.

'Surprise, I'm back early, are you ok?' I called. The surprise was on me when Spence bolted upright with a look of mortification on his face, as the blonde straddling him covered her bare chest with her hands. I felt tears prickle my eyes as I looked from him to her, then back again. Of the two reactions I'd expected to have on seeing him again, pain and humiliation weren't either of them. I shook my head, words not forming as a ball of acid burned my throat, then turned and ran down the stairs. As I grabbed my bag, I could hear him banging about upstairs. I fiddled with the safety catch on the door, my hands shaking as I tried to get out.

'Paige,' he yelled, his feet thudding down the stairs as I burst out onto the street. If that flasher leapt out in front of me again, I was liable to punch him, I was so angry. I ran up the street to my car, trying to retrieve my keys out of my bag as I went, but by the time I'd deactivated the alarm and grabbed the door handle, he'd caught up with me and slammed a hand on the door, stopping me from opening it. 'It's not what it looks like,' he panted.

'Really? Why don't you tell me exactly how you think that looked to me,' I bit, turning around to try and shove him out of the way. I cursed myself for sighing internally as I saw he was only wearing a pair of jeans, that he hadn't even had time to button. I hadn't been hit with an overwhelming sense of love, and I'd not had time to process how I felt about him before I'd been confronted with what I'd just seen, but my sexual attraction to him was obvious.

'Pretty much how this looked to me,' he snapped, slapping the Sunday morning paper down on the roof of my car to show me a headline photo of Alec and me in The Rome Domville restaurant last night, with another report of the Fulham Flasher having struck again just below us. 'I went online after I read this and found dozens of photos of you with him from the last week, including one of you holding hands!'

'He's my friend, I never cheated on you. I'd never have cheated on you, Spence, but I guess you didn't believe in me enough, did you, as you can't explain away what I just saw. Move please, I'm leaving. Box up my stuff and I'll arrange to pick it up off Chunky, we're done.'

'Paige, baby, don't do this. I love you,' he pleaded. I shook my head as I looked up at him.

'People in love don't cheat, Spence. No matter what we had, or may have had before, I can't forgive that.' I shoved him back and threw the car door open, hopped in, and started the engine.

'Paige, you drive off now and we're over,' he warned.

'We were over the minute you invited another woman to your bed, Spence. This is on you, not me,' I snapped. I slammed the door and pulled out into the street, glancing back in my rear view mirror to see him leaning on the neighbour's wall with his head in his hands. I burst into tears and had to pull up a few streets away as I sobbed.

Mission Impossible

A Monday Night in September

'I'm really not sure about this,' I whispered, as Poppie pulled me up the street towards Spence's door, holding a bag of supplies in her other hand. We were both dressed in black jeans and black t-shirts with black hoodies pulled low to keep our faces from being recognised in the dim street light. Not that anyone would recognise us, given we were wearing black face paint too. She'd even insisted on gloves, in case we left fingerprints anywhere.

'Trust me, I never got revenge on Reece for cheating on me and I always wish I had. This will make you feel better.'

'I'm not sure anything would make me feel better right now,' I observed.

'It's been a month, Paige. A month of you hiding away, licking your wounds. I promise you, the knowledge you took some revenge will make you feel better.' She looked around as we approached Spence's house. 'Ok go, let's do this fast just in case they come back early.'

'They're all on the same shifts, they don't finish early, Poppie. It's not like they can say, sorry, we're clocking off early on flexi-time, your building and elderly fat cat will have to burn until the next shift come on, is it?'

'Keep your voice down and get in there,' she ordered, pushing me towards the door.

'I don't know why being so secretive matters anyway,' I huffed as I opened his front door with my key. 'He'll know it was me as the lock's not been forced.'

'Knowing and proving are two totally different things. Don't you watch *C.S.I.*? Drop the key down the back of the hall table, you can say you threw it on there when you stormed out last month and Jean-Claude will give us an alibi if we ask him.'

'Poppie, I really can't afford to get in trouble with the police, not when I'm tabloid fodder as it is.'

'I knew you'd bottle it,' she hissed as I quietly shut the door behind us and pushed the key down the back of the hall table as she'd suggested. 'Fine, I'll do it all. That way, if someone saw us in the area and you have to take a lie detector test, you'll pass.'

'A lie detector test? You watch far too much TV.'

We headed upstairs to his bedroom and I had to quickly close my eyes as I thought of the last sight I'd seen in here, when I'd found him in bed with that blonde. I sat on the floor as Poppie got out her torch and giggled to herself as she stripped his carefully made bed. When I'd purchased myself some new white bedding, I'd got Spence two sets too, to replace the ratty old bedding he'd had when I started to stay over. He was allergic to fabric softener, so he never used it in his sheets, but I did in mine, so Poppie redressed the bed in my set that she'd washed and dried this morning, with treble the dose of softener than normal, so it would make him itchy and blotchy without having a clue why. She grabbed some of his neatly folded underpants and sprinkled itching powder into the crotch before folding them and placing them back as she found them. She was giggling to herself so much, I couldn't help a small smile playing on my lips as I watched her.

'He'll think he has scabies, or crabs, from sleeping with skanky hoes,' she nodded.

'Thanks very much!'

'Not you, that blonde, or whoever else he's been seeing since. Ok, you need to hold the torch for this job,' she warned, handing it over. 'Angle it down low, I'll sit on the floor.'

'You're so evil,' I replied, doing as I was told. She grinned and pulled out a pair of tweezers and a bag of partially defrosted shrimp and proceeded to slip them into the badly stitched hems of the curtains his mum had made for him.

'Whoever came up with this idea, genius,' she chuckled as she finished up. 'The room will start to stink of fish and he'll have no idea where it's coming from. I so wish I'd done this to Reece.'

'Why didn't you?' I asked.

'Because I didn't have an evil best friend to drag me on a secret mission,' she pointed out. 'You're too nice. I mean, you didn't even slap him.'

'Not my style,' I shrugged. She stood up and made her way with her bag to the en-suite. I carefully folded the discarded bedding to take away with us and dump in the nearest bin.

'Now you're sure this is the fake tan that goes on colourless?' she asked as she pulled out the bottle.

'Yes,' I nodded. 'Vivian got it after the debacle with that other one. One thin coat and it develops into a nice tan with no washing off or timers. I've never needed to use it.'

'Great.' Poppie grabbed his tube of men's moisturiser that he loved to slather thickly on his face morning and night and popped off the top. She carefully squeezed the contents into a food bag, which she knotted and dumped back into her bag of tricks, then filled his empty container with the fake tan. I couldn't help giggling at the thought of him heading to work and his face and hands turning darker and darker throughout the day. As if that weren't bad enough, she'd brought a bowl with a spoon and emptied out his charcoal facial mud that he used as part of his weekly Sunday facial routine and mixed some grey ink into it, before syringing it back into the tube. 'Ha! From orange to grey face in the space of a week!'

'Now that I would be happy to see,' I added, finally letting out a proper laugh. He was a real metrosexual man and his appearance was so important to him. 'It's a shame he shaves his head so close or we could have put hair removal cream in his shampoo bottle.'

'Now you're getting the idea,' Poppie grinned, turning to high five me. 'Where's his moist wipes box?'

'I think that's a step too far, Poppie,' I warned as she pulled out the packet of antibacterial and pungent-smelling disinfecting wipes to swap over with his toilet wipes.

'Please, he is an arse, why not teach his arse a lesson by disinfecting it properly. He'll have ring sting for a week.'

'If he comes after me, I'm hiding behind you,' I warned with a pointed finger.

'We've been really restrained in the circumstances,' she advised as she switched them over. 'I mean, we could have scrubbed the toilet bowl with his toothbrush, put haemorrhoid cream in his toothpaste, cut up his clothes, or signed him up for the most expensive online porn site we could find, seeing as you know where to find his bank statements with his account details.'

'Where do you get all of these ideas?' I exclaimed. 'I'm seriously worried about me now if I ever upset you.'

'Never, we've been friends for twenty-three years, Paige. Nothing will ever change that.'

'I really hope not,' I replied as we packed up. 'I promise to come and visit you in jail when you're arrested for this.'

'If I go down, I'm taking you with me,' she laughed, shoving my shoulder. 'There's no one I'd rather be cell mates with.' We both whipped our heads around to Spence's bedroom door as we heard the front door open and shut, then looked back at each other with panic-stricken faces.

'I thought you said they were on shift,' she whispered.

'They were, according to the schedule he emailed me a month or so back,' I whispered in return.

'What do we do? If we get caught, we're in serious trouble.'

'Really? You think? We need to make it to the main bathroom, fast. It has a fire escape window out onto the flat roof of the kitchen.

Sssshhhh a minute,' I warned, grabbing the torch off her and turning it off in case the light could be seen under the door. I could hear the unmistakable sound of someone throwing up downstairs. Great, one of them was ill and there was a one in three chance it was Spence and he'd be coming up to bed any second. We either had to risk it and wait, hoping it was one of the others, or bolt now and risk being seen or heard as we moved from the front of the house to the bathroom at the back, where the door was right at the top of the stairs.

'I need a pee, my bladder and my nerves go hand in hand,' Poppie moaned.

'Well, you're going to have to hold it,' I warned, breathing a sigh of relief when I heard the sound of the television being put on in the lounge. 'Put the torch on again, we need to make sure you have everything, and tread lightly, these old floorboards are a nightmare.'

After quietly bundling everything, including Spence's bedding, back into Poppie's bag, we tiptoed to the door and I grimaced as I carefully turned the handle and opened it to peek out at the upper landing. The TV was on loud enough that our footsteps should be muffled, but we still needed to be careful. Poppie squeezed past me and I shut the door behind me and led the way down to the bathroom. Luckily that door was already open. We slipped inside and I pushed it to, stopping when the hinges let out a noisy squeak.

'You need to leave it open, like we found it,' Poppie whispered.

'And how exactly do you expect me to re-lock the window from the outside when we've gone through that?' I reminded her with a flick to the forehead. 'This bathroom's shared by Chunky and Nobby, I doubt anyone will know who used it last and if they did or didn't leave the door or window ajar. Move it,' I urged.

'Can't I have a pee before we go?'

'No!' I took charge and pushed her over to the large window next to the toilet, unlocked it, and gently swung it open. 'Ok, you go first, don't drop that bag.'

'I don't care about the bag right now, I'm more worried about me falling off a roof, breaking both legs, and wetting myself in the process,' she hissed.

'Well, you should have planned ahead and worn some incontinence pants then, shouldn't you. I told you I didn't want to do this. We could have been at home with a takeout.'

'You go first, I'm nervous with heights.'

'Great, give me the bag.' I snatched it off her and slung it round my neck, letting it hang down my back, and draped myself over the windowsill. Swinging my legs over, I turned to dangle them over the edge, praying I hadn't misjudged the relatively short drop to the kitchen roof. I slowly lowered myself until I felt the roof under my feet and let go. 'It's not too far, come on.'

'I'm not happy about this,' Poppie warned as the soft glow of the moon showed her feet appearing through the gap.

'Join the club.' I moved to the side to let her slither down and land next to me.

'Owwww,' she moaned, rubbing her chest. 'Great, I have pebbledash friction burn on my nipples. Now what? That seemed to be the easy bit, how do we get off this roof.'

'Do I look like I have the answers to everything?' I asked, as I reached up to push the window shut. 'Worst of it is, if we get stuck up here, I can't even call the fire brigade to come and rescue us.'

'We could knot the bedding together and make a rope to climb down,' she offered.

'Which we'd have to leave behind. Plus I don't want my hands on his dirty sheets any more than I have to, thank you. Goodness knows what might be on them.'

'Both excellent points. God, I so need a pee.'

I shook my head and tiptoed to the far end of the roof, to where the kitchen window below looked out over the garden. We had the attached sloping roof of the neighbour's extension to one side, and on the other was Spence's patio. Grass would be a soft landing. I took off the bag and tossed it down, hearing it land with a thud, then sat on the edge of the roof, turned around, and very carefully lowered myself until I was hanging from my fingertips, then dropped, thankful for the slight overhang of the extension roof as I landed on the grass.

'Ok, do the same,' I called up to Poppie as quietly as I could. 'It's not that far.'

'Says the nearly six foot model. I'm going to die, aren't I?'

'You will if you dangle and tinkle on my head at the same time,' I warned as I put the strap of the bag over my head.

'At least you have moist wipes in the bag to clean up with after,' she giggled. She peeked over the edge at me and quickly stepped back. 'O my God, it's so high.'

'Only because you're standing up, it makes it look a lot worse than it really is. Sit on the edge,' I ordered. It took a fair bit of coaxing, including threatening to leave her behind, to get her to do as she was told. 'Does that look better?'

'Yes,' she admitted. 'But I don't know about coming down like you did, what if I scuff up my face on the wall?'

'You won't, there's an overhang. Besides, which of us makes a living from her face? Did it put me off?'

'I'd rather go like this and you catch me.'

'Do I look like Babe Ruth?' I asked, unable to resist the urge for sarcasm. I'd told her this was a bad idea. Why had I let her talk me into it?

'I can't do it if you don't catch me,' she moaned, her voice trembling with genuine fear. 'I'm *scared*.'

'Poppie, I don't know what to do,' I sighed, softening my tone.

'Find a ladder, or maybe a trampoline. I could jump off knowing there was a trampoline to catch me.'

'Or you'd just bounce right over the fence into the neighbour's garden. Besides, where am I going to find a trampoline or ladder? I can hardly knock on someone's door asking for one, dressed like this with my face blacked out. Look to your right, you could climb down the drain pipe.'

'I don't know if I can.'

'You don't have a choice, Poppie. It's that or climb back into the house and try and risk going down the stairs and out of the front door. Whoever's in there might hear you, or head up the stairs as you're coming down. Come on, you managed climbing the ropes at school, you just have to grab it and you can probably slide down it. Just hurry up, I'm amazed none of the neighbours have heard us out here.' I heard her let out a heavy sigh and watched as she shuffled to the corner of the roof and rolled onto her tummy, her feet scrabbling to find a grip on the pipe as she let go of the roof with one hand to grasp it, then the other. I nodded my approval as she slowly started to let herself slide, then held my breath as I heard an unmistakable crack.

'What was that?' came her terrified voice.

'Nothing, just keep going,' I urged, trying to convince her as much as myself.

'You don't sound confident.'

'Poppie, please, it's not far.' I gasped and put my hands in front of my mouth as there was another huge crack and the pipe started to pull away from the wall with a shrieking Poppie attached to it. I watched her falling backwards in slow motion as all of the guttering attached to the pipe started to rip away from the edge of the roof, slowing its descent down.

'I'm going to die,' she screamed, quickly wrapping her legs around the exposed pipe.

'Don't be ridiculous, you're only about six feet off the ground right now.' I ran forward anyway, trying to position myself under where I thought she might land. At least it was coming away slowly, bringing her closer to the grass. I could probably cushion her fall without injuring myself, but I was worried about some of the lights going on in the houses either side of us, not to mention the damage we were doing to Spence's house. Another set of wall grips gave way as I stood below her with outstretched arms. 'My life's flashing before my eyes. Tell Justin I loved him,' she cried in anguish.

'What about me?' I exclaimed, just as the remaining guttering came off the roof and the pipe fell in an almighty racket, dropping Poppie straight back onto me, and we landed in a heap on the grass, the bag below me slightly cushioning the fall.

'O my God,' she gasped. 'I've died, I've really died. I can see God surrounded by a bright white light.'

'No, that would be Chunky looking out of the kitchen window. Quick, get up and move,' I laughed, finally realising the absurdity of our situation. She seemed too shocked to move, so I shoved her off me, quickly stood up, and grabbed her hand, yanking her up. 'Move, he's on his way to the back door,' I urged. She burst into a fit of giggles as I started running, pulling her along behind me. We burst out of the back gate into the narrow grass and mud track that ran between the two rows of houses that backed onto each other. We tore up the long lane, with me looking behind to see if Chunky was chasing us, but relaxed a little to see that so far, there was no one following.

'Stop, stop, I have to pee. I'm amazed I didn't wet myself as I was falling,' Poppie panted.

'We need to get back to your car, just in case. It's not far.'

'I mean it. I'm clenching so tightly my bottom's gone numb and I'm cutting off circulation to my lady parts. I don't want to never have an orgasm again.' She yanked her hand out of mine and quickly dashed behind someone's wheelie bin to pull her jeans and knickers down. I checked up and down the track, keeping a lookout as I heard her starting to tinkle with a huge sigh of relief then a wince. 'Bugger, I think I've just stuck my arse in a load of stinging nettles,' she moaned. 'Can you rummage out those toilet wipes for me for when I'm done?'

'Sure, why don't I open the bag of Spence's moisturiser while I'm at it, then I can massage it into your stinging butt to make you feel better.'

'Thanks.'

'I was messing with you and I'm not rummaging for toilet wipes. Seriously, we need to move, Poppie.' The relative silence was suddenly broken by a load of loud barks that started to get closer.

'O God, it's the police, they're here already and they've set the dogs on us. Noooo, I can't stop, I'm mid flow and I can't stop.'

'Pee faster,' I urged, not able to see anything approaching yet, but the barking was getting closer.

'I can't get arrested with my knickers around my ankles and weals on my backside, Paige.'

'Like that adds extra shame to a criminal record. Hurry, Poppie,' I ordered, shoving a tissue from my jeans pocket into her hands. 'Ok, if you're not done now, we've had it. I can see the dog.'

'Go, go, go,' she yelled, taking me by surprise by bolting out of her hidey-hole, trying to drag her knickers and jeans up. I didn't need any more encouragement, so I started to run, looking behind me when I heard another shriek to see she'd landing face down in the dirt, with her bare backside in the air and her jeans around her ankles. She screamed as the dog leapt on her. 'Get it off me, get it off me,' she howled as I burst out laughing. 'It's licking my bottom, I'm about to be raped, doggie style. Literally!'

'Relax, it's Spence's neighbour's corgi, Clara. She's as soft as a brush, but where Clara goes, her owner isn't far behind.' I lifted Clara off Poppie and gave her a quick cuddle. I'd miss her, she'd always come for a pat when I was heading in and out of Spence's house and she was being walked. 'Go home,' I ordered, setting her back down as Poppie managed to pull herself together and quickly tugged her clothes up. 'Ok, we seriously need to run now,' I ordered, as Clara's name was called. We didn't stop running or say a word until we made it into the safety of Poppie's Corsa, but once we were safely locked inside, I couldn't contain my laughter anymore.

'It's not funny,' Poppie pouted.

'Doggie style, by a female corgi,' I howled.

'Well I didn't know, I thought it was a huge Alsatian or something and you were no help, running off and leaving me behind.'

'You yelled "Go, go, go," so I did.'

'I meant with me, not ahead of me. Honestly, this whole night has been so traumatic. I nearly died, twice. Stop laughing!' she moaned, smacking my arm as I tried to wipe the tears from my face, my body and the whole of her car shaking. 'It's not funny.'

'O yes it is. How many times have you laughed at me and my many calamities? This is total karma, it's so nice not to be the clumsy one for once, but next time you suggest a revenge style undercover mission, count me out. You're more Mr. Bean than Tom Cruise.'

'Cheeky cow,' she muttered, starting the engine and turning on the lights, then leaning over to scratch her backside and finally letting out a giggle. 'You'd better be prepared to ice my bottom as it's really hurting.'

'You pay for the takeout and we have a deal. I'm famished after all that excitement,' I confirmed, reaching for my seat belt.

'Jesus,' Poppie screeched again, pointing out of the windscreen. Framed in the headlights was none other than the Fulham Flasher, in all his glory. She cocked her head as we sat staring at him, not sure what to do, but in the blink of an eye, he was gone.

'You know, he has an amazing body and he's pretty well hung,' I observed.

'Well, what a night,' she exclaimed. 'It sure beat staying in to watch TV. How do we top this?'

The Gorilla

February

It had been six months since Spence had cheated on me. I'd been devastated, even though it was obvious now that he wasn't the right guy for me. My ability to keep picking men that I had no future with was hard to swallow. Regardless of the feelings I still had for Alec, I needed time to grieve over the loss of my relationship with Spence. He'd been a big part of my life and we had been happy for a lot of our relationship. Not having him to occupy my time now though, I'd come to the realisation that he had only masked my feelings for Alec. He was just a very welcome distraction at the time. I wasn't over Alec, I wasn't sure I was ever going to be over him. I'd finally plucked up the courage to contact Alec in October, asking if we could meet. I was ready to tell him that I was single and to ask if he still wanted to give us a try. It had been like a knife in my chest to get a reply to say that he'd just got engaged to Tiffany and they'd brought an apartment together in New York and he was too busy to meet up. That news had hurt like hell and had sent me into a dark pit of depression. Other than putting on a brave face for work, I'd holed myself up in my bedroom, avoiding anything and anyone. I barely ate, to the point my skinnier figure had Jean-Claude up in arms, especially over my refusal to discuss what was upsetting me so much. Eventually Poppie staged an intervention, deciding that I'd wallowed enough and needed to get on with life. My best friend dragged me kicking and screaming back to the real world and slowly everything started to feel a little brighter.

'What are you wearing?' Poppie shook her head as she scanned me.

'What's wrong with it?' I asked, looking down at my knee-length black leather skirt and a short buttoned red cashmere cardigan.

'Ermmmm, nothing if you're going to the dentist for a root canal, everything if you're going out for hot no-strings sex.'

'It's a designer skirt and cardigan.'

'So? Save it for shopping or public appearances. You look nice, classic and elegant, but you need to look hot and slutty.'

'I don't know how to look hot and slutty.'

'Hot you have down pat, whatever you wear. Slutty we need to work on. Right, park your rump on that chair and watch as I go through your wardrobe and come up with some selections. What underwear do you have on? Lingerie or comfy knickers.'

'Comfy,' I grimaced.

'Honestly, I give up.' She shook her head as she ran her eyes over my wardrobe. This was just a basic capsule wardrobe as the apartment wasn't big enough, so the rest of it was kept at Jean-Claude's office building. I had two full rooms there. 'Right, I have an idea. Get those granny knickers off, now. I want you in matching red lace.'

'Yes, Mistress Poppie,' I giggled. She winked at me over her shoulder and tossed a couple of items onto my bed. 'What if he doesn't want sex tonight? You could be going to all of this trouble for nothing.'

'Paige, you have so much to learn about men,' she sighed with a shake of her head. 'They always want sex on the first date, they just hold back trying to be respectful. Trust me, four dates down with no hint of action, you may as well have put him on an old-fashioned torture rack and be twisting the screws.'

'I'm just not sure I'm ready, Poppie. For a fourth date, let alone sex so soon.'

'You're nearly thirty years old and still single, Paige Taylor. Life is rushing past you and before you know it, you'll have missed your chance to settle down and have a family, and I know what that means to you. We're doing things my way.'

'I did things your way and ended up with Spence,' I reminded her.

'Well, I only told you to go and have great sex. I didn't tell you to get serious. That's the beauty of the modern age, women can be sexually adventurous without settling down. Online dating has opened a whole new world of possibilities to us. Have fun while you try and hopefully you'll find a guy you connect with as well as you connected with Alec. Have sex and if it doesn't blow your mind, move on. Don't settle for anyone who doesn't make you feel those butterflies.'

As I didn't do slutty, I compromised and dressed in a black trouser suit, with my red lingerie and some high heels, but left off my top, just buttoning my jacket. Poppie agreed that I looked sexy, but still classy, a look I was much happier with. I turned up at the restaurant and was shown to the table where Kyle was already waiting. I'd been on six dates prior to meeting Kyle, and none of them made it to a second date. They were all far too self-involved, only interested in telling me about their sports cars, gym workouts, and how much money they earned. They also seemed intimidated by me, or by the idea of how much money I made as a model. However, my first date with Kyle had been good. He was more laid back and conversation had flowed easily. I probably wouldn't have agreed to date him if he'd approached me in a bar or club, as he wasn't really my type, but we'd got on well in the emails we'd sent to each other, and meeting him in person had made me realise that I shouldn't discount people immediately. The more I got to know his personality, the more attractive he was becoming.

'Would you like coffee?' he asked, after we finished a delicious-tasting platter of tiny desserts.

'Why don't we go back to yours to have it?' I suggested with a coy smile, feeling bold.

'Mine?' He looked startled and swallowed hard.

'I'm sure you understand that I can't invite people back to mine, not until I'm in an established relationship. For one, the press usually have someone waiting outside.' It was true, my driver had a hard enough job trying to shake them off his trail each time he picked me up to take me anywhere. He'd even had to give Poppie and me evasive driving lessons for when we went out on our own.

'I just … I'm not sure …' He stalled and rubbed his hand over his mouth, looking worried.

'You don't have a wife hiding back there, do you?' I asked, trying to break the obvious tension.

'No, of course not,' he shot back.

'Then what's wrong? Is it me? You're not attracted to me?'

'No, not at all. I mean no, there's nothing wrong with you, obviously I find you attractive. I mean, what guy wouldn't want to be asked to take you home, I'd be stupid not to,' he replied, glancing down at his watch with a frown. 'I guess it would be ok.'

'Don't sound so full of enthusiasm,' I replied, losing some of mine rapidly.

'Sorry, I didn't mean to give that impression. Of course I'm incredibly flattered that a woman as beautiful as you would … O God, have I totally misjudged this? When you said coffee, you were meaning sex, right?' he whispered. I blushed and nodded my head. 'Well, ermmm, ok,' he nodded, standing up and offering me his hand. It still wasn't exactly a morale-boosting response.

I was surprised when we pulled up at his house to find it was a large, double-fronted detached in Chelsea, on quite an affluent street. I texted my driver to let him know where I was and accepted Kyle's hand as he opened the passenger door. He led the way inside and headed straight for the kitchen and flicked on the kettle. I raised my eyebrows. When I'd said coffee, I hadn't meant we had to actually have one. I suspected most guys would be pawing at me right now, but he seemed almost nervous. He passed over a mug of black coffee and took a sip of his own as we stood with the kitchen island separating us. This was seriously painful.

'Are you a virgin?' I asked. He spluttered and spat coffee all over the granite worktop.

'No! Why would you ask that?'

'You seem a little nervous,' I observed.

'Well yes, it's you, you're a famous model,' he replied, turning to grab a dishcloth to clean up the worktop.

'Who's still just a girl. I feel nerves first time, too,' I reminded him. 'Can I use your bathroom?'

'Up the stairs, middle door opposite you,' he nodded. I smiled and put my coffee down and headed up. I'd worked myself up for this tonight. If he wasn't going to make the moves, it seemed I was going to have to. There was a small lamp on in the hall, so I trotted up the stairs, then cursed when I neared the top to realise that the light from it didn't extend all the way up here, but I couldn't see a light switch at the top of the stairs. A window in the landing behind me allowed some moonlight to seep through, illuminating the area enough for me to make out the bathroom door. I headed in, but couldn't find a light switch in there either.

'What is it with this house? Anyone would think I'm dating *Teen Wolf* who can see in the dark. I should have brought some night vision goggles with me,' I muttered. I shut the door behind me and waited until my eyes adjusted slightly to the dark, allowing me to just make out a toilet, sink, bath, and shower. I did my business and washed my hands as I decided maybe he needed a little encouragement. I stripped down to my lingerie, leaving on my heels, so I could surprise him in the kitchen. Poppie would be so proud of me. I carefully folded my suit on the edge of the bath, then made my way over to the bathroom door and opened it, letting out a terrified scream as the moonlight backlit the intimidating shape of a large black haired gorilla standing right outside. His aged leathery face looked menacing, his brown eyes wide and piercing, and when he raised one of his large black-haired hands to his chest, showing me a set of scary-looking smooth, stubby, chunky fingers with dangerous looking talons, I screamed again. Why the bloody hell was a gorilla loose in a house in Chelsea? Not that the distinction of suburb mattered, I'd have been equally terrified and perplexed in Wandsworth or the Royal Borough of Kensington. I mean, gorillas in houses weren't normal, were they? More to the point, was he about to maim me? What I wouldn't give for a bunch of bananas right now to distract him so I could make a run for it.

'Jesus,' it spoke in a gruff voice with a heavy Essex accent. 'You nearly gave me a heart attack.'

'O my God, you can talk?!' I uttered, hastily backing away from it as his dark eyes seemed to scan my body.

'Well, yeah, darling,' it replied. Had I been drinking tonight? I was sure I hadn't had a drink. But here I was having a conversation with a huge gorilla, who seemed to be checking me out and liking what he was seeing. Right now, rather than the bizarre nature of my circumstances, I was more worried at the fact that he seemed to find me sexually appealing. I was about to be seduced by a god damn gorilla. I screamed again as I backed further away, accidentally walking into the toilet and falling backwards over it, then landing on the wooden floorboards with a thump and a moan. 'God, are you ok?' it asked, reaching out one of its large hands to help me up. I gasped as I saw something long and pink pointing at me from between its legs. It had a penis, a really human-looking, hard penis. I managed to scuttle backwards away from it, until I felt my back against the bath. Were gorilla penises supposed to be pink? I'd never looked at one, I had no clue.

'I'm so far from ok, you have no idea,' I moaned, my hands shaking as I shoved myself up onto my knees and tried to get up to make a run for it, but I couldn't seem to find the strength to stand up as he moved closer. 'I'm trapped in a bathroom with a horny talking gorilla who has an erection.'

'What's going on?' came a female voice as the bathroom was suddenly bathed in light.

'Help me!' I screamed, peeking around the gorilla's legs to see a woman with long dark hair dressed in a see-through white negligee.

'Paige?' yelled Kyle's voice as he pushed past her to enter the bathroom. 'O my God. Dad, what's going on?'

'I came to the bathroom for a pee and this woman nearly scared me to death coming out,' the gorilla replied, suddenly ripping off its face to reveal a man in his late sixties, who looked eerily like Kyle.

'You're Kyle's dad?' I gasped.

'You thought I was a real gorilla?' he chuckled.

'O my God,' I moaned, covering my eyes with my hands as I realised his erection was still in fact sticking out of his furry suit. What the hell was going on here? Now his wife was going to be wondering why I was kneeling on the floor in front of her husband who had his bare erect todger hanging out.

'Dad, please put it away,' Kyle groaned. 'Honestly.'

'Christ, sorry, didn't realise.'

'Go, give Paige and me a bit of space, will you.'

'Come and use Kyle's en-suite, darling,' came his mum's voice. 'You must be bursting after all that tea you drank. Nice to meet you, Paige,' she called.

'Yes, great to finally meet you. See you for breakfast?' his dad asked, as if the last few minutes hadn't happened. I had no words right now. I heard the door close, but still couldn't remove my hands from my face. I was mortified.

'God, I'm so sorry. One of the reasons I didn't want to bring you back here. It's a bit embarrassing to admit that at thirty, you still live with your parents.'

'*That's* the embarrassing bit you're pulling from this evening?' I uttered, finally dropping my hands to look at him aghast. 'Not the fact that I just saw your dad's erection, or the fact he was dressed up like a gorilla and saw me half naked?'

'Crap,' Kyle groaned, plonking himself down on the closed toilet seat and shaking his head. 'Saturday night is their fantasy date night. I usually stay out of the way, but I thought they'd be asleep by now.'

'Fantasy night,' I repeated slowly. 'Your mum likes your dad to dress up as a gorilla while he … seduces her?' I really had heard it all.

'She's got a hair fetish,' he gulped. 'That's why she fell for him to start with. See … O God, this is a nightmare. The men in our family tend to have a problem with an abundance of body hair, so my parents took it to the next extreme. Another reason I didn't want to bring you back tonight.'

'Body hair?' I whispered, resisting the urge to shudder. Arm, leg, and the odd bit of chest hair I could handle, but a fur coat really wasn't my cup of tea at all. I'd spent too long around men who waxed it all off for modelling. Hair just looked totally unnatural and very unappealing to me. Kyle stood up and turned pink as he unbuttoned his shirt and removed it. I just stared for a moment at the red, blotchy, and sore-looking mess that was his chest and abdomen, then he turned to show me the same nasty lumps on his back and shoulders.

'I had it all waxed off the other day, as most women don't find it appealing, but it seems I'm allergic to the wax. This date's really not going well, is it?' he sighed.

'I've been on better,' I replied, quickly standing up and marching over to grab my clothes. 'I think I'd better call it a night. I'll ring my driver to pick me up.'

'Can we rearrange for next week?' he asked, his voice full of hope.

'Kyle, I'm really not sure I can date a guy whose father's penis I've seen, it's kind of creepy,' I advised as I pulled on my trousers.

'And you wondered why I was still single.' He let out a heavy sigh of resignation and went to make me another coffee as I pulled on my jacket and rang for my lift.

'A gorilla?' screeched Poppie as I flopped on the sofa and filled her in on my night. 'You must have gone ape.'

'Very funny,' I retorted, laying my head on her shoulder and needing some comfort right now.

‘I’d have gone bananas.’

‘Am I going to get monkey jokes for the next month?’ I pouted.

‘Try the next year,’ she giggled. ‘I’d have been mortified.’

‘I was,’ I giggled in response, finally seeing the funny side. ‘God, my personal life is just doomed.’

‘No negative thinking, Paige Taylor. We just need to get you back on the bike and out on another date, no monkeying around.’

June

'Where are we going?' I asked TJ as he climbed into his Audi convertible and retracted the roof.

'I thought as it's a gorgeous day, we'd head out to the country and have a picnic,' he smiled, revving up the engine. He leaned over and gave me a quick peck on the cheek. We'd been on six dates. He didn't set my heart racing, or have my stomach twisting in nervous or excited knots, but again, just like Kyle, he was easy to get along with. One sure thing he did have going for him was that he was very easy on the eyes. Poppie had confirmed that if she wasn't engaged and happy, she'd have been shoving me aside to date him herself. He had light brown hair with natural sun-kissed caramel streaks, light green eyes with gold flecks that were visible when the sun hit them a certain way, and one of those classically square, masculine faces, with a kind smile. His teeth were a little startling, especially when he did a full-on smile. He'd either had veneers done, or bleached them really white. A little too white.

I sat back as we tore through the streets of London and headed out towards Hertfordshire, enjoying the feel of the sun on my face and the wind in my hair. I could do with putting an engine this powerful into Fi-Fi, it would be great to fly along like this. I'd packed an overnight bag, as I'd agreed to stay over with him tonight and Sunday, as long as he could drop me off at ModOne on Monday morning. I had a new designer who'd cast me for his swimwear range, and he wanted to take my measurements to custom-make the item. Then on Monday night, I was flying out to Vienna for an opera-themed ball gown shoot. I'd thought, approaching thirty, that my bookings would have slowed down, but if anything, I seemed to be even more in demand. TJ leaned over to flick on the radio as we left the hustle and bustle of the city and I reclined my seat. Before I knew it, I was fast asleep.

'Hey, drooling girl, wake up,' he laughed, gently shaking my shoulder.

'Huh?' I moaned, slowly opening my eyes and wiping my mouth. How unsexy of me, I'd dribbled all down my chin. I quickly pulled a tissue out of my denim shorts, licked it, and pulled the sun visor down to wipe the offending marks off my face as TJ clicked a button to put his roof back up. 'Please don't tell me I snored as well?'

'No, just the odd contented sigh now and then. You must have been tired.'

'I am, I've been overdoing it for the last few years with working, events, and appearances. I'm exhausted and in desperate need of a holiday,' I confirmed. I let him help me out of the car, and saw we'd pulled up in the entrance to a field with a stile next to it and a public footpath sign. 'Where are we?'

'It's a short walk along here to the most amazing lake surrounded by trees. It's a great spot for a picnic.'

'I'm glad you told me to dress casually,' I smiled, quickly crouching down to tie the laces of my Converses, which I'd left undone in my rush to get out on time this morning.

I'd put on a long-sleeved t-shirt and rolled up the sleeves. It was turning into a gorgeous day. TJ grabbed the picnic basket while I draped the blanket over my arm, and we headed up the path hand in hand as he filled me in on his day in the exciting world of estate agency. I started grilling him about the best neighbourhoods for me to buy in. Poppie had just set her date to get married, so she'd be moving on soon, and it wasn't like I didn't have enough money to buy my own house, here and abroad if I wanted to. Alec had been good, letting us redecorate to suit us, but I was nearly thirty, I ought to think about putting down roots of my own.

TJ was right about the picnic spot. It was so secluded that I had a feeling I was only one of many women he'd brought here to impress. The silence, other than the chirping of the odd bird and a distant moo of a cow, was a stark contrast to London. It reminded me of my parents' house. I missed them and weirdly, lately I'd found myself starting to miss the peace and quiet of the countryside. I decided it must be an age thing. We ate and I had one glass of wine, which was still pretty much my limit. Poppie found it hilarious that when we went to a swanky club and bottles of champagne were sent over for us, I stuck to water. I found my mind drifting to her wedding arrangements. Someone had cancelled their wedding date in Shrewsbury Abbey, so Poppie had snatched the opportunity to take it with both hands, meaning we didn't have much time at all to get organised. I'd therefore hired her the best wedding planner in London as one of her presents, as we needed all the help we could get to pull this off.

Her parents owned a large detached house in Shrewsbury, so they'd decided to have a marquee in the substantial grounds. I was taking her to ModOne next week, where I'd arranged for one of the hottest wedding dress designers out there right now to measure her and make her the dress she really wanted. She had no idea, she thought we were going shopping for off-the-rack dresses and I couldn't wait to see her face when I surprised her. If I was never going to get married, I was going to make damn sure my best friend had the wedding of her dreams.

'Owwww,' I moaned, when I was suddenly shoved onto my back on the blanket and TJ's teeth clashed with mine as he lunged at my mouth.

'Sorry,' he mumbled between kisses. 'I couldn't wait. I want you so badly, Paige.'

'We're outside,' I reminded him, trying to catch his rhythm and cringing as his tongue slathered all over my chin and top lip. Given my lack of partners, I hadn't exactly been all that adventurous. Getting arrested for public fornication in the country wasn't on my list of to-do items.

'So, I came prepared,' he replied as he continued to lick my face in a style not dissimilar to the giant rollers in a car wash, before he brandished a condom triumphantly. I silently cursed. If this was the extent of his kissing prowess, it didn't inspire confidence in his abilities in the sack. I wasn't sure I was willing to risk taking it any further. I'd end up in a neck brace again, or worse.

'Stop, stop,' I cried, when he decided to ramp up his idea of sexiness by sucking on my chin so hard it was actually quite painful.

'Aren't you enjoying that?' he asked, breaking away and looking at me puzzled.

'As a matter of fact, no. You're telling me other women did?'

'My ex loved it,' he muttered, looking like a petulant child. 'Cow.'

'I'm sorry, are you calling me a cow, or your ex?' I asked. Either way, I wasn't impressed. How was I going to tell him this relationship had run its course and not end up stranded in the countryside without a ride home?

'Cow. Really big and angry-looking cow heading right for us,' he shrieked in an unattractive girlish fashion. Seconds later, he was on his feet, running away from me as if his life depended on it. I propped myself up on my elbows, astounded, and looked over my shoulder.

'O crap, that's no cow,' I exclaimed as I saw the bull charging straight at me, his nostrils flared, head down, and horns looking ready armed and extremely dangerous. I leapt up and started running after TJ, assuming he knew his way back to the car, all of the picnic items forgotten. It was a good thing I had long legs and kept myself in shape, I could see TJ already panting and clutching his side. Some man he was, abandoning me and putting his own life first. I could hear the bull charging behind us, but didn't look back. I was gaining on TJ and quite frankly, right now, I'd be happy to overtake him and let him get pronged in the arse for leaving me behind. 'Run faster,' I gasped as I caught up with him.

'I'm trying,' he moaned. 'Why's that cow so annoyed? I thought they were friendly and docile.'

'It's a bull, not a cow.'

'Seriously?' His eyes went wide as he rubbed the sweat off his forehead. I shook my head, thankful my time in the country had taught me something. I pushed on, passing him as we were yards away from the stile and safety. For a moment, I felt bad for thinking of vaulting over it before him, even though he'd spared no thought for my welfare when he charged off without me, so I turned to see how much time we had.

'It's nearly on us,' I cried. I yelped as I tripped on a clump of grass and my ankle rolled on itself, causing me to stumble. It took me a few seconds to right myself, and TJ shot past me, screaming as if he was about to be murdered.

He botched trying to climb over the stile the first time as he was so nervous, and he fell back onto the floor, then lunged at it again. I grimaced as I put my weight on my ankle and forced myself to make the few steps to safety. If I made it out of this alive, he was so dumped. By the time I got to the stile, he was straddling it, forcing me to step up and virtually sit on the rough bramble hedge to the side. I hissed as the thorns and branches scratched at my bare legs. I caught a glimpse of the bull out of the corner of my eye, digging his hooves into the soil and trying to slow himself down when he realised he'd reached a dead end, but he crashed into the hedge, barely missing my leg. The force of it knocked me off my perch and I screamed as I fell backwards, feeling something sharp and very painful tearing at my backside and catching in my shorts.

'Hurry up, Paige,' TJ yelled. I tried to look around to find him, wondering why I could see his feet and the wheels of the car first. It took a moment to realise that I was upside down, my bottom and legs suspended in the air.

'Hurry up?' I hissed. 'How the hell am I supposed to hurry up, I'm stuck in the damn hedge. Come and help me.'

'What if it breaks through,' he called from a safe distance. 'It's vicious, it could kill us.'

'It's not getting through, but if you don't come and help me, I might just kill you when I next see you,' I warned. I struggled as I tried to get myself down, but winced as I felt a sharp pain in my backside again.

'O my God,' TJ uttered as he gingerly approached me. 'You have a barbed wire fence stuck to your backside. Does it hurt?'

'No, of course it doesn't. Honestly, I don't know why I bother going to a luxury spa when I could hang upside down on a barbed wire fence, with good old Hertfordshire thorns in my skin and mud in my hair,' I retorted, giving him a glare. He managed to help me get down and upright, and winced when he checked me out from behind.

'I think I'd better take you to the hospital, you have blood running down the back of your legs and that barbed wire looks pretty rusty. You're limping, too,' he observed, leaping a few feet in the air as the bull on the other side of the fence snorted his disapproval at our escape.

'Bit late for chivalry,' I muttered under my breath as he opened the passenger door.

'Right, my car's new and I really don't want blood on the upholstery. As I was forced to leave the picnic blanket behind, there's nothing for you to sit on. I'll lower the front seat and you'll have to lie on your stomach, ok?'

It was nearly one a.m. by the time I was called through at A&E. As if having to lie on my front on a metal trolley in the crowded London waiting room, with my butt cheeks virtually on display through my shredded shorts and knickers, wasn't degrading enough, I could see everyone sniggering as they looked at me. I'd begged TJ to leave me, saying I could ring Poppie or Jean-Claude to come and pick me up when I'd been seen, but it seemed he needed to regain his manhood for his earlier display of cowardice and he insisted on staying with me. I was surrounded by mainly drunks at this time of night, who were so rowdy I think they were prioritised ahead of me just to clear them out.

'What happened to you?' asked the nurse as I was finally taken to a private cubicle to be examined.

'I twisted my ankle trying to run from a bull, then fell off the top of the hedge and ripped my backside on a barbed wire fence,' I sighed.

'Hmmm,' she nodded. 'We'll need to x-ray that ankle, it's quite swollen and bruised, and I'll need to remove your shorts and underwear, I think you might need a few butterfly stitches there. What about your chin?'

'My chin?' I twisted my head from my flat-on-my-stomach position to look at her.

'You have a huge bruise on it. Did you hit your face as you fell?' she asked, handing me a small mirror to have a look.

'No,' I groaned. 'That would be my date's idea of sexy foreplay.'

'Seriously?' She tried to keep her laughter under control as I nodded and rolled my eyes, then looked back at the red and purple bruise developing where he'd sucked it.

'I wouldn't be seeing him again if that was me.'

'Trust me, I won't be,' I confirmed.

I hobbled out at three a.m. with my bandaged and sprained ankle raised as I tried to work out how to balance on a pair of crutches. I also had eight stitches in my bottom. I just hoped if they scarred, that Vivian had some decent concealer, or I was going to have to be airbrushed on any shoots from now on. I was seriously tired and irritable.

'Come on, I'll take you home to mine as it's closer. You need some rest,' TJ stated when he saw the state of me. 'What happened to your chin?'

I gritted my teeth and shot him a look, so he just grabbed my bag and walked ahead of me back to the car. I wanted to go home, to my own bed, but I was too tired and sore to argue. It took all of my strength not to pass comment when I saw he'd managed to secure a large incontinence pad to put on his car seat to protect his precious upholstery. Not that sitting on my tender backside was an option right now. I had to shuffle onto my side as he put my crutches on the rear seat. We made it into his one bedroomed apartment and he fetched me a glass of water to wash down two of the painkillers I'd been prescribed.

'So, I suppose sex is out of the question?' he asked, a hopeful look on his face.

'It is with me,' I quickly replied, astounded at his nerve. I was even more astonished that instead of offering me his bed, he set me up on his sofa with a spare pillow and blanket. I made a mental note to block his number and email when I got home tomorrow.

I woke up a few hours later, desperate for the toilet and ready for another set of painkillers, and struggled over to his bedroom by hopping. His en-suite was the only bathroom in his small apartment. He was snoring like an express train and I thanked my lucky stars that I'd seen what kind of man I was dating before I'd actually spent a night in his bed. I headed into his en-suite and closed the door, searching for the light, then squinting as it dazzled me. I took a shocked gasp to be confronted with a glass of water on the sink unit with a set of teeth floating in it, a set of brilliant white, instantly recognisable as TJ's, teeth. He was in his thirties and he had no teeth? I'd just known they were too white the moment I'd set eyes on them. I couldn't help laughing to myself. How the hell did I keep ending up with men like this? If this was the damage he could do sucking on my chin with them in, I hated the idea of what he could do if he was to gum me without them. I decided it was time to call it a day on dating. There was only so much I could take and I was well past my limit. I sneaked out and rang for a taxi, eager to get out of here and home.

I made it into my apartment and knocked over a vase as I bumped the table with one of my crutches, shrieking in surprise as Justin came charging out of Poppie's bedroom wearing a pair of boxers and brandishing a hairbrush.

'Paige, it's you,' he sighed with relief. 'We weren't expecting you home, I thought it was a burglar.'

'And you were going to brush him into submission?' I chuckled.

'Only thing I could find that might inflict some pain,' he grinned, jabbing it to prove his point. 'Poppie, it's only Paige, and I think she might need your shoulder right now,' he called over his. 'Are you ok?'

'Just peachy, another dating disaster to add to the list.'

'O my God,' Poppie exclaimed as she came out wrapping her dressing gown around herself. 'What happened?'

'Chin suction, a bull, and a barbed wire fence,' I replied, spinning on one foot to show her my patched-up bottom.

'Seeing him again then?' she asked, trying to keep a straight face.

'I'm never seeing anyone again. I can't even sit down, my bottom's so sore,' I pouted.

'I'll get dressed and go and get you a rubber ring to sit on,' offered Justin. 'The shops will be opening soon, I can grab us a takeout coffee and breakfast while I'm out.'

'Thanks, babe, you're the best,' Poppie smiled and pursed her lips, and he dipped his head to kiss her tenderly. I sighed as I watched them. Was I ever going to have that? A kind, caring, and considerate boyfriend, with all of his own teeth, no hairy back, parents with fetishes, or cheating tendencies? Surely that wasn't too much to ask? Right now though, it was looking seriously doubtful. 'Come on, you look exhausted, let's get you to bed. You can lie on your side and I'll prop your ankle up and you can tell me all about it.'

'Thank you,' I whispered, feeling really dejected. As usual, she couldn't help herself and laughed as I filled her in on my disaster.

'O, Paige, I'm so sorry. You really don't have much luck, do you?'

'Is it me? Is there something wrong with me?'

'Of course there isn't. You're as beautiful on the inside as you are on the outside. Some people just don't find their Prince Charming straight away, they have to search for him.'

'I've had enough searching,' I sighed. 'I think I'm better off on my own. I can look into sperm donors or adoption and have a baby that way, without all of this drama.'

'Don't say that. Try again. Justin has a friend at work who's really nice. I've met him and I think he's perfect for you. He's attractive, intelligent, and I'm pretty sure he has all of his own teeth. The only downside is he's got a rather old-fashioned name.'

'Is he called Archibald and lives up to his name with no hair?'

'He has his own hair,' she smiled. 'At least I think it's his own, some wigs now are so good you'd never know and I haven't checked out his back for fur, but he's so nice. He's a year or two younger than us and he's single. His girlfriend moved out about eight months ago to take a job abroad and it's taken him a while to get over her. Let us set you up on one date, see if you get on with him. Your bad luck has to run out at some point, right?'

'If it goes wrong, that's it, I'm never dating again,' I warned. 'What's his name?'

'Gordon,' she grimaced.

'Gordon?' I groaned.

'He's super buff, he was a champion sprinter, nearly made it to the Olympics a few years ago. They call him Flash Gordon. Please say yes, I can't bear to see you so miserable.'

'Fine, I'll go on a date with Flash, but only when my bottom's healed enough to sit on. I can't take the humiliation of going on a date carrying a giant inflatable rubber ring.'

'Yay!' she clapped, beaming.

'Ok, I need to take my painkillers and have a quick nap before Justin gets back.' I knocked them back with the glass of water Poppie handed to me.

'Chin, chin,' she giggled. I smacked her with a pillow and ordered her out of my room.

Flash Gordon

July

Giorgio walked around Poppie, frowning as he inspected the first draft of her wedding dress, then shouted something at his assistant in Italian as Jean-Claude and I sat sipping a glass of champagne as we watched. It was my thirtieth birthday weekend celebrations. Today we were dress fitting, then going out for a late lunch, followed by cocktails. Later we were meeting up with Justin, Vivian, Shauna, and a few models, including Dominic and his boyfriend Calvin, to head to the hippest new club in London to dance the night away. I smiled as I popped a chocolate truffle into my mouth. Flash was going to meet us later as well. We'd been seeing each other for five weeks, and so far I had to admit that Poppie was right. He was perfect. On one of our dates, I'd even suggested going swimming so I could check out his body hair situation, or hopefully lack of it. He'd passed inspection with flying colours, earning additional points for a well-toned six pack and defined pecs that I couldn't wait to run my hands over.

It had been nearly a year since I'd had sex. I was a born-again virgin. Archaeologists would be in awe if they discovered my vagina had been untouched for so long. It was unheard of for an attractive thirty-year-old woman in my industry to be single, let alone to not be having sex. It would be the greatest find of the millennium. Desperate as I was to have sex again, I wanted it to be perfect. This time, I was not ending up in a neck brace, or being cheated on. We hadn't talked about sex, or formally diarised a date to do the deed, but I'd already decided this weekend wasn't the time. I didn't want my first time with him to be when I was drunk and woke with no recollection of the event, or worse, found out I'd puked all over him mid act. Tomorrow I was headed home to Shropshire to spend my actual birthday with my parents, and I wasn't coming back until late Sunday night. I didn't want to take him with me to meet them in case it didn't work out. So the following weekend was when I'd mentally pencilled it in. I couldn't wait.

'What has you smiling so much today?' asked Jean-Claude as he observed me with a curious look on his face.

'My best friend is getting married, in what's going to be the most amazing dress,' I nodded, flicking my head over to where she stood on a pedestal, with Giorgio pinning up the bottom of it. 'It's my special birthday weekend, I get to have fun with you all tonight, see my parents tomorrow, and I think I actually have a boyfriend that might go the distance.'

'I thought you weren't dating again after that toothless, and spineless, poor excuse for a Matador?' he frowned.

'I wasn't going to, but Poppie insisted her friend was just my type and it's been going really well.'

'Why didn't you tell me?!' he demanded, standing up and plonking down his champagne on the table.

'I wanted to be sure he was right for me before I started letting people know. And I really think he might be. I was going to introduce you to him at the club tonight. Why are you so cross with me?'

'Honestly, Paige, this is getting ridiculous,' he snapped, gesturing emphatically. 'First I have you losing your curves that made me fall in love with you in the first place and Vivian has to work wonders on concealing the bags under your eyes from all of your tears as you got over that ... *imbecile*, Spencer. I think things are finally getting back to normal and you go on a date with King Kong, then turn up needing more concealer on your bottom for scars that will never fade from the last encounter. I ask you, what next?'

'I'm sorry, I didn't realise it was in my contract that I had to ask your permission to date,' I snapped in response. What was this?

'You are ruining all of my plans,' he muttered, storming out of the room, French expletives leaving his mouth as he slammed the door.

'What was that all about?' called Poppie.

'I have absolutely no idea,' I replied earnestly, with a shake of my head. 'If he wasn't gay, I'd think he was upset that I was seeing someone else instead of him.'

'Do you want me to go and have a word?'

'No, leaving him alone when he gets in a mood is the best thing. He'll be over whatever riled him up in a while. Honestly, it's not like I cause a load of problems at work with my ... lack of a love life, is it?'

'Maybe he had another model lined up for you.'

'No more models,' I replied, shaking my head firmly. 'Been there, done that.'

'And got a crick in the neck to prove it,' Poppie giggled, earning herself a stern Italian glare as her body moved while Giorgio was working.

'Designers,' I mouthed with a roll of my eyes.

I was sitting in one of the booths of the VIP area of the club, feeling incredibly merry. Two glasses of champagne at ModOne, then three cocktails before we came here, despite having an amazing pasta lunch, had my head spinning. Dom was making us all laugh with stories about his best friend Coco, who it seemed had as much luck dating men as I did. Until now, that was. I sighed happily as I spotted Flash talking to one of the bouncers and pointing over the private dance floor at me. He was dressed in his navy suit, fresh from a late night at work in the financial district, and was looking really dapper with a pair of braces. I bolted out of the booth and ran across the busy dance floor as he headed over, throwing my arms around his neck and kissing him passionately.

'Wow, that's some greeting,' he grinned, slipping his arms around my waist, his brown eyes sparkling.

'Don't tell anyone, but I'm a little drunk and I've actually missed you, though I don't know if I'm allowed to say that after only five weeks of dating,' I whispered, putting my finger over my lips.

'I'd encourage you to say it as I've missed you too, and wasn't sure if I was going to be pressuring you by saying it first. Happy birthday.'

'It's not actually until tomorrow, I'm still only twenty-nine. I don't want to be thirty, it will make me a cougar dating a twenty-something,' I pouted.

'I'm twenty-eight, Paige, it's not like you're in your forties or fifties. Besides, I kind of like having a hot older model as a girlfriend.'

'You think I look hot?' I batted my eyelashes at him, feeling a little flirtatious and adventurous with a few drinks in me.

'Crazily hot,' he growled, cocking his head to run his eyes down my body. I had a designer black mini dress on, which had a high neck front, long sleeves, and a sequin mini skirt, with a plunging back that exposed my spine all the way down to the arch of my back. It was a good thing my girls were still pert and buoyant as I couldn't get away with a bra in this. I'd teamed it with a pair of peep-toe, laser-cut knee-high boots that made me over six foot tall. 'But then, I always thought so.' He grabbed my hand and led me to the middle of the dance floor, then tugged me back towards him, crushing me against his chest as his hands slid to my bottom and he started to move to the pounding music. And he could move. His stock was rising rapidly by the minute, not to mention something else I could feel rising as we gyrated sexily to the beat. 'Stay with me tonight,' he whispered throatily in my ear.

'You've no idea how much I want to, but I'm drunk and I want to remember our first time,' I replied, weaving my fingers into his blond hair as his lips moved up and down my neck, completely melting me. 'I don't have a great track record when it comes to dating, I don't want to mess this up. I really like you.'

'I really like you too, Paige. Excuse me for a minute, I need to pop to the gents, then I'll go and order a bottle of champagne.'

'Kiss me first,' I ordered. He did and I squealed with laughter as he lifted me off the floor and spun me around while he did. 'Stop, stop, you'll make me sick, I'm already giddy.' I grinned as I watched him walk away, cocking my head to check out his toned backside as he disappeared. I spun around a little too fast for someone in my state wearing a pair of ridiculously high boots and felt someone quickly clasp my elbow to steady me as I fell against them.

'Ok, lady?' the older guy asked.

'Perfect,' I beamed. 'Thanks for that.'

'Anytime, babe,' he grinned. I yanked my arm out of his grasp as I saw him eyeing up my backside. I was about to head back over to our booth when I did a double take at the entrance to the VIP section, sure I'd just seen Alec standing there. My stomach fluttered and my heart started racing as I scanned the area looking for him. I could see the back of a tall, broad blond heading towards the stairs down to the ground floor where the regular clubbers were. I started pushing my way through the crowds trying to catch up with him. What was he doing here? Why wouldn't he come and say hello? I hadn't seen him since he walked out on me in Rome, nearly a year ago. I ran down the stairs, clinging to the banister tightly. Alcohol, stairs, heels, and Paige Taylor weren't a great combination.

'Alec?' I yelled, still not totally convinced it was him as I watched the blond hair heading towards the VIP club entrance. I shrugged off another lecherous guy in the corridor, who mumbled something about my dress looking better on his bedroom floor. Did guys really think chat up lines like that worked? I burst out of the double doors to the surprise of the bouncers, not to mention the queues of people lined up waiting to get in. I ignored some of the flashbulbs going off as some of the press who hung out here waiting for celebrities started taking my picture, and looked left and right. If it was Alec, he was heading up the street, away from the club. I started running after him, narrowing the gap before I started calling his name. When he looked around, and I saw that it was in fact him, it was as if I'd just run into a brick wall. I heard a crack as the heel of my boot snapped and I landed with a bump, right on my backside on the rough pavement below me.

'Paige, are you ok?' he called, running back towards me.

'No,' I moaned as everything around me spun like I was on a carousel. 'I'm drunk, I've broken my boot, my bottom hurts, and I'm nearly thirty!'

'Yet you still manage to look amazing,' he breathed as he crouched in front of me and held my chin, sweeping his thumb over my lower lip. 'Happy birthday, drunk Paige.'

'Thanks,' I smiled, trying to focus on his divine blue eyes. 'What are you doing here? Why didn't you come and say hello?'

'I was in London and Jean-Claude mentioned you were coming here to celebrate. I thought I'd come and wish you a happy birthday.'

'But you didn't. You were in the club and you walked away.'

'I didn't want to intrude, you were with your boyfriend and looked like you were having a good time.'

'I was, I am, no, I was, I mean I am having a good time, until I just fell over and now I'm not, except it's really nice to see you, so I guess I am.'

'I'm so confused with that statement,' he laughed. 'But it's really nice to see you too. Come on, let's get you up, people are starting to look.'

'Broken boot,' I pointed.

'So, let's take them off and get you upright. Where's your boyfriend?'

'He went to the toilet. O no,' I groaned, putting my head in my hands.

'It's bad for him to go to the toilet?' Alec asked as he unzipped my one boot and carefully pulled it off.

'No, but talking of toilets, I can smell poo. Is it you?'

'Do I smell of poo? I sincerely hope not, or I'm never buying this aftershave in duty free again,' he chuckled, unzipping my other boot as I stared at him. Every single time I thought I was over him, I saw him again and it just reminded me how much I wasn't. I wondered if it was possible to have two great loves of your life. If Alec could be my one unrequited love and Flash, or someone else, would be my second. I sincerely hoped so, because living for another twelve years without anyone to love but a man who was in love with someone else wasn't living at all. 'Ok, up you get, take both of my hands.'

'I'm sure I can smell poo.'

'How drunk are you?' he asked as he hauled me up.

'Two glasses of champagne and three whole cocktails,' I nodded, reaching out to grasp his jacket lapels as the floor felt like it was moving under my feet.

'That's a lot for you,' he confirmed, his fingers holding my upper arms and his thumbs rubbing up and down them as we held each other's gaze. 'Does anything hurt?'

'My bottom's a bit sore. I had to have stitches after being chased by a bull.'

'Never a dull moment with you, Paige Taylor,' he advised with an adorably sexy half smile that showed me one of his gorgeous dimples. 'Are you really ok? Happy, I mean. You looked happy before, but now I see you close up, your eyes look sad.'

'They were expensive boots,' I replied, not willing to admit that every time I saw him, I was filled with equal measures of happiness and despair.

'I was being serious, Paige. I worry about you. I told you that all I ever wanted was for you to be happy.'

'I am,' I nodded. There was no point telling him how I really felt, not now that he'd set a date with Tiffany. You didn't set dates unless you were madly in love. It seemed he'd finally got over me. He was obviously happy in his new life now, I somehow had to leave him behind and be happy in mine. 'Really happy. He's a nice, genuine guy. He has his own teeth, which is a step up from my last date, and he doesn't live with a horny gorilla.'

'Wow, a real catch indeed then,' Alec laughed.

'Are you happy too?'

'Me?' he frowned as he looked at me. 'Of course I am, Paige. Why wouldn't I be?' he asked.

'You look kind of sad, too.' I reached up to touch his face, then thought better of it and pulled my hand away. He bit his lower lip, then opened his mouth to say something.

'Paige?' Flash's voice called from behind me. 'Is everything ok?'

'Your boyfriend's coming, I'd better go. I hope you have a great day tomorrow.'

'Don't go, come and join us. Jean-Claude and Pascal are there, Poppie and Justin and a whole load of others you know.'

'I really ought to be going,' he repeated, kissing me on the cheek. I closed my eyes and breathed him in. I had no idea when I was going to see him again. But maybe it was better if I didn't. How was I ever going to move on if he kept dipping into my life, reminding me of what I'd lost.

'Hi, Gordon Keller, Paige's boyfriend, and you are?' Flash asked as he slipped a hand around my waist in a territorial, staking-his-claim kind of way and extended his other hand.

'Alec, Alec Wright, old friend and fashion photographer. Nice to meet you, Gordon. Paige was just catching up on a job we have coming up, when she broke her boot. I was about to escort her back inside, but now I know she's in safe hands, I'll leave you to it. Take care of her, will you, she's had too much to drink,' he advised, slightly stretching the truth to avoid me getting the third degree.

'I will, don't worry.'

'Bye, Paige.' Alec gave me one of his gorgeous dimpled smiles, making my heart ache.

'Bye, Alec.' I forced one in return as he turned and strode off. We were never going to collide. It was a stupid dream by two young kids who didn't know that life didn't always work out the way they wanted it to.

'Are you ok? Do I need to be chivalrous and offer to carry you back inside as you have no shoes on?'

'No,' I smiled, picking up my boots from the floor. 'I'll be fine, but it was really sweet of you to offer.'

'We'd better get back, everyone was wondering where you'd run off to.'

He held my hand as we headed back, the bouncers gesturing us past the queue and in through the VIP entrance, and we went to join our group who were all laughing and joking. I smiled, I was lucky really. I had a great job, an amazing group of friends, and a new boyfriend. Life wasn't all bad.

'What happened?' Poppie asked, eyeing up the boots dangling from my hand.

'You know me, why stay standing when you can fall over on a regular basis.'

'What's that smell?' Dom frowned, sniffing the air. 'It smells like … dog shit.'

'I could smell it before, too. Have I trodden in it?' I asked, lifting up my feet for him to check and looking up surprised as everyone started laughing. 'I have, haven't I? I've trodden in dog poo.'

'No, but you sat in it,' Poppie giggled. 'It's all matted in your sequins. That will never come out.'

'No,' I moaned, cranking my neck to see. Yet more humiliation, my boots and dress ruined in one night, and I was going to be thirty in a few minutes. This was a new low, even by my standards. 'I'm going to have to go home to get changed.'

'No you don't,' Flash advised, shrugging off his suit jacket and slipping down his braces.

'What are you doing?' I asked as he started to unbutton his shirt.

'You can wear this, it's probably longer than your dress and I can button up my jacket. That way the night's not ruined.'

'Well hello, Flash Gordon,' Dom chuckled. 'Have you thought of getting into modelling? That's a pretty toned body you have there.'

'Mine's not good enough for you?' Calvin tutted, with a scowl at him.

'Happy doing what I do,' Flash replied, handing his discarded black shirt to me as Poppie slipped out of the booth and took my hand.

'Come on, let's go and get you changed. You're not safe to be left on your own. Especially not at your age. Is thirty middle aged?' she asked our friends behind us.

'Thin ice,' warned Jean-Claude as he sipped on his champagne.

'Thank you.' I kissed Flash as he pulled his braces up. 'You saved the day.'

'It's what superheroes do,' he grinned.

Jean-Claude's driver dropped Poppie, Justin, and me off outside our building, and waited while Flash got out to kiss me goodbye.

'I'll call you tomorrow, birthday girl,' he murmured against my lips.

'Great, maybe we could arrange a sleep over soon,' I suggested, holding my breath as I waited for his response.

'How about next Friday? Come to stay at mine, we can order takeout.'

'Great, give me the address and I'll be there.'

'69 Beatrice Street, Fulham. You know how my job is. To save you sitting waiting, I have a spare key under the second flower pot on the right. Turn up, let yourself in, help yourself to wine or whatever, but hopefully we can meet up before then.'

'Hopefully,' I confirmed, kissing him again.

'For goodness sake, put him down, I'd like to get home,' Jean-Claude moaned out of the limo window. He really was in a mood today, I had no idea what had got into him.

'Thanks for the loan of the shirt.'

'It looks better on you,' Flash grinned.

'And you look better without it,' I winked over my shoulder as I headed inside, still clutching my broken boots. They were too expensive to throw away, someone somewhere would be able to fix them.

Friday

I settled myself back on his bed, trying to arrange myself in the sexiest pose possible, hoping he wasn't going to be too late in from work, or I was going to wake up with crusty drool all over my face and messed-up hair. After heading home for my birthday weekend, then working away on a photo shoot, I hadn't seen Flash all week. I hadn't even had time to text him. I hoped that me being here, dressed the way I was dressed, was going to be a great surprise when he got in. Poppie had sourced me a kit that contained the longest wide black satin ribbon, which came with instructions of how to tie it on your naked body, to "gift wrap" yourself for a partner. It covered my breasts, lady parts and the middle of my backside, but everything else was bare. I couldn't wait to see his face when he found me lying here like this. I quickly reached up to drape my long hair down my chest and rubbed my glossed lips together in an attempt to pout them sexily. I was ready.

I woke up with a start when I heard the front door go. Damn it, I'd fallen asleep waiting for him. I glanced over at his alarm clock to see it was already nine thirty, he had worked late. I flicked on the bedside lamp and checked my cheek and chin for drool, before raking my fingers through my hair and checking that my bow was in position as I heard him running up the stairs.

'Surprise,' I called as he threw open the door. The surprise, however, was on me, to see a man wearing a long green mac and a balaclava. I screamed and scrambled up the bed, huddling against the headboard as I tried to protect some of my modesty, my heart pounding with terror.

'Shit,' the man mumbled.

'Flash?' I uttered, recognising the voice. I stared in horror as he reached up to remove his mask and ran a hand through his dishevelled hair. It took a moment or two for me to process, then accept the reality, that I was dating none other than the Fulham Flasher.

'What are you doing here, Paige?' he demanded, the anger in his tone obvious even without the glare I was receiving from his dark brown eyes.

'We agreed I'd come over tonight,' I said quietly, trying to gauge his mood. How did I do it? How did I keep picking these men? Did I have some kind of pheromones that only attracted arseholes, freaks, and perverts? Did he just flash, or was he a sexual terrorist? Did he attack women? Was I about to be raped and butchered by the man that five minutes ago, I could have seen myself with long term?

'No, we agreed next Friday.'

'Which is tonight.'

'No, if I meant this Friday, I'd have said this Friday, I said next Friday, meaning the week after.'

'If it's already Friday and you say next Friday, you mean the next Friday on the calendar, which was this Friday, not the week after … stop trying to distract me! I'm dating the Fulham bloody Flasher, Flash. What the hell is wrong with you?'

'Nothing's wrong with me,' he bit, stepping closer to the bed and tossing his balaclava on the floor. 'There's nothing wrong with being naked, as nature intended. People are too hung up on covering themselves up. We're all sexual beings, I have a great body, why shouldn't I show it off?'

'Join a nudist club then, instead of streaking around Fulham flashing it to unsuspecting women and nearly giving them a heart attack! You've flashed me twice, for God's sake. It's perverted and wrong.'

'I disagree.'

'Well, if it's so above board, why do you wear a mask? Or flash at all? Just run around naked. My God, I thought I'd finally found a nice, normal guy.'

'I *am* normal,' he yelled, his face turning puce with anger.

'No, you're not. Please don't tell me that you've sexually assaulted women, too?' I scrambled off the bed, putting it between us as he moved closer. I was scared now. I'd read an article some psychology professor had written about Flash recently, saying it was often a sexual gratification thing, that they got off on exposing themselves, but it could be a catalyst for sexual and violent behaviour once the initial thrill of flashing wore off.

'Where do you think you're going?' he asked, edging his way around the bed and advancing on me.

'I want to go home and I want to get you some help. This isn't normal.'

'You're going to call the police, aren't you,' he hissed.

'No, of course not,' I lied with a nervous gulp, trying to work out my best escape route from the house. It was the same style terraced house as Spence's, except it had been converted into two flats, with Flash's upstairs. I wasn't sure I could outrun him and make it downstairs and outside, so my only choice was to stay and fight, or try and get to the bathroom and lock myself in. I could scream for help out of the window. I bolted, just as he lunged at me and landed face down on the bed, buying me a few extra seconds to get out of the bedroom and race down the corridor to the bathroom. I slammed the door shut and quickly turned the key, then turned on the light and took in the room. I dragged a small bathroom unit over to wedge under the door handle, right as he started pounding on the door and shouting at me. What the hell had I got mixed up in?

I opened the bathroom window and looked out, hoping there was a flat roof for me to jump out on again. There was a roof, only it was a pitched one with ridged tiles. I hesitated for a moment, wondering if it was better to just scream for help, but risk Flash battering the door down to get to me, or climb out, dressed in only a black bow. I groaned as I came to the conclusion that getting out was safer than staying inside, as he continued to kick or shoulder the door. I eased myself over the windowsill and gently dropped, so that I was straddling the roof, one leg either side.

'God damn it, can tonight get any worse?' I moaned as I saw I'd caught my bow on the catch of the window and it had unravelled. Now I was topless, and very nearly bottomless, straddling a roof in the dark. I quickly scuttled back, leaving my ribbon and the last of my dignity behind as I heard an almighty crash. 'Help!' I screamed, looking left and right for an escape route.

'Get back in here now, Paige,' Flash ordered as he appeared at the window and I tried to cover myself up.

'Climb back in with the flashing pervert who has obvious psychotic tendencies? Sign me up, that's one mission a girl would be crazy to refuse,' I hissed, fear and anger vying for the top emotion battering my mind and body right now.

'Don't make me come out there and get you,' he warned.

'Unless dragging naked screaming women off a dangerous and slippery roof is one of your additional hidden talents, I think I'm quite happy out here, thank you very much. Help!' I screamed again.

'I warned you,' he glowered, lifting a leg up onto the windowsill. Crap, he was probably crazy enough to try it, and kill us both in the process. The sloping roof dipped down to meet another neighbours on the left, so I decided to chance it. I swivelled and slid down it into the gulley, praying I wasn't about to rip my bottom to shreds on the edges of the slate tiles, then scrambled up onto their ridge. The next neighbour along had a flat roof, then there was a wide gap to the next flat roof. I looked to my right. Flash had made it out, dressed in a pair of jeans that he'd not had time to do up, but he was looking pale as he lowered himself to sit on the ridge.

'What's the matter? Scared of heights?' I called, scooting forward and banging on the neighbour's bathroom window, hoping someone would hear me.

'I'm serious, Paige, get back here now. I'm not going to be arrested for this.'

'I think you'll find you are,' I warned. I noticed a light come on two windows to my left. It was now or never. I slid down the other side of the roof, landing on the flat one. Now I just had to get across the gap. I'd always been good at long jump at school, but I didn't exactly have a good run up to this one. I heard a gasp and the sound of Flash sliding down the first set of tiles. I didn't really have a choice. I threw myself across the gap and landed with a heavy smack on the rough covered flat roof opposite, my skin burning where I'd scuffed myself. I quickly scrambled up and ran to the lit window. I could see an elderly naked man having a pee and screwed up my face. What was it with me and naked guys tonight? I banged loudly on the window and he jumped in the air, letting go of his todger mid flow. It was like watching a firefighter's hose, albeit a wrinkly one, being left unattended. It bounced and jerked violently, pee spraying up the wall and over the floor as he yelled in surprise. 'Help me, please,' I screamed.

I looked over to my right. Flash had made it up onto the second ridge and was contemplating either following me, or making a run for it. I looked back through the window to see the old guy peering gingerly at the glass, probably not able to see me as it was so dark out here.

'Please help me, I'm being chased by one of your neighbours, he's the Fulham Flasher. Please let me in,' I pleaded. I quickly placed an arm over my bare breasts and cupped my groin as he opened the window a fraction and peeked out. 'Hi! Sorry to scare you, but I really need to come in, he's not far behind me.'

'Barbara?' he yelled, looking back at the bathroom door. 'Did you put any brandy in my cocoa? I think I'm hallucinating. There's a naked supermodel on the kitchen roof asking to come in.'

'A what?' came a surprised female voice. I looked behind me again to see that Flash had made it onto the other flat roof and was considering jumping.

'Please,' I begged. 'Please let me in.'

'Why are you out there again?' he asked.

'The Fulham Flasher is chasing me.'

'Are you the Fulham Flasher? You're the one naked on my roof.'

'I don't have a penis!'

'For all I know you could have, I can only see your face.'

'Do I look like a man? Seriously?' I screamed again as Flash leapt across the roofs and landed with a thud on mine. I scrambled on all fours up the neighbours sloping roof and cursed. The house next door didn't have an extension. I had nowhere left to go. 'Call the police,' I yelled as I crawled on all fours to the edge of the roofline, wondering if I'd just given him a heart attack to see me in all of my glory. If I hadn't, Barbara was likely to be in for a very lucky night tonight, once she'd scrubbed her bathroom clean, that was. I sat down and turned around to face Flash as he cleverly climbed up to sit with his back to the old guy still peering out of the window, making sure he couldn't see his face.

'Nowhere left to run, Paige,' Flash taunted.

'Gordon Keller is the Fulham Flasher, he lives at number 69. Quite ironic for a sex offender, don't you think?' I yelled at the top of my voice. 'My name is Paige Taylor and if I die by falling off a roof tonight, I want it known that Gordon Keller pushed me.'

'I'm not seeing things. It is her, Barbara, it's Paige Taylor the supermodel,' the old guy yelled over his shoulder as he opened his window wide. 'She's naked and on the Jones's roof right now. They won't be happy, they only just got that leak fixed and had the scaffolding taken down.'

'Now you open the window?! Call the police, Gordon's trying to kill me,' I hollered, noticing other lights starting to come on. Better late than never. Did everyone on this street sleep with ear plugs in? Flash looked around, seeing that we were gathering attention, and his face turned even paler in the moonlight. 'What's the matter, lost your nerve now? Only capable of scaring defenceless women with your mask on?'

'What's going on?' someone yelled out of their window.

'Paige Taylor the swimwear and lingerie model's naked on the Jones's roof,' yelled the old guy back.

'That's the news you share?' I uttered, totally astonished. 'The Fulham Flasher is chasing me over rooftops and lives a few doors up from you, but you tell everyone I'm sitting here with nothing on?'

'It's not every day we see a celebrity around here, let alone a naked one. Don't worry, Barbara's called the police. Sit tight, love,' my naked wrinkly friend called. I heaved a sigh of relief to see Flash slide back down to the flat roof in a bid to get away and drop out of sight between the two buildings. The air was suddenly filled with excited chatter as more people started opening their windows and asking what was going on. I felt like a monkey on display at the zoo, except a monkey had the luxury of fur. I was sitting here naked. I could do with Kyle's dad's gorilla suit right now. Preferably after it had been boil washed and dry cleaned. God only knows what might be matted in that fur.

'Don't worry, I have no intention of going anywhere, but Gordon's making a run for it.'

'Flash, ah-ah,' someone sang out of the window, making me glare in their direction. If someone even thought about blasting out *Queen* on their stereo right now, I was liable to lose it.

'Come on, love, it's safe now. Barbara's getting you some clothes, come on in.'

'Have you put some clothes on?' I called, thinking I'd rather stay out here than face a wrinkled, naked pensioner.

'Late night naked tinkle again, George?' his neighbour called. 'Did you get your prostrate checked last time you went to the doctor? You never said.'

'It was Dr. Beth, I didn't want her inspecting my backside,' George replied.

'Better than Dr. Ramani, no bloke's going near my prostrate,' someone else called.

'George, get away from the window and put some pants on,' a woman, presumably Barbara, scolded. 'It's private, we don't need the whole street to know about your prostrate problems.'

'I think they do now,' I called. I grimaced as the clouds parted and suddenly the whole area was illuminated by the bright glow of a full moon.

'Hello love,' she smiled as she stuck her head out of the window. 'I'm Barbara, nice to meet you. We had no idea Gordon was seeing a supermodel, did we George?' she asked over her shoulder.

'No, Barbara. Bit of a shock, to be honest.'

'Bit of a shock,' she nodded, looking back at me. What were these people on? *That* was the news they were shocked about, their neighbour dating me? It was ok for him to go around flashing his penis, but dating me was the shocker? 'We ought to get you off there, the Jones's only just had their roof fixed, terrible leak they had. Took ages to repair. We're so glad the scaffolding's down, aren't we, George?'

'Yes, Barbara.'

'So glad, Paige, honestly it was a real eye sore. Are you coming in? It's a bit fresh with the window open letting in the draught.' She waited for my answer as I went to move, but it was as if my body had totally frozen. I didn't want to be sitting up here naked, with the whole street hanging out of their windows watching me, but my brain and limbs weren't communicating. As if this wasn't embarrassing enough, if I did manage to crawl over and slide down to their flat roof and climb up through their window, everyone was going to see me completely naked. I could already see some people taking pictures or filming me on their phones.

'I can't move,' I called.

'Don't worry, darling, I called the fire brigade to come and get you down, they should be here any minute,' someone yelled, right around the time I heard sirens in the distance. My shoulders slumped in defeat. It seemed my humiliation wasn't over yet.

'George! Stop staring at her and go and put some pants on, you'll need to open the side gate for them to get in the back garden,' Barbara ordered. 'Sorry, Paige. It's all very exciting for us. In fact, it's the most excitement we've seen in a long time. It's not every day you see a naked woman on your neighbour's roof, let alone a celebrity.'

'I should hope not,' I replied. I sat patiently waiting as everyone yelled back and forth, and it wasn't long before I heard noise down in the garden below me, then the sound of a ladder being put up against the house.

'Sit tight, sweetheart, I'm coming to get you,' someone called. I groaned. If I thought my public humiliation couldn't reach the lows of my fake tan rescue, I was wrong. Of all the firemen in the world to come and rescue me, it had to be Spence, didn't it.

'Please could you bring some clothes up?' I called.

'Paige? Is that you?'

'Yes, Spence, it's me and I'm sitting up here naked and would very much like to cover up and come down, in that order.'

'You know, if you wanted to see me again, you could have just asked,' he chuckled as I heard him climbing the ladder.

'As if, after you cheated on me,' I retorted.

'I think you got your own back, my room stunk of fish for weeks and we're not even going to mention what you messing with my toiletries did to my face.'

‘Got my own back?’ I asked, playing for innocence as he climbed onto the flat roof below me, then scrambled up to sit opposite me.

‘I actually thought it was that crazy clingy girl I made the mistake of sleeping with while I was with you, but now that I see you out here, on another roof, I’ve revised that assessment. Shuffle towards me, away from the edge, and put your arm out, you can have my jacket again.’

‘Thank you,’ I whispered, the night’s events suddenly hitting me, making my lower lip tremble and my eyes start to fill up.

‘Why exactly are you out here naked?’

‘Because I have shitty taste in men,’ I replied, deciding that flashing my breasts was the preferable option as I moved my arm to slip it into one of the sleeves he was holding for me.

‘I’ll say if you’re dating old George Barnsley now,’ he laughed. I switched hands and let him feed my other arm through his jacket and quickly pulled it around me, doing it up tightly. It took a bit of coaxing from him to get me to hold his hands as he lowered me down the tiles onto the flat roof, then slid down to join me. By the time he’d carried me down the ladder, amidst the cheers and hollers from all of the watching neighbours, I completely broke down and started sobbing. That was it, the final straw. I was never dating anyone ever again.

A Line In The Sand

August

I sat at the edge of the infinity pool of the private hotel villa I'd rented in Grand Cayman, dangling my feet in the crystal clear water and looking out at the ocean. For the first time in a long time, I felt free and relaxed. The Monday after my disastrous date with Flash, who'd thankfully been caught at his office trying to get a change of clothes and scrape together some money, I'd heard that Alec and Tiffany were getting married the same day as Poppie. I thought I'd hit rock bottom before that news, but that had taken me to a level I could never have imagined existed. I guessed I'd hoped that he'd only proposed to her because he couldn't have me, because he thought I'd moved on. But then if that was the case, he would have fought for me when I saw him in London, and he wouldn't have set a date. I'd never felt so low in my life, so I'd booked a month's vacation in this exclusive hotel complex and had left the same day.

I'd sent Jean-Claude an email, left Poppie a letter, and recorded a brief message on my parents' answering machine, then I'd fled, leaving my phone behind. I just wanted a time out, away from work, away from everything, to recharge and re-evaluate my personal life. I was going to lose some modelling jobs and let down some clients, but it couldn't be helped. I hadn't had a vacation in forever and with all of the inevitable media attention after my relationship with Flash and my naked roof experience, it was as good a time as any to escape. I had to accept that my dream of Alec and me finally colliding was never going to happen, and being alone to deal with that was what I needed. As long as I was back in time for Poppie's wedding, everything else could wait.

I headed indoors to get the frozen watermelon chunks I'd prepared this morning out of the freezer. I took them back out to the pool to feast on as I soaked up the sun. The weather was glorious, my natural tan was quickly developing, and I'd already had three weeks to mull over my life and make some decisions, the biggest one being that my dating days were over. I couldn't take any more disasters, especially not from men I'd grown close to that had let me down so badly. My heart couldn't take any more breakages. There were only so many times you could glue something back together before another fracture rendered it useless. Marriage was never going to be in the cards for me, but that didn't mean a family couldn't be. I'd already looked up a number of highly respected donor clinics in London, and that was going to be first on my agenda when I got home, along with looking for my own house. A house I could bring up a daughter or son in. The thought made me smile. It might not be the way I thought I was going to have a child, but having a baby was all that mattered. Someone to love unconditionally, something that was all mine.

I pulled my hair back and adjusted my bikini, then grabbed my mask and snorkel and headed down the steps to my own private section of beach, lined with palm trees. The swimming pool was amazing, but nothing beat swimming in the ocean and watching all the brightly coloured fish, turtles, and the odd stingray lazily swimming below me. I felt bad that I'd been here for so long and not looked up Toby, but it had been nearly ten years since we'd dated. It was a lifetime ago, just like my relationship with Alec. It was time to leave the past behind and move on with a new phase of my life. If I was going to become a mother, I'd need to cut back on my modelling, make sure I gave my baby all the time, love, and attention it was going to need. I didn't need to work anymore, but it would be nice to keep my hand in as long as the industry wanted me. I waded out into the water, pulled on my mask, bit down on my snorkel, and started swimming further away from the shore. I lost track of time as I bobbed around in the water, delighting in the sights I was seeing. I sat up to tread water and removed my snorkel as I sucked in a lungful of air. I frowned as I heard the unmistakable sound of my name being yelled. I looked around, back at the shoreline, to see someone jumping up and down on my veranda, waving frantically. I squinted in the sunlight. Was that Jean-Claude? What was he doing here, and more to the point, how had he found me?

'Paige, get out of the water!'

'What?'

'Get out, now. Jellyfish!' he screamed. My blood ran cold. Although no jellyfish sting was pleasant, one from a box jellyfish could be deadly.

'Where?' I yelled, not sure what direction to move in.

'Behind you, moving towards you fast. Swim!'

I didn't need any more encouragement. I put my face down into the water and started to power back to the shore, thankful I was a strong swimmer. I tilted my face for air every three strokes, just the way Toby had taught me to do to make me a better swimmer when I lived out here. There was no point looking behind me, or up at Jean-Claude, it would only slow me down and I couldn't swim any faster than I already was. I cried out as I felt something wrap around my lower leg and a burning pain shoot through it, but I kept on going. I was so close to the shore, I couldn't stop. I nearly cried as I felt my feet hitting sand and stumbled as I dragged myself up and tried to wade as fast as I could, feeling another sting on my other leg.

'Hurry, Paige, hurry,' urged Jean-Claude, who'd made it down to the beach and was standing back from the waves lapping at the dry, golden sand. I looked over my shoulder and gasped. The water was filled with them, I'd never seen so many. The burning in my legs was intense, but I wasn't feeling any other side effects. I had to hope I was lucky and this wasn't a deadly variety. I limped out of the water and used my last bit of strength to run up the sand, collapsing face first at Jean-Claude's feet. 'O my God, are you dead?' he exclaimed.

'I feel like I am. My arms and legs ache, my lungs are burning, and I've been stung,' I moaned, spitting some sand out of my mouth. I quickly rolled onto my back, my eyes wide with horror as I heard the unmistakable sound of a zip being undone. 'What are you doing?'

'I need to pee on you. It's a well-known fact that urine helps a jellyfish sting.'

'Put your todger away,' I gasped. 'You are not peeing on me! There's no scientific evidence that it helps. Go to the kitchen and grab the balsamic vinegar.'

'You want me to make you a salad? Shouldn't I be ringing for an ambulance?'

'Vinegar helps a sting, Toby used to use it. Please hurry, it hurts like hell and I'm too tired to move.'

'I'm not leaving you here. What if they come out of the water after you? I shall carry you up the stairs and into the house.'

'Come out of the water? What jellyfish horror movie have you been watching? They don't have legs.'

'You won't have legs if I don't get you treated, those welts look nasty,' he observed as he crouched down and I put my weary arms around his neck. He lifted me up and shook his head as he looked down at me. 'Always in trouble, Paige Taylor. You will be the death of me one day. Running off without telling anyone where you're going and nearly being eaten alive. When will you stop testing my patience?'

'I'm sorry, I just needed a break,' I sighed, flopping my head against his chest.

'Then you tell me you need a break,' he said softly. 'You don't run away. I've been worried sick, Poppie too.'

'How did you find me?'

'Please, there's nowhere in the world a famous model can sneak off to without someone posting online they've seen her. Someone in the hotel must have leaked the news as it was all over the internet yesterday that you'd surfaced here.'

'You've come to drag me back to work?'

'No, I've come to be with my friend who's obviously having a rough time. Sssshhhh, darling. No more talk for now, we need to get you treated. We'll have time for talk later.' He dipped his head and kissed my forehead, making tears form behind my eyes. I should just have been honest with him that I needed a time out, instead of running away like that.

'Owwww,' I moaned, as he misjudged the angle of the white wooden gate onto my veranda and nearly knocked me out on the gate post. I heard excited yaps and tried to look down as we skirted the swimming pool. 'You've brought Chi-Chi with you?' I asked.

'Pascal is in Venice working, and I was not leaving Chi-Chi with the dog sitter for a week,' he replied. We both screamed as Jean-Claude staggered and lurched sideways, catapulting us both into the pool. I quickly took a breath of air before I hit the water with a smack, went under, and came back up to the surface. Jean-Claude popped up beside me screaming. 'I can't swim, help me! I'm drowning!'

'You're in the shallow end,' I giggled, standing up to prove it as he floundered. His face turned red as his arms stopped flapping and he slowly rose up, fully clothed, his linen suit ruined. 'You can't swim? That's something we're going to rectify this week. What just happened?'

'Chi-Chi got under my feet, the little monkey. Where is he?' he asked as he searched the edge of the pool. He let out another scream as he looked behind me and covered his mouth with his hands. I quickly looked around to see Chi-Chi in the water, struggling to keep afloat as his little legs paddled for dear life. I was exhausted, my legs were burning with pain like I'd never felt before, my temple was throbbing from where I'd just been bashed, but the damn chihuahua had made it over to the deep end, so I was the only one who could rescue him. I started swimming towards him as he let out a few barks and slowly started to sink, with Jean-Claude frantically crying in the background. Three weeks on my own with no disasters and now look at me. Chi-Chi sank as I got closer, so I went under and twisted onto my back, coming up under him and cradling him to my stomach as I kicked for the surface. Using one arm, I struck out for the side and lifted him up, carefully lying him down on the warm tiled floor as Jean-Claude came running over and dropped to his knees beside him. 'He's not breathing, Paige, he's not breathing. What do I do?' he howled.

'I really don't believe this,' I uttered as I used every last ounce of strength to haul myself out of the water. I rolled over, sat up, and grabbed Chi-Chi's back legs, lifting him in the air and shaking him a few times until a stream of water came out of his mouth. I then lay him on his side and felt for a heartbeat, relieved I could still feel one. A shudder ran through me as I parted his mouth with one hand, ignoring his pink floppy tongue hanging over the edge of his tiny razor-sharp teeth and the ripe odour of doggie breath as I gave him mouth to mouth. After a few breaths, his legs started to move and before I knew it, he was licking my lips with all of the enthusiasm and vigour of TJ the chin sucker.

'Paige, you saved him, you saved him,' Jean-Claude sobbed, throwing his arms around me as Chi-Chi leapt up and started yapping as if nothing had happened. 'How can I ever thank you?'

'By getting me that vinegar and ringing the doctor,' I replied, patting his back as I tried to wipe the doggie drool off my face. 'I think you'd better ring a vet as well to check him over.'

I lay on the recliner, looking up at the thousands of sparkling stars, with my sore legs raised and a plaster on the cut on my head, while Jean-Claude chatted to the butler who'd come to clear away our room service meal. Chi-Chi was fast asleep on the sofa inside, no worse for wear after his ordeal. Jean-Claude appeared and handed me a glass of iced water before laying down on the sun lounger next to me with a glass of white wine.

'Now we talk,' he advised. 'Why did you run away?'

'Why do you think?' I laughed. 'My personal life is a disaster. Of the last two men I kissed, one is awaiting trial for indecent exposure and the other is a small canine in serious need of some doggie breath mints. He's never going to impregnate anyone with breath like that.'

'His breath does not smell.'

'Then you go and give him mouth to mouth if you love him so much.'

'I love you, Paige. Talk to me, running away doesn't change your life.'

'No, but it gives me some perspective. I'm just not destined to be in a relationship, I've accepted that now.'

'But you want children.'

'I do, but I don't need a boyfriend or husband for that. Once Poppie's wedding is over, I'm going to make an appointment to look into artificial insemination.'

'Paige,' he sighed with a tut. 'This is no substitute for having a child naturally in a loving relationship.'

'You think I don't know that? I've tried, but I've been on so many bad dates, I give up, Jean-Claude. It's never going to happen for me.'

'I agree, you've had more bad luck than most, but it's a numbers game. The more bad dates you have, the closer you get to the perfect man for you.'

'But that's the problem,' I cried, full of frustration. 'I've already met him, I fell in love with him, but he doesn't want me.'

'Who is this imbecile that doesn't want a beautiful and intelligent woman?'

'It doesn't matter,' I muttered, feeling my cheeks turn scarlet at the thought of Jean-Claude knowing how pathetic I was, loving a guy who didn't love me in return. 'The fact is he exists and no one else will ever compare to him, so I quit. I give up. I don't need a man to be happy or to have a family, and I refuse to settle for anyone who will always be second best, so I'm better off on my own.'

'Who are you talking about, Paige,' Jean-Claude demanded, swinging his legs off his lounger as he sat up to face me.

'Just some guy, you don't know him,' I lied.

'You're lying, Paige Taylor. I've worked with you long enough to know when you're lying. Mon Dieu, is it Alec? It is, isn't it? You're *in love* with Alec,' he gasped.

'No,' I retorted, struggling to sit up so I could get away from his piercing stare and impending Gestapo interrogation.

'Not so fast!' he ordered, shoving me back down on the lounger. 'Paige, this is serious. I'm right, aren't I?'

'Fine,' I snapped, knowing I was never going to get away with continuing to lie to him. He'd known me too long. 'You're right, but it doesn't matter, does it? He doesn't feel that way about me and I've accepted that.'

'I have never committed violence, let alone considered it against a woman, but I could shake you right now, woman,' he bit angrily.

'What did I do? You wanted to know.'

'How long have you felt like this about him?'

'From the moment I saw him thirteen years ago.'

'Then why did you say nothing? He has no idea that you ever felt that strongly about him, or that you still do.'

'Life got in the way of us starting anything, then each time we saw each other, we were with other people. It was just never our time. After Spence and I broke up, knowing that no one would ever live up to my ideal of Alec, sent me into a real black hole, until Poppie insisted on me dating again to try and get over him.'

'Your period of depression and weight loss was because of Alec, not Spencer?'

'Yes.'

'My God, Paige, why did you not tell me this?' he cried, raising his hands towards the inky sky in frustration.

'Why would I? It was my pain, no one else needed to know, and he was obviously happy with Tiffany after all, as he went and got engaged to her. Telling you, his best friend, that I was in love with him would just make things awkward.'

'He wasn't *that* happy with Tiffany! She was always second best next to you,' Jean-Claude snapped, quickly standing up to pace the floor. 'My God, Paige. After he flew to Rome and told you he wanted you, it broke his heart when you told him you were happy with Spencer and could see yourself falling in love. Thinking you'd moved on, he decided to move on with his life as well. When he heard that you and Spencer had broken up, he was going to fly back to be with you and I told him not to, I told him that you were so in love with Spencer, you were grieving for him and it wasn't the right time, that you needed space to heal. Now I find out that all along it was Alec you were pining over, that it's my fault you're not together!'

'No, Jean-Claude!' I moaned, putting my head in my hands.

'How was I supposed to know? You never told me how you felt about him, Paige. You didn't even tell me that you'd started dating again. I thought you were single after you broke up with TJ, so I worked really hard to convince Alec to try again, to come to London for your birthday. He told me he was finally happy with Tiffany, but I said maybe one look at you would be all it would take again for his feelings to come rushing back. Then you announced you were dating and happy when he was already half way across the Atlantic! When he saw you with Flash, he fled back to New York, unwilling to put himself out there and have you break his heart again. The last time we spoke, he told me that he'd finally moved on, that he was putting you behind him and was going ahead with his wedding. My God, all of this could have been avoided if you'd just been honest with me, or with each other.'

'He still wanted me?' I whispered, the pain in my legs suddenly being replaced by a blossoming pain in my heart. 'He really wanted me?'

'He always wanted you, Paige. Why do you think he settled for someone who looked like you? A poor imitation at best, but she reminds him of you.'

'So all of this time I've been unhappily dating, trying to get over him, I could have been with him?'

'Yes,' Jean-Claude sighed. 'But now he is getting married, he's reassured me that he's doing the right thing, that he's actually happy with Tiffany now. I think you've left it too long to confess your feelings for him.'

'Why did you tell me this?' I demanded, shooting up to my feet. 'This doesn't help, Jean-Claude. Knowing how close I was to having him over the years makes everything a hundred times worse than assuming he'd moved on with her and never felt that strongly about me at all.'

'I didn't mean to hurt you, Paige. I'm just so shocked to find that you've been covering up your feelings for him for so long. I'll ring him, tell him how you really feel.'

'Don't you dare!' I snapped. 'I've taken all the humiliation I can in one lifetime. If he's going ahead with this wedding, he's obviously in love with Tiffany and he's let me go. Admitting how I really feel about him now, to have him reject me just like he did all those years ago, would break me for good, Jean-Claude. Don't do that to me! Don't you *dare* do that to me.'

'Come and lie down, you've had a traumatic day. The doctor said you need to rest.'

'I need to be alone, I know you mean well, but I can't … I just can't.' I ran from him back into the villa and into my suite, locking the double doors behind me. I threw myself onto my bed and started to sob, harder than I'd ever cried in my life.

'You look simply stunning, the most beautiful bride that ever lived,' I sniffed as I adjusted Poppie's veil, feeling overcome with emotion. 'And in about thirty minutes, you'll be married to your very own Prince Charming.'

'Don't cry, you'll make me cry and I can't walk up the aisle in tears already.'

'I'm sorry, I'm just extra emotional as my best friend is getting married today.'

'And the love of your life is, too,' she said gently, catching both of my hands in hers. 'It's not too late. Until he says I do, you can ring him and tell him how you really feel.'

'I can't, Poppie,' I replied with a shake of my head. 'I'm so unhappy without him that I've taken a vow of celibacy. If he was in love with me, he wouldn't be walking up the aisle with another woman. Why can't you or Jean-Claude see that? It's over. I'm going to be fine, I have a whole new life to plan, but today isn't about me, it's about you. So, that's enough on the matter.'

'You're as stubborn as a mule, Paige,' she sighed.

'I know,' I smiled, putting on a brave front. 'Come on, your dad's outside and he's fit to burst with excitement and pride, so God knows how poor Justin is feeling.'

'He's there, right, he's turned up?'

'Of course he has, things like that would happen to me, not to you,' I grinned, handing her bouquet over and linking arms with her as we headed to the door.

We made it to the Abbey about fifteen minutes early, so after pictures with me had been taken, and while pictures were being taken of Poppie and her dad outside, I rushed over to the The Peach Tree to use their toilets. I cursed and hopped from foot to foot as I waited for the afternoon tea brigade to empty their bladders of Earl Grey and coffee. I checked my watch, it was nearly three p.m. The wedding service was due to start, I hadn't expected to have to queue so long. I was on the verge of screaming "*Irritable bowel sufferer, bottom explosion pending*," when finally a stall was vacated. I rushed my pee and was careful not to splash water all over my pretty bridesmaid's dress. Poppie's dress was gorgeous, layers and layers of toile, a tightly fitted bodice, and a wide gold sash around her waist that flowed down her back and out across her train. The gold just offset her blonde hair and brown eyes perfectly. I was in a matching gold, off the shoulder dress with three-quarter sleeves and a full skirt that stopped just above the knee, which was teamed with a pair of jewelled gold shoes to match Poppie's. Both of us had jewelled pouches that dangled from our wrists, in which I'd stuffed my phone, some tissues, and my lip-gloss. I washed my hands really gently, making sure I didn't splash any water on myself. Paige Taylor was not going to create a scene today. All attention needed to be on Poppie, not me.

'Sorry, sorry,' I called as I dashed across the road to find everyone else had gone in and Poppie and her dad were patiently waiting outside. 'I'm here now. Where's Sarah?' I asked. The wedding planner I'd organised had been like a constant shadow from the moment we opened our eyes this morning.

'Letting Justin know I'm not standing him up,' Poppie giggled. 'She said to make your way in, the organist will start as soon as you enter.

'Good luck,' I smiled, leaning in to kiss her cheek. 'I'm really going to miss not living with you.'

'Paige!' she moaned, fluttering her hands. 'Don't start me. Dad, do you have a tissue?'

'Sure, baby, look at me. Let me dab, can't have you walking up the aisle with mascara everywhere.'

I sighed as I watched them smiling at each other, her dad licking the edge of his pocket-handkerchief to carefully wipe her tears away. I felt awful that I was doing my dad out of this moment. I rushed through the grand arched entrance to the Abbey and waited for the organ to start, then slowly walked up the aisle, trying to remember I wasn't on the catwalk and to slow my speed and sass down. I smiled as I passed the first group of the congregation, who were all facing my direction, and cringed as the unmistakable sound of Taylor Swift's *We Are Never Ever Getting Back Together* emanated from my bag. I'd added it as my ringtone in Grand Cayman to help me focus on moving on. I just hoped Justin didn't think my ringtone was some kind of omen, that I was only heading up the aisle to tell him that his bride wasn't three minutes late, that she was actually never coming.

'Paige, Paige.' I could hear people whispering behind me, trying to let me know, like it wasn't obvious. I was carrying a bouquet in one hand and my small bag had such a tight opening that I couldn't wrestle my phone out without stopping, and there was no way I was delaying this wedding for another moment, so I gave up trying to find the mute button and managed to make out the red reject sign glowing and tapped that instead. 'Paige,' someone else hissed loudly.

'Alright, alright, I'm sorry but it's stopped ringing now,' I whispered over my shoulder as I carried on walking. I gave Jean-Claude and Pascal a little wave as I passed them and saw both of them trying to stifle their laughter. I straightened my shoulders. So what if I had a break up song on my phone? it didn't just apply to Alec, it could apply to anyone I'd ever dated or kissed, including Chi-Chi. I made it to the top of the aisle and smiled at Justin. He looked happy and nervous all rolled into one. 'She's coming,' I mouthed, giving him a reassuring smile and receiving a relieved one in return.

'Thank God,' he mouthed back, then grimaced as he flicked his eyes at the vicar to see if he'd heard him blaspheme. I took my position, slightly facing the congregation, and trained my eyes on the door, waiting for Poppie to come through as the organist started playing the wedding march. I could still hear people sniggering, the front few rows seemed to be pointing at me as they laughed. Honestly, it was only Taylor Swift, it wasn't like I came up the aisle with Black Sabbath or Slipknot blaring. I ignored them all and focussed on Poppie's happy face as she headed towards us. My eyes widened in horror as she shook her head and started laughing, looking straight at me. What had I done now?

'What?' I whispered as she steered her dad towards me, instead of walking up besides Justin.

'Nice purple knickers,' she giggled, handing me her bouquet.

'How did you know I was wearing purple knickers?'

'Everyone knows, Paige, you've walked up the aisle with your dress tucked into them and your bottom on display.'

'No, seriously?' I craned my head to look behind me as she pulled and freed the taffeta and smoothed it down for me. 'I'm so sorry.'

'It wouldn't be the same to have a day without a Paige disaster, but on the plus side, at least you didn't fall over and you weren't wearing a G-string to really flash everyone,' she grinned, kissing my cheek. I handed her bouquet back and quickly glared in Jean-Claude and Pascal's direction, to see their shoulders were shaking with laughter. I was so getting them back for that later. I teared up as the happy couple faced each other to make their vows. Poppie was crying, her parents were crying, my parents were crying, even Justin was on the verge of tears.

'Sorry, sorry, sorry,' I whimpered as my phone started ringing again. I pulled my bag off my wrist and tossed it up over the heads of family in the front rows to Jean-Claude. Pascal leapt up to catch it so he could turn the phone off.

'You do realise that wasn't the bride's bouquet, right, darling,' Jean-Claude laughed, making the whole church burst into laughter as well.

We laughed our way through the evening meal in the white and gold-decorated marquee at Poppie's parents' house, and I was led to the dance floor by Justin's best man, Callum, who worked with him in the same financial firm that Flash had.

'I'm so sorry about Gordon, none of us had any clue,' he said as he twirled me around.

'It's not your fault, I just have a way of attracting them.'

'You'll find your Prince Charming one day, Paige. Elisa's three years older than me and she never thought she'd get married. One day a really nice guy will sweep you off your feet.'

'All the good ones are married though,' I said sadly. It was lunchtime in New York and my Prince Charming was no longer available. The final nail in the coffin of Alec and Paige had been hammered. 'Will you excuse me, Callum?' I asked, kissing his cheek and dashing off the dance floor. I just needed a few minutes to grieve, then I could put on my happy face again and join the after party.

I ran out of the marquee and bent down to pull off my shoes, clutching them in one hand by the heels. I headed down the immaculately manicured lush grass to the river that ran along the bottom of the grounds. I sat on the bench next to a weeping willow, which overlooked the river and a small jetty where a rowing boat was moored, and smiled. Poppie and I had spent many school holidays down here. I pulled my feet up onto the bench and hugged my knees to my chest, closing my eyes as I thought of all the happy moments I'd had with Alec, wondering if he remembered any of them with fondness, too. I let myself wallow for a few minutes, then sighed and wiped a few stray tears from my eyes. I was about to get up when I remembered my missed calls from earlier. I'd not turned my phone back on. I pulled it out of my bag and powered it up to see I had six missed calls now, all from the same number. Alec's number. How bizarre, and he hadn't left any messages for me either.

'Why are you calling me, Alec?' I asked my phone. 'Today of all days? It's your wedding day, the happiest day of your life.'

'No, it wasn't, because I realised that I was making the biggest mistake of my life. That I was about to marry the wrong girl to try and get over the right girl, so I came to see if she was still available and might think about giving me another chance.'

'Alec?' I whispered, not sure if my ears were playing tricks on me. I slowly looked behind me, my breath catching in my throat to see him standing there, wearing formal wear, with his cravat hanging loosely around his neck. I dropped my phone on the bench next to my shoes and bag and stood up, turning to face him. My hands started shaking, my heart was racing, and my stomach fluttered as I drank him in. I was going to be in love with this man until I took my last breath, there was no point fighting it.

'I don't care anymore if you're seeing someone else again, Paige. I'm fed up of waiting for the right time. I should never have told you it was ok to take that job in Grand Cayman. I should have put my foot down and told you that I was going to be everything you ever needed, that you'd never regret turning it down to stay with me, and we could have had so many happy years together. But I could see in your eyes that you weren't ready to make the same commitment to me back then, so I tried to make it easier for you and I let you go. I've had to live with that regret ever since. I won't live with regrets anymore. If you're seeing someone now, I want you to break it off, to give me a chance, because no one will ever love you the way that I've loved you from the moment that Daisy showered you in cow poo,' he stated earnestly. I laughed as happy tears started to roll down my face.

'Do you really mean that?' I asked, my heart soaring with hope.

'I *love* you, Paige Taylor, and I'm never going to be happy until I make you Paige Wright. The only question is whether you feel the same about me?' He bit his lower lip nervously as he gazed at me, emotion swimming in his gorgeous blue eyes.

'That's one question you *never* have to ask me, Alec Wright,' I replied, throwing myself at him, my arms wrapping around his neck as I kissed him. He laughed and lifted me off my feet and spun me around.

'Really? Tell me, Paige, I need to hear it,' he demanded forcefully between kisses that rendered me to the consistency of melted butter.

'I love you, I've loved you from the moment I first set eyes on you, and I don't want to live with regrets anymore either.'

'God, Paige, you've just turned the lowest day of my life into the best one ever,' he groaned, one hand reaching up to clasp the back of my head as he kissed me so passionately I saw stars. He broke away, both of us panting for air. 'Why did you never tell me that you were in love with me?'

'Because you were a serial dater travelling the world, Alec. I didn't think you were the settling-down type, then you broke my heart when I heard you'd moved in with Tiffany. When you came to Rome to say you wanted to be with me, I thought I was happy with Spence. By the time I realised I wasn't and I'd got over that relationship, you'd gone and got engaged and refused to meet me! I really believed you were happy with her, that you'd moved on, so I didn't think it was fair to tell you that I was still in love with you. I tried to make it work with other guys to get over you, as I had no idea that you still felt anything for me.'

'I was so gutted that you turned me down in Rome, I guess I was scared of putting myself out there again, of admitting that I was still in love with you and having you break my heart all over again, so I convinced myself that I was happy with Tiffany to try and get over you. I was so close to telling you how I felt again in London for your birthday, but you looked so happy with that guy that I bottled it. Tell me we'll never be that stupid again, that we'll be honest about our feelings for each other from this moment on.'

'I promise,' I confirmed, kissing him again, feeling happier than I had in my whole life. He pulled me off him and set me down on the grass, then quickly dropped to one knee in front of me, making me gasp.

'I meant what I said before. Marry me, Paige, don't make me waste any more of my life waiting for you. It's our time to collide right now, let's not waste this opportunity.' He choked up on his last few words as he slipped a dazzling diamond solitaire onto my finger.

'O my God, that's not Tiffany's ring, is it?' I exclaimed, making him laugh and shake his head. 'What? It's not so funny. I've stolen her husband-to-be on his wedding day and he's proposing to me in the outfit he was going to get married to her in.'

'You can't steal something that was always yours, Paige. You've owned me and my heart from that day in the cow stall. And no, it's not Tiffany's ring, though I did purchase it from Tiffany & Co in New York before I flew back here to find you. Please, Paige, I've waited for you for thirteen unlucky years, the longest of my life, don't subject me to even thirteen more seconds of misery waiting for your answer.'

'Don't you think we ought to have sex first? We might not even be compatible,' I giggled.

'The way we kiss? The way my skin vibrates whenever you're near, the way my heart pounds so hard I think I might die, the way I can't breathe whenever I look at you? There's no way we're not compatible, but I promise you we'll get plenty of practice in before the day, just to be sure,' he winked. 'Starting tonight, in the Signature suite in The Domville. I'll wait for my answer until morning if you need to be sure, but no longer.'

'I don't need to be sure, Alec, I already know. I want to be Mrs. Wright, it's all I've ever wanted, but I'd better warn you that I want at least two baby Wrights in the not-too-distant future.'

'We have a deal then,' he laughed, quickly standing up and clasping my face as he gazed down at me with indisputable love in his eyes. I had a feeling that look had always been there, but I'd been too scared, or too distracted, to see it. 'You have never looked more beautiful,' he murmured.

'Because I'm finally happy, because you've made me happy. Promise me you'll never break my heart, because I only have one and you own it. You've always owned it, Alec.'

'I promise, as long as you promise the same in return.'

'I do. Come on, much as I'd love to just make out with you down here for the rest of the night, my best friend just got married, we can't miss her night.' I squealed with laughter as he swooped me up into his arms and headed over to the bench to let me gather up my belongings. He carried me into the marquee and Poppie screamed as she saw us and started jumping up and down and clapping her hands. I grinned and held up mine to show her my ring.

'Best. Day. Ever,' she cried. Dad put his arm around Mum and squeezed her tightly as they both smiled at me, Dad giving me a slight nod, his seal of approval.

'Don't you think you two should slow down a bit?' called Jean-Claude with a grin that threatened to crack his face. 'It's only been thirteen years getting you to this point, we don't want to rush into anything, do we?'

'Please tell me that we can rush?' I asked, looking up at Alec's handsome, ecstatic face and falling in love with him all over again.

'Only if we do it right. You've missed out on so much, I want to give you a wedding day that you'll never forget.'

July

'Darling, you look stunning. I mean, you always looked stunning, but this …' Mum shook her head and had to grab another tissue and blow her nose forcefully. She was a wreck this morning, and it wasn't helping me keep my emotions in check.

'She's right, Paige. Jean-Claude has outdone himself with this dress,' Poppie confirmed, raking her eyes up and down it.

He really had. He'd never done a dress design before, but he'd wanted to do something special for me for my wedding day. He'd promised me that if I didn't like it, he wouldn't be offended if I chose one of the more prestigious designers, but I'd fallen in love with it on first sight. He'd done a variation of the dress I'd worn to the ball with Alec all those years ago. It was a silver-jewelled halter neck with a sweetheart neckline, and it fanned out with layers of handmade lace with hundreds of tiny diamonds stitched into it. Alec had paid for it, insisting on diamonds and not diamantés. I looked like some kind of fairy tale princess. Vivian had pulled some of my long hair up, leaving the rest trailing down my back, and I was wearing a pair of diamond earrings from Mum and Dad and a diamond solitaire necklace from Poppie and Justin. The florist had been most upset when I'd asked for cornflowers in my small bouquet, but they reminded me of my first date with Alec, so I put my foot down. Poppie, who was my chief bridesmaid, was dressed in a rich shimmering blue that reminded me of his eyes. I'd asked Vivian and Shauna to be my other bridesmaids, I'd spent so many hours with them for work, we'd become really close. I laughed as Poppie pouted when she looked over at them, then down at the huge bump showing in her dress.

'I'm so sorry, I really didn't want to waddle up the aisle on your special day. I didn't think I'd get pregnant so fast.'

'Hey, I streaked up the aisle with my backside on display and my phone blaring for yours,' I laughed. 'Besides, how could I not be happy that my best friend is having a baby in two months and that I'm going to be godmother?'

'Please tell me you'll try for a baby soon,' she pleaded. 'It would be amazing to have children of a similar age. They could end up being best friends like us.'

'Except for the fact that they'll live so far apart,' I sighed.

I'd spent the last ten months living between London, New York, and Rome, doing some modelling jobs wherever Alec was working. We still hadn't agreed on where we were going to call home. Poppie and Justin had moved out of London and returned to Shropshire, to be close to her parents for when the baby was born. The beauty of finance was that as long as he had a good internet connection, he could work from anywhere. I was missing her terribly, and from the moment I found out that she was pregnant and moving home, the appeal of my formerly glamorous and jet setting, yet hardworking, lifestyle suddenly lost its sparkle. Alec and I needed to have a serious conversation on our honeymoon about where we were going to put down roots.

'I have to go, darling. Give me a kiss and I'll see you at the church.' Mum pursed her lips, but I threw my arms around her neck and hugged her tightly.

'Thank you so much,' I whispered earnestly. Despite Alec and me wanting to pay for our own wedding, my parents had insisted, saying that after I'd paid off their mortgage and set them up for life, meaning they could retire early, it was something they wanted to do for me. I knew it wasn't like we were having an extravagant wedding, I only wanted it to be close friends and family, but all the same, I was really touched.

'It's the least we can do after everything you've done for us, darling. I'm just so proud that you followed your heart and stuck to your guns. He's been the only man you've ever wanted, just like your dad was for me. I hope you'll both be as happy as we are.'

'We will be. I know we will be, Mum,' I confirmed. I kissed her goodbye and let Vivian come and check my hair and makeup before we got ready to leave the house and head to the small village church down the road. I'd wanted to keep it low-key as well to avoid all of the press attention. It was our day, not the public's. We deserved at least one day of our lives out of the spotlight of the media. I laughed when Poppie emptied out my jewelled bag and made sure my phone was turned off.

'Nothing is interfering with this wedding,' she said firmly. 'I've even made sure that that cow Ruth wasn't going to be in the area today. I wouldn't have put it past her to barge in and try and ruin your day.'

'You did? I wonder what happened to her. I haven't heard anything about her for a long time.'

'You didn't know? She married Reece, got pregnant, and he walked out on her for another woman he was seeing behind her back. I would say karma's a bitch, but in this case, she already had that covered.'

'Poppie,' I scolded. Yes, Ruth hadn't been the nicest of people, but no one deserved to be abandoned.

'Don't you dare feel sorry for her, Paige,' she warned with a pointed finger and a scowl. 'She didn't have a nice bone in her body.'

'Wow, pregnancy hormones make you one angry mamma bear,' I giggled. 'Remind me never to cross you.'

'I thought you'd learned that after my revenge mission on Spence,' she grinned. 'I can't believe you fessed up and gave him money for his guttering.'

'You know what? I'm getting married today, let's not talk about exes. I want to get to the church and marry him before he changes his mind and runs out on me.' I felt a swirl of nerves stir in my stomach. My head was telling me not to be so ridiculous, but he'd left Tiffany on their wedding day. And I was Paige Taylor, good luck had never been a friend of mine.

'There is no way he's not marrying you today, Paige. Wild … bulls couldn't drag him away from you. The love he has for you is the real deal, so stop looking over your shoulder waiting for the worst to happen. Those days are behind you now. You kissed all of those frogs and now you have your own Prince Charming.'

Dad held my hand in the vintage car as we pulled out of the drive. I looked at him with a frown as we turned in the opposite direction to the church.

'What's happening?'

'It's a surprise, all arranged by Alec, just go with it. I promise you'll be happy.'

I bit my lip as we drove further out into the countryside, past the village hall where I'd first met Alec, back when he was chairman of the YFC and I'd just stare at him in awe. I wished I could go back in time to whisper in that young girl's ear to keep dreaming and never lose hope, that sometimes fairy tales really do come true. Tears stung my eyes when the car pulled into a smart paved courtyard flanked by stables and a large barn that had been done up, with tall white rose bushes in blue glazed pots flanking the walls. It was the farm where I'd come to do my stock judging all those years ago. Except it was no longer a working farm, it had been turned into a boutique wedding venue. Dad helped me out of the car and Poppie rushed over to adjust my veil with a grin.

'What do you think? How gorgeous does it look?'

'Amazing! I had no idea it had been converted.'

'Alec wanted it to be a surprise, we all knew. See over there?' she pointed. 'That's Daisy's old stall, where you groped a cow's arse, got covered in crap, and nearly had your first kiss. It all started here, Paige, fourteen years ago to the day.'

'Are you ok?' Dad asked, looking concerned. I nodded. I was just speechless, totally overwhelmed. It *had* all started here and I couldn't think of anywhere better for it to come full circle. We posed for some photographs, taken by Alec's apprentice, before I was led over to the paddock opposite, where an outdoor wedding had been set up. There were white-painted wooden chairs, with azure organza ribbons tied around the backs, for the guests who were all craning their necks to see us. The aisle was lined with more white rose bushes in blue pots with white wooden duckboards forming a firm surface on the grass for us to walk up. A pergola had been created and decorated with floating white voile panels, white roses, and hundreds of blue cornflowers, and Alec was standing there, his broad back rocking the fitted morning suit he was wearing. I couldn't wait to see his face. A small orchestra started playing as first Vivian, then Shauna, and finally Poppie, headed up the aisle before me. 'Ready?' Dad asked.

'I've never been more ready for anything in my life, Dad,' I confirmed, itching to get up there to see my man.

'I'll always be here for you, Paige. I may be handing you over to another man, giving him the responsibility of caring for you now, but as beautiful and grown up as you may be today, you'll always be my little girl, no matter what.'

'Dad,' I moaned, my eyes filling with tears, matching his. He wiped mine away for me, then his own, and held out his arm. My heart was racing with each step I took towards Alec. I barely noticed our small congregation either side, I just wanted to see his face the moment he turned around and saw me. 'Owwww,' I uttered as Dad moved forwards and I was yanked back.

'What's wrong?' he asked.

'My foot, I can't move it.' I pulled again, but it was like I'd been super glued to the wooden slats below me. I reached down and hitched up my dress and groaned. I'd only caught the slender heel of my designer, silver-jewelled shoe in the gap in one of the boards. 'Seriously? Today? I couldn't just have one perfect, disaster-free day?' I moaned. Dad dropped to his knees and I put my hand on his shoulder as I slipped my foot out of my shoe. I balanced on one leg as he tried to pull my shoe out.

'Careful, careful, these shoes were custom made, they are priceless,' Jean-Claude uttered as he raced down from Alec's side, in his role as best man, to come and assist. 'Gently, gently,' he urged. The orchestra stopped playing and all eyes were on me as the two men argued about the best way to get it out, with Dad asking if anyone had a hammer or wrench at hand.

'Like people turn up at a wedding with one in their jacket pockets.' I rolled my eyes as he and Jean-Claude bickered. 'Leave it, I'm getting married right now, with or without it.'

'You can't limp up the aisle with one leg shorter than the other, darling,' Jean-Claude chastised. 'It will ruin the whole effect of my dress.'

'Then I'll take off my other shoe and go barefoot,' I suggested.

'And drag my dress on the ground? No, no, no,' he uttered, looking horrified.

'I'll carry her up the aisle,' Dad offered.

'You're fifty-two, Dad. I'm not having you carry me up the aisle, you'll have a heart attack.'

'I'm very fit for my age, thank you very much,' he retorted with an offended look. 'Just ask your mother, she has no complaints.'

'No complaints at all,' Mum winked from the front row. 'He'd put some teenagers to shame.'

'Seriously? We're discussing your sex life in public? Today?' I groaned. I was just going to have to stomp up the aisle barefoot with my dress hitched up.

'Allow me,' came Alec's voice. I looked up to see him standing in front of me, his blond hair styled into that perfect mess I loved so much, his blue eyes shining with happiness, offset by the cerulean cravat he was wearing. 'If anyone's carrying my stunning bride up the aisle, it's going to be me. It's the only way I know she'll make it in one piece. I've waited long enough, I'm not waiting any longer.'

'I'm so sorry, it was all supposed to be perfect today.'

'It is,' he smiled. 'You're here, looking simply breathtaking and missing one shoe. If I can't play Prince Charming to your Cinderella today, when can I?' he asked, bending down to gather me up in his arms. I swooned as I put my arms around his neck and looked up at him. 'This is it, last chance to change your mind,' he whispered as he walked me the short distance to the waiting celebrant.

'I'm right where I want to be, are you?'

'Of course I am, Paige. This is where I fell in love with you, there's nowhere else in the world I'd rather be today. Look over there.' He flicked his head to where a black and white cow was chewing on some grass, with a blue ribbon around her neck. 'Even the cow who started all of this has come to celebrate.'

'That's Daisy?' I laughed. 'She's still alive?'

'Seventeen years old, with the most enormous family of her own. Her old stall where you judged her is now the bedroom of the honeymoon suite. I finally get to kiss you in there tonight, like I wanted to that day. I'm also hoping that we'll be starting a family all of our own in there later, too.'

'Mr. Wright,' I grinned. 'You do know how to woo a girl, but I'm warning you that much as I love that Daisy's here, if she takes one step towards me with that flatulent bottom of hers, we'll be having barbequed beef for lunch tomorrow.' Daisy lifted her head and let out a long, low moo of disapproval.

'Can we proceed?' asked the celebrant.

'Wait, wait,' huffed Jean-Claude as he appeared at Alec's side, brandishing my missing shoe. 'I prised off the wooden slat with the starter crank from the wedding car to free it.'

'Thank you,' I beamed. Alec carefully set me down and slipped my shoe onto my bare foot, grinning up at me from his kneeling position.

'See, perfect fit. There's no disputing you're my Cinderella now.'

'I always was, we just took our time getting to the ball,' I reminded him.

For once in my life, with the exception of Daisy farting and making everyone laugh as I was trying to say my heartfelt vows, the rest of the day went without a hitch. The sun stayed shining as we had canapés out in the courtyard before heading in to the gorgeously decked-out barn for our formal sit-down meal, followed by much dancing and laughter. I refused any alcohol, but for a tiny sip for the toasts. I still couldn't handle it and there was no way I was ruining my wedding night. I didn't object when Alec took my hand and we sneaked out, leaving everyone else to enjoy their night as we headed to our cosy suite. Everyone was stopping over in the en-suite rooms of the converted farmhouse, so we were all having breakfast together in the morning before Alec and I headed off on our two-week honeymoon.

'Do you want your wedding present now, or shall I save it for when we're away?' Alec asked, slipping his arms around my waist as we stood in the exact spot he'd fallen on me all those years ago.

'Let's save it, like I'll save mine for you. Right now, the only gift I want to unwrap is you.'

'Your wish is my command, Mrs. Wright,' he murmured, gently kissing my lips.

'Say that again,' I begged, sure I'd never get tired of hearing it.

'Mrs. Wright, can we stop talking and get on with the baby-making portion of the evening?'

'Something you never need to ask me,' I replied, then giggled as he tackled me to the bed with a growl. He'd not been wrong about our compatibility in bed, or in the shower, bath, car, or anywhere else we were constantly doing it. He blew my mind. Even Spence wasn't a patch on Alec, and I thought I'd had it good with him at the time. I really was the luckiest girl in the world.

'Stop, stop,' I laughed as he dove under the clear water again to catch my feet and pull me under. We'd been horsing around like teenagers for the last thirty minutes and I was exhausted. He hauled me against him with one arm, as he swept my wet hair away from my forehead with his free hand and kissed me.

'Do you surrender?'

'Always to you,' I confirmed, kissing him back. 'Come on, let's go and lie down for a while. We've been so busy, we haven't even swapped wedding presents.'

He took my hand and we climbed out of the lake and up the steps to the flat lawn flanked by Cypress trees, below our private villa on Lake Como. I'd told him that I wanted to come to Italy for our honeymoon. Both of us were so well travelled, I wanted to be somewhere with him that was relaxed, with an easy pace of life and good food. He'd suggested his apartment in Rome, but much as I loved the city, much as I loved all of the major cities I'd visited, I was actually starting to crave the quiet now, something I never thought I'd say. So he'd booked this magnificent old villa with no immediate neighbours and a stunning view of the lake and mountains. It even came with its own speedboat, so we could explore the lakeside towns and buy provisions. He grabbed a large towel off the bed in the shaded muslin-lined cabana and wrapped it around me, gently rubbing me dry as he planted tender kisses on my lips. I sighed, full of contentment.

'Wait here, let me go and get my camera,' he ordered. 'Do you need anything? Food, water?'

'I'm good, thanks,' I confirmed. We'd declined the cook and butler that came as part of the package, just wanting to spend time alone. I squeezed my hair in the towel as I watched him jog up to the house, marvelling at his toned, bronzed body. He was the personification of male perfection. Better still, he was all mine. I sipped some iced water and lay back on the bed, propped up by huge, squashy, waterproof cushions as I admired the view. We only had a few days left before we headed home, though where home was going to be, I still had no idea.

'Alec,' I scolded as he reappeared and started taking pictures of me.

'I'm a photographer with a beautiful wife, I can't help it,' he grinned, clicking a few more before coming to lie beside me. 'You look so sexy, bare faced and in this skimpy bikini, though I think you need to lay off the creamy pasta, your stomach's bloated.' He bent down to kiss it, and I smiled as I reached over into my bag and pulled out his carefully wrapped present.

'Happy belated wedding day, Alec.' I handed him the tiny parcel and he put his camera to one side and sat up as he started to tear at the paper. He looked at the item in his hand, then back at me, confused. I laughed and turned over the long, thin piece of plastic, to let him see the pink words "Pregnant" that showed in the small window. His mouth opened and closed a few times, no sounds coming out. He shook his head and reached up to wipe some tears from his face. 'I'm about thirteen weeks. I didn't want to tell you until I was past the dangerous phase, but we have the scan when we get home next week, so we'll know more then.'

'We're having a baby?' he whispered, the emotion in his voice making my eyes fill with tears, too.

'We are. Is that ok? I didn't think I'd get caught so soon.'

'Is that ok? Other than you agreeing to marry me, it's the best news I've ever had in my life, Paige.' He put the stick down and grabbed my face, making me laugh as he peppered it with kisses. 'I'm going to be the best dad that ever walked the face of this earth, I promise.'

'I know you will be. Will you mind if we have a boy or a girl?'

'I don't care. Whatever we have, we can try again for the other. God, I love you,' he sighed, letting his lips meet mine. I sank back on the cushions, pulling him down with me as we lost ourselves in our bubble of bliss for a moment. He eventually propped himself up on his side and put his palm on my stomach. I covered his hand with mine as I smiled up at him. I hadn't even told Mum or Dad or Poppie yet. I knew I was pregnant on our wedding day, when she'd said she'd love me to be pregnant at the same time, but Alec deserved to know first. I frowned as I tried to work out what felt different. Ever since Alec had turned up on Poppie's wedding day to claim me, nothing had felt the same. 'What's wrong?'

'I'm just … I'm so happy,' I nodded. The realisation that this was what I'd always longed to feel like hit me hard, and tears rolled down my cheeks. 'Before you came for me, I didn't know life could be this good, it's all a little overwhelming.'

'Neither did I, but this is it, Paige. We've had our share of misery and disasters. Now we're together, it's going to be like this all of the time, I'll make sure of it. Can I give you my present now?'

'Don't tell me you're pregnant, too?' I teased. He laughed and kissed the tip of my nose, then wiped away my tears.

'I don't think we can expect two miracles in one day, you've already given me one.' He bent down to kiss my stomach again, then reached for the flat, rectangular wrapped gift he'd returned with, which he handed to me.

'What is it?' I asked as I took it off him to find it was flexible.

'Well, open it and see,' he chuckled. 'If you don't like it, if I've made a mistake, be honest. I just want to make you as happy as you've made me.'

I peeled back the paper and my eyes widened with surprise to see the quality brochure he'd carefully wrapped. It was an exclusive estate agent's brochure, showing a stunning sandstone and timbered Jacobean house, set in extensive grounds in the Shropshire countryside, not far from Mum and Dad, or Poppie and Justin. I looked up at him to see him nervously chewing his lower lip, then back down at the brochure. I opened it to see the pictures of the large, beamed sitting room with a huge inglenook fireplace and the contemporary open plan kitchen-dining-family room. There was also a cloakroom, utility, and pantry downstairs, then a cellar with a huge study and wine storage. One side of the first floor had two large en-suite double bedrooms with a landing so vast it could double up as a playroom or second lounge. The master suite was on the other side with an enormous dressing room and bathroom, and on the top floor was another large double bedroom in the eaves with its own en-suite and skylights, perfect for guests. The matching Jacobean stables next to it had been converted into an indoor pool and gym, with another study and two en-suite rooms above it. It was breathtaking.

'So?' Alec eventually asked as I tried to take it all in.

'You want to buy this for us?' I asked, tearing my eyes away to look up at him.

'No, I've already bought it for you, for us. Don't you like it?'

'Alec, it's beautiful, a really gorgeous family home. I love it, honestly I do. I could see Christmas's here with all of our loved ones around a roaring fire. But it's in Shropshire, in the countryside, not New York or London where you need to be.'

'I need to be wherever you are, Paige, and I know that you've started craving a quieter life, close to your family and best friend. It's close to my family too, and the grounds are extensive enough for me to have a helicopter pad. It's a short flight to the nearest airport and I already checked that they can accommodate my plane. I can still travel to anywhere I need in the world from here. You can come with me when I'm working away, or if you choose to stay at home, I know you have family nearby to keep an eye on you.'

'You really don't mind moving back to the country?'

'No,' he replied, his serious face reassuring me. 'Much as I've loved living in cities for most of my life, I want our son or daughter to have fresh air and plenty of space to run around in. To get the chance to experience nature and the countryside, just like we did. I can't think of anywhere else that I'd want our child to grow up. Do I need to sell it and we'll look for somewhere together?'

'No,' I answered as I shook my head vehemently. 'This is perfect, I love that you've thought about what suits us as a family.'

'Thank God,' he smiled with a sigh of relief. 'I wasn't sure you were serious about being ready to move out of London.'

‘I am, especially now that I’m pregnant. I want to take a break from work and focus on us and our baby. I can always do the odd shoot if I miss it, but it’s not like we need the money.’

‘It’s not,’ he laughed. He was commanding extortionate fees now, making money faster than he could spend it, but we weren’t extravagant with it. ‘We’ll go and see it when we get home and think about any kitchen and bathroom alterations you want to make. I think the current dressing room will need to be properly kitted out for all of your clothes and accessories, and we can discuss décor and order furniture. I want to be in before the baby arrives so you can put your feet up and relax for the last month or two of your pregnancy.’

‘You were so worth the wait,’ I told him as I clasped his face and poured all of my love for him into a long, deep kiss.

‘Keep buttering me up like that, Mrs. Wright, and baby two will be happening before you’ve had a chance to draw breath.’

‘I have no problem with that at all,’ I replied, then giggled as he forced me back down onto the bed to kiss me into another blissed-out stupor. We hadn’t just collided, we’d merged. I had no idea anymore where I ended and he began, and I never wanted to find out.

Epilogue

'What are you wearing?' I laughed as I opened the heavy old oak front door to see Poppie dressed in black with camouflage stripes on her face. 'Who are we pulling a revenge prank on today?'

'Get ready, fast, we don't have any time to waste. This is a serious undercover mission,' she ordered, handing over a small tin.

'You're not going to tell me what this is about?' I asked as she herded me up to my bedroom at top speed.

'No, you have to see this with your own two eyes. Bring one of Alec's cameras with a zoom lens and some binoculars, just in case.'

'I don't own binoculars. What's going on?' I demanded as she riffled through my dressing room and threw a pair of black jeans and a black sweater at me.

'Less talk, more action, Paige Wright. Move it, I'll be waiting in the car with the engine running.'

'I'd better let Alec know I'm going out. I told him I was staying in to have a blissfully quiet pamper night.'

'No need. He's having a pint with Justin in *The Cock and Bull*, as usual on a Thursday. You'll be home before he even knows you were missing.' She shot off down the stairs, leaving me standing there in a confused daze. I did as I was told, except for the black facial stripes, and headed downstairs to Alec's studio in the cellar to grab one of his cameras. Poppie was waiting, as promised, with the passenger door to her BMW X5 open and the engine running. I'd barely had time to close the door when she wheel span out of the gravelled forecourt and up my drive.

'Are you trying to kill me?' I exclaimed as I hastily tugged on my seatbelt, my voice reverberating as she shot over the cattle grid.

'No, but you might kill me when we get there, for showing you this.'

'Poppie, seriously, what's going on? Who's upset you and why would I be cross with you?'

'No one's upset me and this is something you need to see, rather than be told,' she replied, slamming through the gears as she shot along our long drive flanked by fields and trees. We allowed the farmer to let his sheep graze on our non-landscaped land to help keep the grass down, and right now, I was worried that a poor, unsuspecting sheep was going to amble into Poppie "spawn of Lewis Hamilton" Cavendish's path and be catapulted into the air feet first, then crash through the ceiling and land in my lap. I'd planned on a roast turkey for lunch on Sunday, not roast road kill lamb.

'Slow down,' I urged as she hit the next cattle grid and nearly took off. 'I'm only forty-seven, I'm too young to die.'

'I hate you sometimes,' Poppie muttered. 'Why do you still get to look fresh faced and gorgeous at forty-seven and I look old, lined, and haggard?'

'You don't look any older than me, Poppie,' I laughed. 'One bonus of me having been in the beauty industry for so long is I was given all the creams and potions to keep us looking younger than our years. Men don't seem put off by our age either. I saw that twenty-something model flirting with you at the Gala ball in London last weekend.'

'He was hot, wasn't he,' she nodded, flashing me a grin. 'Nice to know I've still got it sometimes.'

'You've always got it. And you've also got a handsome and very attentive husband who will always love you, no matter how many lines you develop as we age. Seriously, what's going on?'

'A few more minutes and we'll be there. You have to promise me to stay calm and not to freak out, ok?'

'Of course, because nothing reassures me more than you warning me not to freak out,' I responded sarcastically. My mind boggled at what she could possibly be taking me to see that she thought might upset me. If I didn't know my husband so well, I might think she was taking me to show me proof of him having an affair, but my bad luck had run out the day Alec and I had finally got together. Even though we were both much older, we were more in love and happier than ever. 'I'm about to lose some nails in your leather upholstery,' I warned as she took another narrow country lane hairpin bend at speed.

'O stop moaning, this is a way less risky mission than our breaking and entering when we exacted revenge on that cheating arsehole, Spence,' she retorted. I saw the pub sign for *The Cock and Bull* flash past and a glimpse of Alec's Porsche Cayenne sitting on the forecourt. Poppie slammed on the brakes and I jolted forwards with a gasp as she swung left, into the village hall car park.

'You've just given me a double mastectomy and quite possibly a couple of fractured ribs,' I moaned, rubbing where the seatbelt had cut into my chest.

'Sssshhh, stealth is the name of the game from this moment on,' she warned as she cut the lights and proceeded to drive in the dark to the furthest corner of the car park.

'How can you see where you're going?' I whispered.

'I can't,' she replied, 'but who parks at the back of the car park? It's too far to walk to the door.'

'What about the hedge?'

'What hedge?' she asked, turning to face me as there was a horrendous screech of twigs on metal as she ploughed straight through it into the field on the other side. 'Shit, who put that there?'

'Poppie,' I giggled. 'What's got into you?'

'I'm nervous, seriously nervous,' she replied as she slammed the car into reverse and managed to completely miss the BMW-sized hole in the hedge and fence that she'd already made and carved a new one, before coming to a stop on the gravel car park. 'Oops. If Justin asks, the brakes momentarily failed. Ok, why don't you have your face paint on?'

'For starters, it was black boot polish, which you're going to have a hell of a time washing off. Secondly, I want to know why we're at the village hall dressed like burglars.'

'Grab your camera and come with me. Tred quietly, we don't want to alert anyone to our presence,' she warned as she slipped out of the car.

'Right, as no one will have heard you hand brake turn into the car park or drive through the hedgerow, twice.'

'Ssssshhhh!' she scolded, grabbing my hand and crouching as she scurried forwards, trying to keep to the shadows as we approached the windows facing the car park. 'Leg it,' she shrieked as the security light pinged on and we were bathed in a dazzling brilliant white glow.

'Leg it where? I can't see a damn thing and I've no idea what we're doing,' I replied. She grabbed me and yanked me forwards, slamming me against the expanse of rough stone wall between the two long lit windows. 'Ok, very slowly and carefully, angle the camera to take some pictures of the room inside, then check them and tell me what you don't see.'

'Ok,' I said slowly, none the wiser. I jumped as she suddenly grabbed my arm.

'Make sure the flash is off, we need to stay incognito.'

'Have you been tested for senile dementia?' I asked.

'No, why?'

'Because right now I really think you ought to be. We look like a couple of elderly perverts spying on the kids at KFC.'

'YFC,' she tutted. 'And I've got senile dementia?'

'I know that, I'm just dreaming of chicken. Now that I'm older, it's harder work to keep in shape. I have to eat healthily most of the time, so on my one night off a week, I like to gorge on fried chicken and chips, then a huge slab of chocolate, in secret. Instead of that, I'm on some *Expendables* covert operation with you, so covert even I don't know what I'm doing here,' I hissed as I took some pictures. I pulled the digital imager up to study the shots, with Poppie looking over my shoulder. 'Ok, I'm looking at a room full of youngsters enjoying themselves. Where's the scandal?'

'Tell me what, or who, you don't see?' she repeated. I frowned as I scanned the faces again. Everyone was facing me, but for the club president and secretary, who always sat facing the room. I gasped and looked around at her.

'Where's Daisy?' My sixteen-year-old daughter, who was supposed to be in there right now, was missing.

'Exactly. Now don't kill me when you see who else is missing,' she advised as I looked again.

'Jeremy!' I exclaimed, shooting her a look. 'Where has your son gone with my daughter, Poppie?'

'Who says he's gone somewhere with her? She might have been the one to drag him into the kitchen at the back for a snog,' she retorted.

'They're snogging in the kitchen?'

'Please don't yell, but they were last week,' she grimaced.

'Right, I'm going in,' I stated with grim determination. She was only sixteen, too young to be snogging anyone, let alone my godson. They'd practically grown up together.

'Please don't, I wanted you to see for yourself instead of telling you as I knew you'd be angry. They're so sweet together. He really cares about her, he wouldn't do anything to get her into trouble. You'll understand when you see them. Come with me.'

'Are they having sex?' I asked, my heart breaking at the thought of it. Her dad would go mad if he found out.

'No, of course not, what kind of boy do you think I raised?' she scolded as she pulled me around the side of the hall and we squeezed past some bushes to the rear. She pushed me down into a crouching position and we scuttled along sideways, like fast-moving crabs, until we were under the window. We gripped the windowsill and slowly pulled ourselves up until we could see into the room. I drew in a sharp breath to see Daisy gripping Jeremy's bottom, as he held her face in his hands, kissing her. Actually, kissing her made it sound sweet. What he was doing to my daughter wasn't sweet, he was eating her alive. Right how I'd have been chowing down on my illicit fried chicken if I'd been left in blissful oblivion. 'How adorable is that?' Poppie moaned, wiping some tears from her eyes as we dropped back down out of sight.

'Adorable? If he goes at it any harder, he'll swallow her whole. No wonder she's been stealing my Vaseline, he's sucking the top layer of her lips off each week. How long has this been going on?' I demanded, ready to march in there and drag her out.

'Just over a month, apparently. He's always had a soft spot for her, Paige. I warned him not to even think about kissing her until she was sixteen. He came home the night of her birthday party with stars in his eyes, saying she'd let him kiss her and told him that she thought he was really cute. He was so happy. Please don't be mad, he adores her. In fact, he's told me he loves her and one day he's going to marry her.'

'She's only sixteen, Poppie,' I sighed.

'And? If they were shagging like rabbits, I'd be up in arms as well, but they're not. They're just teenagers who've fallen for each other, who make out. We were doing it at their age. In fact, I was doing worse.'

'You were,' I nodded. 'I wasn't though, I was eighteen before I kissed Alec.'

'You'd have kissed him earlier if you'd had the chance and don't tell me you wouldn't. Please don't put your foot down, he's so happy. I've had a long chat with him about not rushing things. What harm can it do?' she urged. I shook my head and we pulled ourselves up to watch them again. Jeremy was tucking her long dark hair behind her ear as she gazed up at him with eyes full of adoration, just the way I was sure I did with Alec, then he dipped his head and planted a tender kiss on her forehead. I felt my eyes fill up with tears as I watched. My little girl wasn't a little girl anymore. She was turning into a woman, a woman who was already falling in love with the son of my best friend. I guess there were worse things that could happen to her.

'What exactly do you two think you're doing?' came Alec's voice from behind me.

'Shit, busted,' muttered Poppie, as we sheepishly turned to face him and Justin, who both stood with their arms folded as they shook their heads. 'How did you find us?'

'My son rang me to say he'd seen a couple of perverts taking pictures through the window, then sneaking around the back. Obviously we ran over from the pub immediately to confront them. Imagine our surprise to find you two spying through a window, dressed up like you're on a bank heist. Care to elaborate, Paige?' Alec demanded.

'We're not perverts, obviously,' I replied, quickly standing up and dragging Poppie up with me, trying to block his view of our daughter in the room behind. 'We were … we were … why don't you tell him what we were doing, Poppie?' I suggested, warning her with my eyes not to let on.

'No, you're so much better at storytelling than me, you go ahead,' she nodded, giving me an evil smile.

'Paige?'

'We'd heard rumours of real life perverts sniffing around the children, so we were testing out the clubs defences and security measures,' I stuttered.

'Right,' he nodded with a chuckle and a bemused shake of his head. 'Here was me thinking you were spying on our daughter and Jeremy kissing in the kitchen.'

'You knew?' I gasped, waiting for the fallout.

'Of course I did, Justin asked my permission for Jeremy to ask her out at her birthday party. I said as long as there was no hanky panky, I was fine with it.'

'And you didn't tell me?!'

'Because I knew how you'd react,' he said softly. 'She's a sensible young woman, not a little girl anymore, and she really likes him. Look, Paige, really look at them,' he urged, stepping forward to turn me around to see they were kissing again. 'Don't they remind you of us on our first date? We had obstacles thrown in our way, and we were miserable being kept apart from each other, I don't want that to happen to my daughter. If Jeremy can make her happy now, I say let him. We can worry about the future when the time comes.'

'She does look happy,' I sighed, putting my hands over his as he pulled me back against him.

'So am I forgiven?' Poppie asked.

'You are,' I nodded as the four of us watched our eldest children, who were totally oblivious to our presence.

'Not by me you're not, Poppie Cavendish,' Justin stated as he wrapped his arms around her and kissed the top of her head. 'Not only did you interrupt my one and only pint of beer a week, you'd better explain to me why our car has a section of barbed wire fence and a load of bushes attached to the back of it.'

'To balance out the ones at the front?' she offered with a giggle, making us all laugh. We left Daisy and Jeremy in peace and headed back to the front of the club.

'My dad caught the perverts,' came my fourteen-year-old son Xander's gleeful voice from behind us. 'O, hey Mum, what are you and Auntie Poppie doing here?' he asked, looking confused. 'Were you reinforcements?'

'Totally busted,' I laughed as the entire club, including Daisy and Jeremy, came out to stare in astonishment at Poppie and me all dressed in black.

'Never a dull moment with you, Mrs. Wright,' Alec chuckled. 'Part of the reason I fall more in love with you every day.'

The End

Win A Signed Paperback

I am offering one lucky reader the chance to win an exclusive signed, and personalised, first edition paperback copy of *Until We Collide,* a £10 or $15 USD Amazon Gift card, and some signed swag.

To be in with a chance, all you have to do is leave an honest review for *Until We Collide* on Amazon, even if it's only a sentence or two. They are so important to authors in helping other readers find our work. Once done, simply complete the following GoogleDocs form to register your details and to allow us to verify your entry:

Competition Google Docs Form

I will close this giveaway on 31st August 2016.

Terms and conditions are detailed on the attached form.

This giveaway is open internationally.

I will also announce the winner's name on my Facebook account, in case your email is changed in the meantime, or my message goes to your junk box and you miss it.

Thank you and good luck!

Charlotte x

Next Release

My main genre for writing is humorous erotic romance, under the name C.J Fallowfield. However, I plan to release a romantic comedy novel, penned under the name of Charlotte Fallowfield, in February of each year.

To be kept up to date on progress of my rom-coms, to see exclusive teasers and cover reveals, and to receive information about any giveaways I'm running, then simply sign up for my bi-annual newsletter here:

Newsletter Sign Up Link

About Charlotte Fallowfield

My website holds the most comprehensive information about me, as well as my current and up and coming releases, but you can also follow me via my other social media sites.

Amazon UK

Amazon USA

Facebook

Goodreads

Twitter

51164920R00104

Made in the USA
Charleston, SC
16 January 2016